THE COMPLETE TALES OF SHERIFF HENRY, VOLUME 2

The Apes of Devil's Island

BY JOHN CUNNINGHAM

The Darkness at Windon Manor

BY MAX BRAND

The Exploits of Beau Quicksilver

BY FLORENCE M. PETTEE

The Flying Legion

BY GEORGE ALLAN ENGLAND

The Golden Cat:
The Adventures of Peter the Brazen, Volume 3

BY LORING BRENT

The Opposing Venus: The Complete Cabalistic Cases
of Semi Dual, the Occult Detector

BY J.U. GIESY AND JUNIUS B. SMITH

The Radio Menace

BY RALPH MILNE FARLEY

The Ruby of Suratan Singh: The Adventures
of Scarlet and Bradshaw, Volume 2

BY THEODORE ROSCOE

The Vengeance of the Wah Fu Tong:
The Complete Cases of Jigger Masters, Volume 1

BY ANTHONY M. RUD

THE SHERIFF
OF TONTO TOWN

THE COMPLETE TALES OF
SHERIFF HENRY, VOLUME 2

W.C. TUTTLE

ALTUS PRESS
2018

PUBLISHING HISTORY

"The Sheriff of Tonto Town" originally appeared in the September 14, 21, 28, October 5, 12, and 19, 1935 issues of *Argosy* magazine (Vol. 258, No. 4–Vol. 259, No. 3). Copyright © 1935 by The Frank A. Munsey Company. Copyright renewed © 1962 and assigned to Steeger Properties, LLC. All rights reserved.

"Suspected by Henry" originally appeared in the December 7, 1935 issue of *Argosy* magazine (Vol. 260, No. 4). Copyright © 1935 by The Frank A. Munsey Company. Copyright renewed © 1963 and assigned to Steeger Properties, LLC. All rights reserved.

THANKS TO

Gerd Pircher

Visit altuspress.com for more books like this.

TABLE OF CONTENTS

THE SHERIFF OF TONTO TOWN

A dying man who has just discovered a rich
Arizona mine brings puzzling and dangerous
problems to Sheriff Henry Conroy

CHAPTER I

A QUEER GUN

"DOC" SARGENT'S DARKLY handsome face was flushed with anger as he stood in the doorway of the sheriff's office, glowering at Henry Harrison Conroy, the sheriff, who sat at his desk, his spurred boots against the top edge, his knees almost touching his chin.

"It wasn't any of your damn business anyway," declared Doc Sargent hotly. "You can't do things like that, Conroy."

Doc Sargent was the most immaculate gambler in the State, with his perfectly tailored black suits, hand-made shirts, hand-made shoes. He was also very clever, with his long, flexible fingers.

Henry Harrison Conroy had spent all his life, except the last few months, on the vaudeville stage, only leaving the profession when his last contract had been canceled, and an uncle had died, leaving him the J Bar C ranch in Wild Horse Valley.

Henry had made the best of it. He didn't believe in inspecting the dental work of gift horses.

Henry's nose was known from one end of the country to the other; and it was still as large and as red as ever. His face was moon-like, his head was almost bald, his eyes squinty, and his body was of tub-like proportions.

He never asked for the office of sheriff.

As a joke, his name was proposed for nomination; and he was elected—by one vote.

"I can't do things like what?" queried Henry.

1

"Judge" Van Treece, tilted against the wall in a much whittled chair, chuckled softly. Judge was sixty years of age, tall and gaunt, being six feet four inches tall, with a long, lean face and pouchy eyes. Whisky had driven Judge from practicing law. When the voters of Wild Horse Valley played a joke upon themselves by electing Henry sheriff, Henry decided to give them additional laughs; so he appointed Judge as his deputy, and made Oscar Johnson the jailer. Just now Oscar was sitting on the cot, apparently paying no attention to the conversation. Oscar had the body of a Hercules, faded blond hair, a button-like nose, and small blue eyes.

DOC SARGENT'S eyes shifted to Judge, who had chuckled.

"Do you see anything funny in this, Van Treece?" he asked.

"It has its element of humor," admitted Judge.

"Well, I don't see it," said Doc coldly.

"I am just wondering if you are expecting me to break down and cry?" said Henry slowly. "The fact still remains that the young man was being fleeced, Mr. Sargent. He sold that property for the sum of four thousand dollars. That is a mighty lot of money for a young cowboy to have.

"You happened to know that Mr. West paid him that much money. I happen to know that Mr. West now owns the Tonto Saloon. The idea was, I believe, to separate that young cowboy from his four thousand as quickly and as painlessly as possible. Well, I believe you have at least half of it, Mr. Sargent. Let well enough alone."

"That's all right," said the dapper gambler easily. "But you openly accused me of crooked dealing."

"Rather," corrected Henry, "I congratulated you on your

Regan slammed
the gambler
against the table.

perfect technique in palming cards. For many years, in vaudeville, I have watched the cleverest sleight-of-hand perform-
ers—magicians, if you please—and none of them—"

"What the hell has that got to do with the case?" demanded
the gambler. "I say that I dealt a square game. Was it my fault
if that fool cowboy overplayed his cards?"

"Nor the cards," added Henry. "They were good hands, I'll
admit. In fact, I have never seen three aces beat three kings as
many times. Queerly enough, you always drew to one pair, while
the young cowboy had his set of threes before the draw. But"—
Henry squinted close at the gambler—"that was all right, until
I saw how you got that third ace."

"You lie, if you say—"

Wham! The little office shook from the concussion of a
forty-five revolver, and a section of the door frame, adjacent to
the head of Doc Sargent, splintered off and went flying into
the street.

Henry went over backwards, struck the wall and slid slowly
to the floor, feet in the air, while Doc Sargent seemed to fade
out, so swiftly did he leave the immediate vicinity of the office.
Henry grunted, turned over to his hands and knees, and slowly
got to his feet. His overwrought leather belt had busted, and
he made a frantic grab to hold up his overalls, as he glared at
Oscar Johnson.

Judge sat there, as one petrified, merely his eyes shifting.

"You—you fool Swede!" gasped Henry. "I—I've busted my
belt!"

"Yah, su-ure," agreed Oscar blandly.

"In the name of everything, what happened?" gasped Judge.

"Das ha'ar gon," replied Oscar, "von't stay cocked."

Henry blinked at the heavy revolver in Oscar's big hand. He
looked at the splintered doorway and shuddered.

"You say that gun won't stay cocked?" queried Judge. "Wh-
why, didn't you know it wouldn't? What were you—"

"Please, Judge," interrupted Henry, "let me handle it. Oscar, why won't that gun stay cocked?"

"Va'l"—Oscar's blue eyes looked innocently at Henry—"mebbe it vars because Ay pulled de trigger, Henry."

Henry tugged up his overalls, let loose with one hand, and rubbed his nose carefully.

"Very few of them will stay cocked, under those circumstances," he said slowly. "But, Oscar, you might have killed that man! Don't you realize—oh, no, of course you don't; you wouldn't."

Henry shrugged his shoulders and looked at his upset chair.

"That Terrible Swede is going to kill somebody—some time," said Judge wearily.

"Ay hope to ta'l you," agreed Oscar.

HENRY WALKED over to the doorway and looked out at the street. Doc Sargent was nowhere in sight. In less than sixty days Tonto City had changed from a sleepy little cow-town to a boom mining town of over five thousand. The magic lure of a big gold strike was bringing in more people every day.

"You can't stand there forever, holding up your pants, Henry," said Judge.

Henry turned and came back to his desk.

"Forever is a long time, Judge," he said sadly. He picked up his cartridge belt and buckled it securely around the top of his overalls. He heaved a deep sigh and sat on a corner of his desk.

"At times I weary of Tonto City," he said. "I want the old town again, Judge. I want to sit down in the shade and let the rest of the world pass by. Look at it now. Wild-eyed, hard-faced men, painted women. Garish-fronted buildings, roaring honkytonks; a city of tent houses, shuddering to the jar of dynamite blasts. I hate it, sir."

"So do I," nodded Judge. "But, sir, our combined hates of the present condition of Tonto City only serve to make us both look a little older. If you don't take that gun away from Oscar, and keep it away from him, I am going to have a complete physical breakdown."

"Ay bought das ha'r gon," stated Oscar belligerently, "and it belongs to me. Das ha'r town is gettin' so damn tough, Ay must have a gon—yust like any yailer."

"I suppose he is right," sighed Henry. "After all, Judge, if you are fated to die by the gun, what difference who fires it?"

"I don't want to die accidentally," said Judge.

"Life is an accident—why not death?" queried Henry.

"Ay am no accident," denied Oscar.

"You, my dear Oscar, were a mistake," smiled Henry.

"Yah, su-ure," agreed Oscar blandly. He shoved the big gun inside the waistband of his overalls and sauntered out.

"A Swedish accident, goin' out to happen," sighed Henry.

"With a gun, he is positively a menace to all of Arizona," declared Judge. "He will go across the street, swagger for an hour in the Tonto Saloon, ogling all the girls, and come back bursting with egotism. I imagine he'll be very popular over there, since he nearly murdered Doc Sargent."

"I suppose," sighed Henry.

"And another thing, Henry. You are new to this country. I've been here ever since the Huachuca Mountains were holes in the ground. That is, they were still slight depressions when I arrived. I know the pulse of the West. Now, in that little matter—"

"Check that with the rest of the scenery," interrupted Henry. "For the tenth time, you are going to explain to me that I am not supposed to act as a dry-nurse to embryo gamblers. That my business is to be the sheriff, acting only in cases of law-breakage. That I must ignore crooked dealing, fixed roulette wheels, and loaded dice. All this must I do, in order that the world may stay bright to my vision and my body remain per-pendicular."

"Quite right," nodded Judge. "Minding one's own business is the best life insurance in this country, sir. I have seen many a test case. Let Jack West and his hired help operate the Tonto. I'm sure they will not interfere in your operating the sheriff's office."

"In other words," smiled Henry, "they will promise not to make any arrests as long as I refrain from running gambling games, selling liquor, or operating a honkytonk in the county jail."

"Something like that," agreed Judge.

"And you," said Henry accusingly, "a man of your age, steeped in the lore of Blackstone, a gentleman in spite of an uncontrollable thirst, can sit there and calmly explain to me just why I should shut my eyes to crooked practices. My dear Judge, I am afraid you were educated in law—not in justice."

"It is merely common practice to mind one's own business, Henry. The world laughs at a crusader."

"And so we talk in circles, Judge," smiled Henry. "Talking, even in circles, is a dry occupation. Were I to mention a drink—"

JUDGE WAS already out of his chair, and arm in arm they went to the Tonto Saloon, which now bore the gaudy sign:

TONTO SALOON
GAMBLING PALACE AND PLACE
OF ENTERTAINMENT

Miners, just off shift, with the muck of the mines on their clothes, rubbed elbows with seedy-looking prospectors, cowboys, speculators, and the general following of a new gold strike.

Where the Tonto Saloon had been one low-ceilinged room, it was now a big three-room establishment, each room far larger than the original cow-town saloon.

Jack West owned it now, and Jack West also owned the richest mines in the district. Although few men in Wild Horse Valley had ever seen Jack West, his operations were well known. Twenty years ago he had discovered and sold the Three Partners mine for over a million. This was in the Maricopa district, two hundred miles from Tonto City. Stories had been told in which

West and a partner, in a quarrel which almost ended fatally, played one hand of poker for ownership of the Three Partners—and West won.

"To you, sir," said Henry Harrison Conroy.

"And to you, sir," replied Judge Van Treece.

Drinking, with them, was a ritual; and always amusing to the rough element of Tonto City. Standing near them was an oldish man, poorly dressed, and with a terribly scarred face. It was really one continuous scar, which began high up on his forehead above his left eye, extended down the bridge of his nose, where it went at a right angle, cutting deep into his right cheek, and then looped down around his mouth, like an inverted question mark. His eyes were almost concealed under his beetling brows.

"It is not my custom," remarked Judge, "to belittle whisky, no matter how humble its origin, but that," pointing at the bottle, "is hardly fit for human consumption."

"Your trouble," smiled the bartender, "is the fact that you have been drinking prune whisky. The liquor in that bottle is pure stuff."

"Not rye—just stuff," nodded Henry. "I detest that word 'stuff.' It reeks of pillows, mattresses. Judge, will you have another—er—stuff?"

"Not from that same bottle, Henry. Have you something in bonded liquor?"

A commotion outside caused them to step back to the doorway, where a crowd had gathered. Danny Regan and Slim Pickins, the foreman and a cowboy from Henry's J Bar C ranch, were in the ranch buckboard, and several men were crowded around the rear of the equipage, where a man was stretched out, his feet hanging over the rear.

"Is Dr. Bogart there—in the saloon?" asked Danny.

"Here he comes now," called a voice.

Dr. Bogart was hurrying across the street. He took one look at the injured man, and ordered Danny to take him down to the house where Dr. Bogart lived, which he also used as an office. Danny whirled the team around and drove swiftly away.

"Dynamite accident," said one of the men. "Badly busted, I reckon."

THE CROWD separated, going about their own business. Henry saw the scar-faced man, standing there on the sidewalk, looking down the street where the buckboard had disappeared around a corner. In all his life Henry Harrison Conroy had never seen such hate depicted on a human countenance as was on the face of this scarred person.

Henry looked curiously at Judge, who had also noted it. Finally the scar-faced man went slowly across the street.

"Danny will come back to the office, Judge," said Henry. "We'll get the details of this accident."

They walked back and sat down in the office.

"You noticed the scar-faced man, Henry?" queried Judge.

Henry nodded slowly.

"I did, Judge; and if the devil has a worse expression, I hope the preachers are mistaken about damnation. No doubt, some of it was due to that scar."

"Undoubtedly," agreed Judge. "But that scar flamed scarlet, while the rest of his face turned gray. He saw the man in the buckboard. I saw him take a look, and then he drew back."

Danny and Slim came back in a few minutes and tied their horses in front of the office.

"We found him beside the road, a mile this side of the ranch," explained Danny. "He'd fallen off his old horse. Couldn't talk much, but managed to tell us that a delayed blast went off on him. He got on his horse and headed for a doctor, but fainted from loss of blood. Henry, the poor devil is all busted to hell."

"That's certainly hard luck," said Henry. "Who is he, Danny?"

"We never asked him. It was mighty hard for him to talk."

"I was scared to help him pack into the house—scared he'd

fall to pieces," said Slim. "He kept mumblin' somethin' about strikin' it rich."

"That's right," nodded Danny. "He kept sayin' somethin' about jewelry ore. What's that?"

"A common expression among miners and prospectors," said Judge. "It refers to very rich stuff—sparkling with gold, or silver."

"Perhaps," said Henry sadly, "he has found the end of the rainbow; and in his delirium he sees the pots of gold, or a dream-vein, studded with the stuff he gave up his life to find."

"Frijole Bill sent in a jug," said Slim. "I'll get it."

Frijole Bill Cullison, the little cook at the J Bar C, spent much of his spare time distilling prune-juice, of which he sent a generous share to the sheriff's office staff.

It was never more than a few days old, but its kick was tremendous. Oscar Johnson preferred it to any other beverage.

"WE MUST hide this from Oscar," said Judge. "Of such stuff is total wreckage manufactured. And don't forget, Henry— Oscar has a gun which won't stay cocked."

"My gosh, you didn't give the Terrible Swede a gun, didja?" exclaimed Danny.

"No; he bought it for himself," replied Henry.

"And that Swede is as lethal as a quart of nitro-glycerine," sighed Judge. "I'm afraid to sneeze in his presence."

"Why don't you fire him, Henry?" asked Danny. "Send him back to the ranch, where he can't do worse than to break the neck of a horse or two. Hire a good jailer."

"Oscar rises or falls with the office," replied Henry.

"It is no use, Danny," sighed Judge. "Henry won't listen to reason."

"Reason!" snorted Henry. "If I did, I'd fire all three of us. God knows the job is dreary enough, without taking away my greatest source of amusement. You underestimate Oscar. Oh, I am perfectly aware that he does everything wrong. But I have a system. I tell him to do something *wrong*, and he will invariably do it *right*."

"But," reminded Judge, "you have managed to keep guns out of his hands, Henry. If he gets a dozen drinks under his belt, he will take a shot at everyone on the street."

"That isn't possible, Judge."

"Why isn't it possible?"

"Because I only let him have five cartridges."

"I reckon we better go back to the ranch, before Oscar starts usin' up his allowance," said Danny seriously. "And please keep him away from Harper's Millinery Store, Henry," added Danny. "The last time Oscar got drunk he went over there and tried on six hats. Leila and her mother tried to get him to quit it, but he wouldn't budge. He said, 'Ay am tryin' to find purty hat for Yosephine. You see, any hat dat looks goot on me will be yust right for Yosephine.'"

"Did he buy one?" asked Judge.

"Can yuh imagine Oscar lookin' good in a woman's hat?"

"Or Josephine?" added Henry. "I could only imagine her, standing on the prow of a Viking ship, her yellow locks flailing in the wind. To my mind, she is wasted, making beds in the Tonto Hotel, or poking the muzzle of an insect gun into the folds of a mattress. She is a fit mate for a fighting Swede."

"And she'll get one, too—if she ever quits throwing chairs and crockery at Oscar," chuckled Judge. "The last time, she missed Oscar and crippled a traveling salesman. It cost the hotel ten dollars to square the fight. They tried to make Oscar pay the ten—for dodging—but he asked me for legal assistance, and I responded."

"I witnessed that scene," remarked Henry thoughtfully. "As a matter of fact, I do not believe she ever threw that chair at Oscar. That traveling salesman made a smart remark to Josephine as he came into the dining room. It requires considerable time for Josephine to digest any remark. She was very thoughtful for a time. At least time for the salesman to have forgotten her existence. Oscar merely happened to be standing in the line of fire.

"In the parlance of horseshoe pitching, it was a perfect ringer. The salesman staggered out of the dining room, with the back of the chair suspended around his neck, the seat of it dangling in front of him, and he was beating time on it with his fists, like a snare-drummer."

The two cowboys chuckled at Henry's description.

"We'll be going back now," said Danny. "Did that feller Werner come in to see yuh yet, Henry?"

"Not yet, Danny. Who is Werner?"

"He's that new butcher. He's tryin' to contract with several of the mines. He was goin' to talk prices with you. We might sell a lot of beef to him."

"I'll be looking for him, Danny."

AFTER THE two cowboys drove away, Judge opened the jug, and they each took a big drink.

"By gad, sir!" exploded Judge, half strangled, "that is liquor! It warms the cockles of one's heart."

Henry squinted thoughtfully, his lips puckered.

"Warms the cockles of one's heart, eh? It may warm the cockles of your heart, Judge; but that one drink cauterized a corn on my left foot. It is the compound tincture of red-hot pokers. Whew!"

Again they bowed to each other and drank again.

"Not bad at all, sir," admitted Henry. "It is like getting your head chopped off—it only hurts the first time."

"A grand boy, that Danny Regan," said Judge, apropos of nothing.

Henry nodded solemnly, his eyes squinted close, as he considered Judge for several moments.

"Aye, a grand boy," admitted Henry. "Judge, old friend, I have something to impart to you; something I have told no one as yet."

"Except to Mrs. Harper," corrected Judge soberly.

"Well, well!" Henry's solemn face became wreathed with smiles. "You guessed it, Judge?"

"Not exactly, Henry. I knew it was either an upset physical condition—or love. Your own remark settled the question. When is it to be?"

"You won't mention it to anyone, Judge?"

"I never betray a trust, sir."

"Well," smiled Henry, "we haven't set a date. We haven't even told Leila and Danny; but we hope to make it a double marriage."

"Wonderful! Henry, she is an estimable woman; I congratulate you."

"Thank you, Judge—thank you. I—I feel so damn foolish."

"Then you look exactly as you feel. Let us have a drink. Hold out your cup. Good. Well, sir—to an old fool."

"To you, Judge."

CHAPTER II

DEAD MAN'S SECRET

"**I'VE WAITED TWENTY** long years to kill you, Parke Neal; and now I find yuh dyin'. Damn yore soul, it ain't square. But you never did play square with me. Six hours late—after twenty years."

The scar-faced man's voice broke huskily, his gnarled fingers clutching his knees. In the dim lamplight that terrible scar looked like a fresh wound. The dying man, bearded and unkempt, his hands twisted in the clean sheet, blinked at the ceiling.

"I'll take yore word for who yuh say yuh are," he whispered hoarsely. "Things is kinda blurred. But you ain't Tom Silver. He had black hair, a handsome face. Wild Tom Silver. Where yuh been, Tom?"

"In the penitentiary, damn yuh. I follered yuh to Yuma—to kill yuh. I saw where yuh registered for a room; and I went to that room in the dark—and shot yuh full of holes. But I killed the wrong man, damn yuh. I killed the man in room twenty-eight—and you was in twenty-three."

The dying man closed his eyes for several moments, his brow knitted.

"I 'member," he whispered. "A man named Condon. But they said a man named—it wasn't Silver—"

"I never gave my right name. I didn't want anybody to know. Oh, I knew you was in love with my wife, Neal. I seen you give her money. I took it away from her and threw it in the street. Jack West knew I was goin' to kill you."

"You fool," whispered the dying man. "Jack West sent me to her, with the money. I never tried to steal yore wife. It was dog-cat-dog, after we found the Three Partners mine. West wanted it all—and mebbe I did, too. After you disappeared, me and West fought. He beat me out of my share, Tom; robbed me with crooked cards. But he's rich now, Tom. He owns most of the mines in this valley—owns everythin'."

"What about—the woman?" asked Silver. "Don't lie, Neal. There was to be a baby—soon. Don't lie to me. Where's the woman and the baby?"

"She's—she's—Hold me—up."

Tom Silver reached over quickly and lifted Neal's head and shoulders, but it was too late. The door opened, and Dr. Bogart came in.

"He jist died, Doc," said Silver.

The doctor made an examination, and drew the sheet over the dead man's face.

"I knew it was only a matter of a short time," he said. "He was badly broken—poor devil. And just when he had made his strike."

Silver looked quickly at the doctor. "Strike?" he said curiously.

"So he said. Perhaps it was an hallucination, caused by his accident. He said it would be worth millions; bigger than the Three Partners."

The doctor leaned over the bed and looked all around. "He wanted pencil and paper," he said. "Seemed to want to write something."

The oil lamp guttered smokily, and the doctor turned to the table. "I'll fill the lamp," he said, and went out.

Tom Silver stepped over to the bedside, pawing swiftly at the bedding. In the folds of a blanket he found two sheets of paper and a pencil. One sheet contained writing, but Tom Silver did not stop to read it. Tucking it in a pocket, he replaced the pencil and unused paper.

THE DOCTOR refilled the lamp, and found the paper and pencil. "Too badly injured to write," he remarked. "I—don't see how he lived as long as he did. But these old prospectors—"

Someone was knocking on the door.

"Come in," called the doctor.

The door swung open and a woman stepped inside.

She was tall and slender, shimmering with silk. The yellow lamplight glistened on the gold of her hair as she came forward. She was beautiful, in spite of her make-up. She glanced at the sheeted figure on the bed and shook her head.

"Dead?" she said throatily.

"He died a few minutes ago," replied the doctor.

The woman nodded slowly.

"I didn't know about it until a short time ago," she said.

"You knew him?" queried the doctor.

"I staked him twice," she said simply, turned and walked out, closing the door.

"Who is she, Doc?" asked Tom Silver.

"They call her Lola," replied the doctor. "She's—she sings—

and deals faro for the Tonto. They say she's hard as the devil. I don't know about that."

"She staked him twice," said Tom Silver. "She—she ain't very old, Doc."

"Too young to be doing what she's doing. It must be a hell of a life for a girl."

"That's right. Well, I'll be goin', Doc."

Tom Silver walked down the slope to the main street, where he entered the Tonto Saloon. The games were running full blast. Over at the long bar, a drunken miner was trying to sing to the music of a tinkling music-box. Silver sat down against the wall, hunched to a comfortable position, and drew out the crumpled paper he had filched from the dead man. The penciled scrawl read:

> I struck it rich, but Doc says I'm dying. I hereby give my mine to Lola, the faro dealer at the Tonto Saloon. It is located—

Parke Neal had died before telling where the mine was located. Perhaps his fingers had failed him, or he had forgotten. Tom Silver crumpled the paper in his hand, staring with unseeing eyes.

"Lola," he muttered. "Lola. That's what I called my wife."

With a trembling hand he shoved the paper deep in his pocket. Some men at the bar were talking about Parke Neal, and Tom Silver listened.

"I tell yuh, it's richer'n hell. They was some samples in his saddle bags. You talk about jewelry!"

"But where did he find it?" asked the bartender.

"Who knows?"

"Yuh could look for his recordin' and see."

"It ain't recorded. I'll betcha there's been a dozen men over at the recorder's office, tryin' to find out."

"Well, I'd shore like to see a vein as rich as the Three Partners. There was a mine for yuh."

"Don't I know it!" laughed a miner. "I've worked there. West sold it for over a million. Mebbe you fellers don't know it, but there's been bad blood between Neal and West for years. Neal was a partner of West, and Neal claimed West froze a deck of cards on him and beat him out of his share of the Three Partners."

"It wasn't that—not alone," chimed in another. "They had a lot of trouble over a woman."

"Who got the woman?" laughed the bartender.

"I dunno who got her. That's a hell of a long time to remember about another man's woman. Well, here's hopin' Parke Neal strikes it rich—wherever he's gone."

TOM SILVER walked out of the saloon. The stage from Scorpion Bend was just pulling into town, and Silver walked slowly up to the stage station, where a crowd usually collected to look over the new arrivals. Two huge lanterns lighted the front.

A huge, well-dressed man was on the seat with the driver. He was of middle age, but powerfully built, with a face as hard as carved granite. Tom Silver shoved in close to the front of the stage, looking square at the big man.

It was the supreme test. If Jack West could not recognize Tom Silver, no man could. For a moment the hard, gray eyes of Jack West searched the scarred face, but there was no sign of recognition. Twenty years in prison, plus a dynamite blast, had given Tom Silver a perfect disguise.

Jack West went straight to the Tonto Saloon, where he met Doc Sargent, and they went back to Sargent's private office. They had a drink of private stock liquor, and Sargent tossed a piece of ore on the desk in front of West, who examined it critically.

"Where did that come from, Doc?" asked West curiously.

"Do you remember Parke Neal?"

West's lips tightened for a moment.

"No need to ask me that question, Doc."

"Neal found that ore, West. He was smashed up in a blast, tried to get to a doctor, but fell off his horse along the road. A couple of cowboys from the J Bar C found him and brought him in here. Later some fellows found his horse, and that is one of the samples he had in his saddle bags."

"My God, Doc, that's rich stuff! Even a small vein—Wait! What about his mine—isn't it recorded?"

The dapper gambler shook his head slowly.

"That's the rub, West; he never recorded it. Never left a scrap of paper to show where it's located."

"He's dead, eh?"

Doc Sargent nodded. "Died less than an hour ago, over at Dr. Bogart's house. But here's something, West. Lola staked Neal. When she heard he was hurt, she slipped out of here and went up there. Whether she was there before he died, or not, I don't know."

"She staked him, eh?" mused West darkly.

"Twice, I believe."

West looked curiously at his boss gambler.

"Why did she stake him, Doc?"

"Oh, I don't know. Maybe she was playing a hunch. She has plenty of witnesses to the fact that she staked Neal. Unless the claim was recorded, she hasn't any legal right to it, of course."

"No claim in the world," said West coldly, as he examined the piece of ore again. "Look at the stuff, Doc! It's rotten with gold."

West laid the ore aside and helped himself to another drink.

"What else is new, Doc?" he asked.

"I damn near got killed today."

"You did? How'd that happen, Doc?"

The gambler told West about the poker incident, and what happened at the sheriff's office when he went to remonstrate with the sheriff.

"I've heard about that sheriff and his gang," said West. "They told me in Scorpion Bend that Tonto City had three of the craziest peace officers in Arizona."

Doc Sargent nodded gloomily. "And they can drink more liquor than any other three people in the State. The Swede gets wild; but the other two merely become more dignified and courteous."

"How in hell do they manage to operate their office?"

"Just about like they did today; drive you away with a bullet."

"Not so good," said West. "I'll be down here quite a lot now, Doc. I've got things workin' good at Maricopa; and I'll have more time. Maybe I'll have a little talk with this sheriff. He'd better understand that what goes on in here is none of his business; and if he don't keep his nose out of my business— there'll be a new sheriff."

CHAPTER III

BRASS KNUCKLES

IT WAS MID afternoon next day when Lola came to the Tonto. She did not go on shift until early in the evening. Men turned to stare at her, but she paid no attention. Doc Sargent was sitting alone at a table, staring moodily at an empty whisky glass on the table. He glanced up at Lola and motioned for her to sit down.

"You don't look very happy," she said quietly.

Doe smiled sourly and shook his head.

"Drinking whisky, too," observed the girl. "Rather unusual, isn't it, Doc?"

The handsome gambler laughed shortly. "I needed a bracer, Lola."

"Nerves?"

"Maybe. Yes, I guess it's nerves."

"Or," suggested Lola, "was it reaction from that shot yesterday?"

"No, it wasn't that."

Lola looked at him thoughtfully and a smile flashed across her eyes. "Not the little lady of the millinery—I hope."

Doc looked curiously at her.

"You hope?" he queried.

"So that *is* the reason. Yes, I have seen you over there. But isn't she engaged to marry that good-looking, red-headed cowboy? Danny Regan is the name, I believe?"

"Good-looking!"

"Well, he is good-looking; clean-looking, anyway. He has a wonderful smile—and how he can ride! I don't blame the little milliner."

"You're a lot of satisfaction," grunted Doc. "You wouldn't marry me, you know."

"Why should I marry you, Doc?"

"Oh, I don't know."

Doc Sargent looked narrowly at Lola for several moments.

"If you think this Danny Regan is so wonderful, why don't you take him yourself?" he asked.

"Take him?" Lola laughed heartily. "Doc, you talk as though such things were as easy as drawing a card off the deck. Anyway, the young man is engaged to marry a very charming young lady; so your question is answered."

"Neither of them means a thing to you, eh?"

"Certainly not. But why such a question, Doc?"

"Will you do me a favor, Lola?"

"That depends on the favor. What do you want?"

"I want that girl—Leila Harper. I want to marry her."

"Oh, I see-e-e. I suppose you want me to go over to her and tell her what a wonderful husband you would make."

"Hardly. I want you to make a play for Danny Regan."

"You want me to make a play—for Danny Regan?"

"That's it, Lola. If Leila even thought—"

"Hold it!" snapped Lola. "You're dealing off the bottom again, Doc. I see what you mean. My advice to you is to confine your crooked dealing to the poker table."

Doc Sargent flushed hotly.

"So you think I'm crooked, eh?" he sneered. "Listen to me! One word from me, and you'd lose your job so damn quick that—"

Lola laughed across the table at him.

"Try it, Doc," she said easily. "And after you've told Jack West that I wouldn't be a party to your crooked work—he might tell you that he pays me more salary than you are getting. Stick to cards, and leave love to—well, to people who don't deal cards."

BOTH OF them were so absorbed in their conversation that they had paid no attention to those about them. As Lola started to get to her feet she looked square into the eyes of Danny Regan. She and Danny had never exchanged a word. Danny rarely took a drink, and most of his gambling was confined to bunk-house games.

He was standing close behind Doc Sargent; and Lola had no idea how long he had been there.

"Thank yuh very much, ma'am," he said to her calmly.

Doc Sargent turned quickly in his chair and looked up at Danny. Doc prided himself on his poker-face, his steel nerves.

"Have a drink, Regan," he said calmly, and the next instant he was lifted bodily from the chair and slammed back against the table. Lola merely stepped back and said:

"Watch for that derringer—vest pocket."

"I got it the first grab," said Danny easily.

He whirled Sargent around, his left hand twisted in the gambler's collar, choking him.

Sargent was helpless, his hands clawing impotently at Danny's clenched left hand. The crowd was aware of the trouble, and came shoving in.

Danny merely gave them a sharp glance as he said, "Keep back—all of yuh; this is my job."

Danny did not see Jack West come from the rear of the room. He was behind Danny now, and his huge left fist smashed with stunning force against the side of Danny's head, knocking Danny almost into the crowd, where he sprawled on the floor, blood running from his face.

Doc Sargent was sprawling across the table, trying to pump air into his tortured lungs, while the crowd stood around and dumbly looked at Danny. Tom Silver was one of the crowd. West turned to the bartender and said:

"Throw some water on him and tell him to go home."

West turned, grasped Sargent by the arm, and led him back to the office, where he closed the door.

Danny was on his feet in a few minutes, but still dazed and bleeding. The bartender mopped him off with a wet towel.

"Ye felt the weight of Jack West's fist, me lad," said a grizzled miner. "Th' big felly hits ha-ard."

"Yuh don't need much weight to yore fist if yuh wear knucks," said Tom Silver.

Danny looked curiously at him. "So that's what cut me, eh?" he said.

"No fist was ever hard enough to gouge like that. Yuh better have the doctor fix yuh up."

Danny nodded and turned away. At the doorway he stopped and looked back. Lola was near the same spot, looking at him. He smiled weakly and lifted his hat before he went out.

Back in Sargent's office, Jack West sat down at the desk and watched the boss gambler pull himself together.

"Well, what started it?" asked West.

Doc's voice was husky as he replied painfully, "The damn fool cowpuncher! Lola and I were quarreling a little, and he took it upon himself to interfere."

"What were you quarreling about?"

"Oh"—Doc cleared his throat and smiled wryly—"she intimated that I was crooked. She made me mad."

"Mad?" West laughed. "That's like a kettle gettin' mad because yuh called it black. Don't quarrel with her any more. She's bringin' in the business—and she's a damn good faro dealer. Any mail come here for me?"

"In that top drawer, on the left side."

WEST JERKED the drawer out and removed several letters, which he glanced through quickly. One envelope was sealed, but not addressed.

"Is that yours?" he asked.

"Not mine," replied Doc Sargent.

West tore the envelope open and shook out a newspaper clipping. It was faded and yellow with age, bearing the date line of a small Eastern town. West was reading swiftly, and all the color seemed to drain from his hard features. Finally he clenched his jaw tightly and looked across the table at Sargent.

"You don't know where this came from?" he asked in a brittle voice.

"I never saw that blank envelope before," replied Sargent.

With a hand that trembled too much, West thought he returned the clipping to the envelope. Shoving the envelope into his pocket, he got to his feet.

"I'm goin' out to eat," he said, and walked out, closing the door.

The gambler stepped to the door, opened it a few inches, and saw West leave the saloon. Then he turned quickly, found the clipping under the desk, and proceeded to read:

> Officers are still searching for Handsome Jack West, who, it is alleged, beat his wife almost to death a week ago, and robbed her of eight thousand dollars, which she had received on a sale of her home.
>
> Since the murderous assault by her husband, Mrs. West has been confined to a local hospital, and the doctors fear that she

will be permanently crippled. Mrs. West has one child, by her former husband, Henry Woods.

Doc Sargent whistled softly to himself. There was nothing to show what year this happened, but the clipping was very old. He folded it carefully and placed it deep in his pocket. Sargent was not above blackmail; in case he needed a little extra power.

"Who in the devil ever put that in the desk?" he wondered, and helped himself to a big drink. "Anyway," he decided, "I better put it in a safe place right now."

Feeling very well satisfied with himself, in spite of a sore neck and a torn shirt, Doc Sargent sauntered out to the bar, where he had a drink. The bartender leaned across the bar, speaking confidentially with the boss gambler.

"Doc, who is that scar-faced hombre over there by the chuck-aluck table?"

"I don't know who he is. He sure carries a brand. What about him?"

"Oh, nothing much, except that he told Regan that West had on brass knuckles when he hit him."

Doc smiled thinly. "West usually wears 'em, I understand."

"I know—but this is different. West is used to fighting with miners. Cowboys don't take kindly to brass knuckles."

Doc shrugged his shoulders indifferently.

"What of it?" he asked.

"Nothing—mebbe. They tell me that Regan is a fast gunman."

"Well, that's no skin off my nose. What became of my der-ringer?"

"Regan got it."

"Quite a boy—this Regan," mused Doc thoughtfully.

JACK WEST came back to the Tonto and walked quickly through the big room, going straight back to the office. Doc Sargent's eyes narrowed as he watched the broad back of his employer disappear through the doorway. He turned back to the bar and was talking with the bartender when West came up to him.

"Come back to the office, Doc," he said.

West closed the office door and stepped over near the desk.

"You saw me take a newspaper clipping from an envelope a while ago, Doc," he said slowly, his eyes narrowed.

"Yes, I did," replied Doc. "You put it back in the envelope and put it in your pocket."

"You saw me do that?"

"Why—yes, I saw you. What about it, West?"

West turned and knelt down beside the desk, searching the floor. He opened desk drawers, examined them, and searched the floor of the little office. Finally he got to his feet and leaned against the desk, a puzzled frown between his hard eyes.

"That's damn funny," he muttered. "It's gone."

"Why, you put it in that envelope," said the gambler.

"I thought I did. Doc, I'd give a cold thousand dollars for that clipping—*and no questions asked.*"

"A thousand dollars? Well, let me take a look!"

Naturally, Doc's search was futile. Finally he dusted off his knees and looked curiously at Jack West.

"Is there some joke connected with it?" he asked.

"Joke?" West smiled bitterly. "Would I pay a thousand for a joke?"

"Were you serious about that thousand dollars?"

"Yo're damn right! And I'd murder the man who got it—if he ever tried to use it."

"Holy smoke!" exclaimed Doc. "Why, what on earth was it, West?"

West ignored the direct question.

"Who came in here, after I left?" he countered.

"No one, as far as I know, I followed you out."

"Don't you keep that door locked?"

"Not very often. I'll see if I can find out who came in here."

"Drop it. Mebbe I lost it on the street, and it blew away. I hope to God I did. I'll just have to wait—and see."

"If I knew what it was—" suggested Doc.

"If you knew what it was," said West slowly, "and I knew that you knew what it was—you wouldn't live to reach that door, Doc."

"Whew! Thank you for not telling me, West. But that don't show who put it in the desk."

West shook his head slowly, but his mind was working swiftly. Who was there in Tonto City with a knowledge of things that happened in that little Eastern town nearly twenty-five years ago? Who would preserve a clipping all these years, and drop it into his mail? And why? It was a chapter of his wild life that he thought closed years ago.

"I don't know who left it there," he replied wearily. "Forget it, Doc."

"You look kinda sick, West."

"I'm all right—forget it."

"I have a very poor memory," said Doc. "But just as a word of warning—keep an eye on Danny Regan. He knows you wore a pair of brass knucks—and they say he's a *muy malo hombre* with a six-gun."

"Aw, to hell with him!" rasped West. "I know how to handle his kind."

They walked out together, and West left the saloon. His stays in Tonto City had been very short; so he sauntered along the main street, getting familiar with the business places. West intended making Tonto City his headquarters in a short time.

He stopped near the show-window of Harper's Millinery, and was idly watching the street, when a movement in the window caused him to turn his head. Mrs. Harper had drawn back the curtain background, and was arranging some hats. Mrs. Harper had been a beautiful girl, and at middle age she was a handsome woman.

WEST STARED at her, his jaw slacked. It was his second shock of the day. As she lifted her head, he turned quickly away. But he got another good look at her before the curtains dropped into place. With a muttered curse on his lips, Jack West strode back to the saloon.

Doc Sargent was talking with Lola, but West called him back to the office.

"Did you find it?" queried Doc.

"No. What do you know about the Harper people—the hat store?"

Doc smiled sourly. "Not very much, West. Mother and daughter."

"Been here long?"

"Quite a few years, I believe. Lon Harper, the woman's husband, has been dead quite a while, I believe."

"Yo're doin' a lot of believin', Doc."

"Maybe I am. What else do you want to know?"

"How much of a business are they doin'?"

"I don't know that one," smiled Doc. "I suppose they are making a living."

West studied the situation grimly, but made up his mind soon.

"I'm goin' back to Maricopa," he said. "Find out what that woman will take for her business—and agree not to start another store in Tonto City. Don't let my name figure in it. Hell, buy it in your own name. We'll find somebody to take it over."

"In other words," smiled Doc, "you want to own an exclusive on all the millinery in Tonto City."

"Think what yuh please. Pay her more than she asks. *Get her out of Tonto City.*"

Doc Sargent went back to the bar and drank two straight whiskies in succession. The plot was getting too complicated for him. He saw Jack West leave on the northbound stage, and later in the evening, when business was dull, he went over to the faro layout to talk with Lola. By that time, Doc Sargent was half-drunk, which was unusual.

"The boss headed north again," he told Lola. She nodded indifferently, glancing around the room.

"Listen," said Doc confidentially. "How would you like to own a millinery store?"

"You are drunk," she replied bluntly. Doc laughed softly.

"Only half-drunk, my dear. Listen to this, will you? West ordered me to buy out the Harper store."

Lola looked at him curiously. "I suppose it's the whisky," she said.

"No, I'm not drunk. He really wants me to buy them out. He wants to get those two women out of Tonto City."

"Why?"

"Who knows? He told me to pay them more than the place is worth."

"What on earth would he do with a millinery store?"

"Well, he said we could find somebody to take it over."

"That should be easy—in a boom town like this. But why does he want to get those two women out of town?"

"Lola," said Doc easily, "just between you and me, I believe the big boss has a skeleton in his closet—and it has began to rattle a little."

She smiled at him and shook her pretty head.

"I still think you are drunk, Doc."

"You do, eh? Well, I can show you—" Doc hesitated. He was very near to telling her about the newspaper clipping.

"You can show me what?" queried Lola.

"Nothing. Maybe I have had a little too much. Anyway, I guess I better open a game; the poker players are drifting in."

CHAPTER IV

TOUGH LIVER

IT WAS TWO nights after Jack West had gone back to Maricopa. Henry Harrison Conroy, Judge Van Treece and Danny Regan were having supper at the Harper home, which was the rear half of the building used as a millinery shop. Henry, shaved and polished, especially his nose, and with a napkin tucked inside his collar, smiled expansively at the array of well-cooked viands.

The left side of Danny's head was still swollen, and plentifully decorated with court-plaster. No one had told Leila and her mother about the trouble at the Tonto, and they believed Danny had been kicked by a horse.

"Ah-h-h-h!" exclaimed Henry softly. "The odors of Araby. My dear Laura, sit down, so we may form a line of direct attack."

"In moderation, Henry," warned Judge. "Remember what the merchant told you? Nothing in waist measurements above a forty-six."

"Henry is not a forty-six," declared Mrs. Harper.

"Quite correct, Mrs. Harper," replied Judge. "That horse-blanket safety-pin is approximately six inches in length, which gives an additional five inches, at least; and the man continually complains of a tightness around his abdomen."

"That is slander, sir," declared Henry soberly. "I, fifty-one inches around the waist? Absurd!"

"Merely a fallen chest," said Danny.

"Or a bosom, which failed to rise—like Frijole Bill's biscuits," laughed Henry. "Laura, my dear, do not let Judge have that carving-knife! That man is positively penurious in carving a roast. At times, I feel that he received his law training in a barber college. A slice of rare, roast beef must be at least one-half inch thick"

"Oh, very well," sighed Judge, relinquishing the knife to Mrs. Harper. "We can alter the size of the office doorway, I suppose."

"You take a weight off my mind, Judge," smiled Henry.

The dinner, as usual, was a huge success. Henry finished a big slice of apple pie, and leaned back in his chair.

"Just at present," he stated, "I am looking at the trouble of the world through the small end of a telescope."

Danny Regan was unusually quiet during the meal; so quiet that Leila looked curiously at him several times.

"Aren't you feeling well, Danny?" she asked.

"Shore, I'm feelin' all right."

"You've been so quiet."

"With Henry and Judge here, who could get in a word?"

"By the way," said Mrs. Harper, "we have had a strange offer."

"Strange offer?" queried Henry. "An offer for what, my dear?"

"For our millinery business."

"My goodness! Someone wants to buy you out?"

Mrs. Harper nodded seriously. "A gambler wants to buy the shop."

"Heavens above!" exclaimed Henry. "What is happening to the world?"

Danny's eyes narrowed, as he looked at Leila and her mother.

"Mr. Sargent wants to buy it," said Mrs. Harper. "He came yesterday, and said he would be willing to pay us a top price, if we would agree to not open another shop in Tonto City. He wants the exclusive hat business of the town."

DANNY LAUGHED harshly. "What would that tin-horn know about the millinery business?"

"He is likely buying it for someone else," said Judge. "With the town booming, I suppose the hat business will also boom. My advice to you would be to make him pay enough to make it worth while."

"The business is getting better," said Leila. "Our stock is worth very little, and we rent this building; so I don't see where we could make enough on a sale to do us much good. Mother and I do not want to leave Tonto City—and this is a good living."

"Did he make any offer?" asked Henry.

"No, he merely said he would pay us more than the place is worth."

"I imagine that two hundred dollars would cover the stock."

"It would more than cover it," admitted Mrs. Harper.

"And you rent the building, which could not figure on the deal. I believe that forty-eight hundred would cover the good-will. Yes, my dear, I believe a price of five thousand would be reasonable and fair."

"Five thousand!" exclaimed Mrs. Harper. "No one, with any sense, would pay that price."

"My dear Laura, I do not consider Mr. Sargent as a brainy man. He is very nimble with his fingers—very. And anyway," Henry smiled slyly, "I should hate to see a man milliner in a town like this."

"I don't know whether Mother understood, or not," said Leila, "but Mr. Sargent intimated that, in case of a sale, we were to leave Tonto City."

"Leave Tonto City!" Henry was indignant. "The very idea! Leave Tonto City, indeed! I've a notion to go over there and—Laura, my dear woman, your selling price is twenty thousand dollars."

Mrs. Harper laughed and began clearing away the dishes.

"I am afraid that even a gambler would refuse to pay that price," she said.

"No doubt of it," agreed Henry heartily, "but it might serve to smoke an Ethiopian out of the wood-pile."

Danny leaned across the table toward Henry.

"Do yuh think there's some real reason behind this offer—except to get the shop, Henry?" he asked.

"Danny, my boy," smiled Henry, "when tin-horn gamblers develop ambition along millinery lines, it is time for all men to come to the aid of their sex. Laura, may I handle this deal?"

"I wish you would, Henry; I don't know what to say about prices."

Danny went back to the office with them. He had told Henry all about what had happened to him in the Tonto Saloon. Judge knew about it, too; and the three of them sat in the office, trying to puzzle out Doc Sargent's reasons for wanting the millinery shop.

"You are not worrying about Leila, are you, Danny?" asked Henry.

"Well, I ain't very pleased about that slick-haired gambler hangin' around there. He wanted to take her to Scorpion Bend to a dance, and she turned him down. That was when he tried to make that deal with the lady faro dealer. Henry, he's as crooked as a snake; and I don't like this deal he's tryin' to make. He's got some scheme up his sleeve."

"Let me handle the deal, Danny. And don't worry about Leila."

Judge tilted forward in his chair, listening intently. It sounded as though several people were stumbling along the wooden sidewalk, coming toward the office.

"What in the world is coming?" exclaimed Judge.

A MOMENT later Oscar Johnson came stumbling through the doorway, dragging a miner, who was almost as large as Oscar. He dumped the man in the middle of the floor; dusted off his hands and stepped back. The man's left eye was swollen shut, his nose looked like an over-ripe tomato, and there was a lump on the side of his head as large as an egg.

"What on earth happened to him?" asked Henry.

"Das ha'ar yigger," stated Oscar, "vars dasturbing de peace."

"Disturbing the peace," parroted Henry. "Oh, I see."

"Ay vant him arrested; so Ay can put him in de yail."

"I see-e-e," nodded Henry. "Disturbing the peace, and you want to put him in jail. Just whose—er—peace did he disturb, Oscar?"

"Yosephine's."

"Josephine's, eh? He disturbed her peace—and you beat him up."

"Ay did not beat him oop," declared Oscar soberly.

"You didn't? Well, who did?"

"Yosephine."

The culprit stared around, felt tenderly of his sore head.

"What the hell's goin' on around here, anyway?" he asked hoarsely.

"My dear man," replied Henry, "you are charged with disturbing the peace."

"Huh?"

"Of course, you remember disturbing it, don't you?"

"Disturbin' what? My Gawd, what happened to me, anyway?"

Henry turned to Oscar. "What started this trouble, Oscar?"

"Va'l oll I know is vat Yosephine ta'l me. She say dis yigger coom in and set down at table, and den he say, 'Seester, how is your liver tonight?'"

"That's what I said," groaned the injured man. "Sometimes it's good and sometimes it ain't good. Hell, ain't a feller got any rights in this country? I reckon she'd 'a' killed me, if I'd asked about roast beef—I dunno."

"Case dismissed," declared Judge. "This court decides that the man has been sufficiently punished for trying to eat liver in that hotel dining room. I've tried it—and I know. The case is dismissed."

The big miner got slowly to his feet, scowled at Oscar and clenched his fists, but changed his mind and went stumbling out of the office.

"Well, what do you think of that?" breathed Danny.

"Va'l," sighed Oscar, "Ay lost my first customer."

"Oscar," said Judge, his eyes full of tears, "the peace of Tonto City is very, very hard to disturb."

"Ay skal ta'l you, Yudge," admitted Oscar soberly.

Tom Rickey, owner of the hotel, came hurrying into the office, half out of breath.

"What became of that big miner?" he asked anxiously.

"Do you mean the one with the liver trouble?" asked Henry.

"I mean the one Oscar took out of the hotel."

"Oh—that one. I suppose he went back to the Tonto Saloon."

Rickey turned to Oscar. "What on earth happened?" he asked.

"Das ha'ar faller got smort vit Yosephine."

"I see. Do you know who he is?"

"Ay have no idea."

"That man is Lars Swenson, said to be the heavyweight champion of Minnesota."

Oscar gawped blankly at Rickey for a moment.

"Is das man a Svede?"

"Norwegian, I believe."

"Yah, su-ure. Yust a dumb Norvegian. He better stay in Minnesota and fight Norvegians. Where de ha'al is dat yug of prune yuice? Ay feel like big drink."

CHAPTER V

NICK BORDEN

"**SO YOU WANT** a job as a swamper, eh?"

Doc Sargent leaned against the bar in the Tonto Saloon, and looked curiously at Tom Silver.

"I've got to eat," replied the scar-faced Silver.

"Why don't you get out and take a man-sized job?"

"I'm askin' for the only job I'm qualified to do well," replied Silver. Doc laughed and looked around the nearly empty room.

"All right. Forty a month and six drinks a day. What's your name?"

"Just call me Tom; I forgot the rest."

"All right," laughed Doc, and turned to see Henry Harrison Conroy, the sheriff, coming into the room.

"How are you, Sheriff?" he asked pleasantly. "Ripping, I hope."

Henry flinched and looked down at his waist-line.

"Not as yet," he smiled. "This man, Levi, who tailors most of the trousers worn in this country, has slim ideas."

Doc laughed and nodded to the bartender to serve them.

"I am on a little matter of business, Mr. Sargent," said Henry.

"Business?"

"Yes. Quite out of my line as a stalwart bulwark of the law, I assure you. I believe you approached Mrs. Harper, and suggested that she sell you her millinery business."

"Something like that," admitted Doc. "You don't happen—"

"My dear, sir, I never happen," interrupted Henry. "As a matter of fact, Mrs. Harper has asked me to negotiate with you. Perhaps we may arrive at some price satisfactory to all concerned."

"Well," Doc smiled slowly, "we might."

"I hope," added Henry. "Of course, the location is rented; so we may count that out of any deal we make. The stock and fixtures will amount to about two hundred dollars. Does that sound fair?"

"Do you mean that two hundred dollars is the price?"

"Oh, not at all. Business is booming, Mr. Sargent. It is the only millinery business in this town. I estimate that the good will of the place is worth nineteen thousand, eight hundred dollars. Making a grand total of twenty thousand dollars—full price."

Doc had lifted his glass, but now he placed it on the bar and looked queerly at Henry.

"Are you crazy?" he asked.

"I am not exactly certain," replied Henry thoughtfully.

"Why, I could buy the whole town for twenty thousand dollars."

"You could—once," corrected Henry. "Right now, prices are very high. Well, here is to you, sir."

Doc Sargent drank quickly, and sent his glass spinning down the polished bar-top.

"Are you serious?" he asked.

"I am fifty-five years of age, and I have never been more serious in my whole life."

"I guess the deal is off," said Doc.

"I am perfectly satisfied," nodded Henry. "Good-day, sir."

AS HE turned to walk away, a man came into the saloon. He was tall, swarthy and handsome, dressed entirely in black, from his patent-leather boots to his big Stetson sombrero. His black hair was brushed with silver at the temples.

Doc Sargent had walked away from the bar, but had turned and was staring at the tall newcomer. Finally he said:

"So you are the Borden who bought the Smoke Tree mine, eh? *Nick* Borden. I wondered."

The tall man laughed, showing a flash of white teeth.

"Why not, Doc?" he asked casually. "Any law against it?"

"No, I guess not, Nick. Did somebody salt it on you?"

"No, I don't reckon so. If they did, they sure salted it deep, because we've opened a mighty rich vein today. Call up the boys—and girls, too. I'm buyin' the drinks."

"All right, Nick; that's fine. Say, I want you to meet Henry Conroy, the sheriff. Sheriff, this Nick Borden."

Borden gave Henry's hand a hearty shake.

"I've heard about you, Conroy," he boomed. "We'll probably see a lot of each other."

"Very likely," said Doc dryly.

Borden gave Doc a sharp glance, and his lips tightened for a moment. The crowd was moving in for a free drink, and Borden laughed softly as he turned to face the bar.

"This is on Nick Borden," announced Doc. "They've just made a strike on the Smoke Tree."

"Forget the strike," said Borden. "I'm merely buyin' a drink."

AFTER THE drink, Henry slipped quietly out and went to the office, where he found Judge half-asleep at the desk.

"Did you make a sale?" queried Judge.

"I made very little progress," admitted Henry, sitting down on Oscar Johnson's cot.

"Did you find out anything?"

"Yes, I found one thing, Judge."

"What was that, Henry?"

"That I am crazy."

"Well—of course," nodded Judge.

"Kind of you," sighed Henry. "Judge, in your migrations over this land of wide-open spaces, did you ever hear of a man named Nick Borden?"

"Eh? Nick Borden? Why, yes, I have, Henry. In fact—What about him?"

"I just met him at the Tonto. He owns the Smoke Tree mine."

"Well, well! So he's a mine owner. The last time—Let me see-e-e. It was twelve years ago that I defended him. Yes, I believe it was. He was charged with train robbery. Cleared him with a perfect alibi. The day after the robbery, he spent the day with an ignorant old German who was working on a prospect.

"Impressing the old man with the fact that it was Sunday, they spent the day playing cards and drinking Nick's whisky. The German swore to this in court, and Nick was acquitted, because it would have been impossible for him to have robbed the train and still be at the German's claim on Sunday.

Luckily"—Judge smiled slowly—"no one thought to ask the German how he knew it was Sunday."

"In that event," mused Henry, "I do not believe that Mr. Borden will improve the morals of Tonto City."

"Nor corrupt them," added Judge. "As a matter of fact, where are the morals of Tonto City, Henry? Are they something like a flag, which is paraded on the Fourth of July, and fed to the moths the rest of the year? Consider Mr. West, who is destined to be our leading citizen. He became wealthy through—hm-m-m-m. Henry, that poor devil of a prospector who blasted himself off this mortal coil was named Parke Neal, was he not? Parke Neal. Why, damn it, Henry, that same Parke Neal was Jack West's partner in the Three Partners mine!"

"Am I supposed to say 'Ah-h-h-h!' and show my tonsils?" queried Henry.

"That's true—you wouldn't know," replied Judge soberly. "There was a third partner, too. It is rather vague, after twenty years, but there was a third partner. I believe he disappeared—in some way.

"Rumor has it that West forced Neal to play poker for the Three Partners and stacked the deck. West made a million or so. Apparently no one in the country knew anything about the richness of the Three Partners until West made the sale."

"A great mind—apparently," observed Henry.

"Don't forget that cold deck."

"True—we must not forget that cold deck."

"And," added Judge, "unless my memory plays me false, there is no love lost between Jack West and Nick Borden. Borden is not a mining man. At least, I never heard that he was."

"As far as that is concerned," replied Henry, "if you were to ask any member of the theatrical profession their opinion of me as a sheriff—and yet, I am a sheriff, you know, Judge."

"And," observed Judge, "as far as that is concerned, why bother searching for one of your former profession? Query any man in this county."

"Am I *that* bad, Judge?"

"I never like to flatter any man," replied Judge. "But, Henry, you are, or have been, referred to as the Shame of Arizona. They say you can't ride, you can't shoot—Well, why go any further?"

"In other words?" queried Henry soberly.

"They are laughing at you, sir."

"The bad men, too, Judge?"

"Every last one of them."

"At last!" exclaimed Henry. "For fifty years I tried to make the world laugh. I never was a real success, no matter how hard I tried. And now, in the late autumn of my life, I find myself cast in a real comedy rôle. I am merely Henry Harrison Conroy, sheriff of Tonto—and the whole damn State of Arizona is laughing. I am a success!"

"Henry, have you been at that jug of prune juice?" asked Judge.

"Not even once—but I have a distinct leaning, Judge."

"I feel myself about to gravitate," said Judge. "Frijole did well on that last batch."

NICK BORDEN sat at a rough table in his cabin at the Smoke Tree, a solitaire layout spread before him. A half-smoked cigar was clenched between his white teeth, a scowl between his eyes. Placing the deck of cards on the table, he leaned back in his chair, looking at the closed door. There was a Colt revolver on the table, and after a moment of indecision he placed the gun beside his right thigh, where it was partly covered by the rough cushion.

"Bring him in!" he called curtly.

The door swung open to admit Tom Silver, the scar-faced man, while behind him came a tall, hard-faced man, dressed in rough cowboy clothes, who had a gun in his right hand.

Borden looked sharply at the scar-faced man, indicated a chair, and motioned for the other man to stay at the door.

Tom Silver sat down. "What's the idea of the gun-play?" he

asked. "I walk up here to yore cabin, and get a gun stuck in my ribs."

Nick Borden laughed shortly.

"Yo're the swamper at the Tonto, I believe. I couldn't very well mistake that face."

"I didn't come here to talk about my face, Borden."

"You work for Jack West."

"Suppose I do—what of it?"

"Sort of a tough hombre, eh? Yuh better cool off—this ain't the Tonto."

"I don't like to have guns stuck in my ribs."

"Then keep away from places where yo're not wanted."

"I might be wanted here, Borden."

"Yuh might, eh? Just what the hell did yuh come here for; and who are yuh?"

The scar-faced Silver looked keenly at Borden for moments.

"Borden, do you remember the old days around Maricopa—twenty years ago?"

"Twenty years ago? Suppose I do."

"Do yuh remember Tom Silver?"

"Tom Silver? Silver. Why, yeah, I remember there was a Tom Silver. Disappeared, if I remember correctly. What about him, feller?"

"I'm Tom Silver."

NICK BORDEN leaned forward, looking keenly at Silver's face. "What's the joke?" he asked.

"Joke?"

"Yeah—joke. You're no more Tom Silver than I am."

"Do you remember what Silver looked like?"

"Well, kinda."

"Uh-huh. 'Bout my size, black hair, good-lookin'."

"Yeah, that's right, feller. Thinkin' about him causes me to remember him pretty well. Yeah, he had black hair—and if I remember correctly, he was good-lookin'. What's yore game, feller?"

"I'm Tom Silver. No, wait a minute. I went to the penitentiary for twenty years, Borden. A dynamite blast almost killed me. We was doin' some prison road work. That twenty-year stretch ain't no fountain of youth—and when yuh add a dynamite blast in yore face—"

"What was you sent up for?"

"Murderin' a man named Condon, in Yuma."

"Condon? Condon. It seems to me that I remember somethin' about that. But yore name wasn't connected with it—not Tom Silver."

"I went by the name of Tom Jones."

"I see," muttered Borden thoughtfully. "But what are yuh doin' here, Silver; and why come to me?"

"I came here to kill Parke Neal."

"The hell yuh did! Well, a dynamite blast—"

"I know; I was there when he died."

"This is all Greek to me, Silver. Why did you want to kill Neal?"

"I thought I was shootin' Neal—when I shot Condon. I thought Neal was stealin' my wife—there in Maricopa. I reckon Neal told me the truth, when he was dyin'. It wasn't Neal—it was Jack West."

"It's beginnin' to get a little clearer, Silver. So West stole yore wife. Has he still got her?"

"I don't know," replied Silver grimly.

"Figurin' on killin' Jack West?"

"Not until I've made him pay me damn well."

"Oh, he owes yuh somethin', does he?"

"Listen to me, Borden. I happen to know that yo're no friend to Jack West. If yuh was, I wouldn't be here. Remember the Three Partners mine?"

"Who doesn't—in this State?"

"Me and Parke Neal and Jack West discovered that mine, Borden. That is, me and Neal found it; West was too damn lazy to prospect. We was down to our last dollar when we struck it. My wife was in Maricopa, and a baby was comin' soon. We sent West out to record the claim. He got drunk and didn't show up; so we finished the grub and came back.

"I reckon I had too many drinks, and I went home, where I seen Parke Neal give my wife two hundred dollars. They didn't know I seen 'em. I tore the money out of my wife's hands and went out of there, trailin' Parke Neal. He went to Yuma, and I follered. Well, I killed the wrong man—and got caught.

"Borden, Neal told me that West stole his interest in that mine. I've been to Maricopa, and I've seen that old record. Jack West recorded it in his name alone. Damn him, he not only stole my wife, but he stole my third of the Three Partners mine."

"Well, that's quite a story," said Borden slowly. "I've often wondered where West got the name for that mine. Three Partners. You and Neal and West. And yo're workin' for West now."

"I'm as close to him as I can get, Borden."

"I see. But just why did you come to me, Silver?"

"I jist figured that we might be able to help each other."

Borden laughed shortly.

"How could you help me?" he asked curiously.

"By workin' for a man you don't like, Borden. Oh, I know; you're a mine owner—and all that. But you never came to Wild Horse Valley to dig rocks. If yuh happen to need me—or information—I'll be down there rasslin' spittoons and sweepin' up torn cards. *Adios.*"

BORDEN NODDED to the tall cowboy, who stepped aside and let Tom Silver out. Borden looked curiously at the cowboy and smiled thoughtfully.

"I'd shore hate to have a face like that," said the cowboy.

"Yeah, it would be kinda unfortunate," agreed Borden.

"Did yuh believe his story, Nick?"

"Sure; I knew most of it."

Borden swept up the solitaire layout and shuffled the cards slowly.

"Lobo," he said, "I never expected to have a man workin' for Jack West—not even a swamper. *Viva la escupidera!*"

The tall cowboy laughed as he started to roll a cigarette. "I've heard the Mexes cheer 'most everythin', but that's the first *viva* I've ever heard for a cuspidor."

Borden laughed and tossed the cards aside.

CHAPTER VI

JAILER'S WOE

JACK WEST DROVE in from Scorpion Bend that night and arrived in Tonto City about midnight. Doc Sargent turned his game over to another gambler and went into conference with his boss.

"What about that millinery store?" asked West abruptly.

"Twenty thousand dollars," replied Doc. West snorted aloud.

"Mrs. Harper turned the deal over to the sheriff," explained Doc, "and the damn fool made me that price."

"Is the man crazy, Doc? Twenty thousand! Why, the place ain't worth five hundred."

"Two hundred," said Doc. "That's what Conroy said; but the price is still twenty thousand dollars. You could get another building and open—"

"You fool!" snapped West. "I don't want the business."

"I see-e-e," murmured Doc wisely. "You want those two women to get out of Tonto City."

"And that's as far as you need to see, Doc."

"All right," smiled Doc. "But I was wondering if *they* happen to know what you want. That's a pretty stiff price, West."

*Oscar threw West
into the street.*

West glowered, chewing savagely on his cigar.

"What else is wrong around here?" he asked roughly.

"Oh, I guess everything is all right. Business is fine. I suppose you know that Nick Borden bought the Smoke Tree Mine."

"Nick Borden? Is that—you say he bought the Smoke Tree?"

Doc Savage nodded. "That's what he announced in here. He set 'em up to the house, in celebration of a rich strike."

"In the Smoke Tree? Hell, there ain't an ounce of gold in that whole hill. I had experts go over it with a fine-tooth comb."

"Even an expert can be mistaken, I suppose," remarked Doc.

"That's possible; but improbable. Nick Borden owns it, does he?"

"Yes, he bought it from the Rice brothers. I don't know what he paid—he didn't say."

"You bet he didn't! Do yuh know if anybody has been tryin' to find Parke Neal's prospect?"

"Haven't heard a thing about it. Everybody seems to think that Neal was dynamite-crazy; imagined he'd struck it rich."

"I'll put a couple of the boys on that job. They should be able to trace the prospect down. Somebody must have known where he was workin'. I wonder if he told Lola where the mine was located."

"I don't believe he did."

"Has yore friend Regan been in since I socked him?"

"No, he's kept away from here," laughed Doc. "Are you goin' back tonight?"

"I reckon I'll stay here tonight, and have a talk with that fool sheriff in the mornin'. Another thing, Doc; don't forget that I'll give a thousand dollars for that newspaper clippin'—and no questions asked."

"Well, you don't think I've got it, do you?" asked Doc indignantly.

"You're still alive, Doc," replied West. "That answers yore question."

"And no questions asked," mused Doc, after West had left the office. "The man who claimed the reward wouldn't live long. I believe that little clipping is worth many times that amount—and Doc Sargent is going to collect—sometime."

JACK WEST strolled through the gambling room, and entered the honkytonk. Possibly fifty men were in there, drinking and listening to the very rough brand of vaudeville. Lola sang her song, and came back from the stage, meeting West near the door.

"Yore voice was beautiful tonight, Lola," he told her.

"I suppose it is improving," she said. "Whiskey fumes and tobacco smoke are wonderful for the voice."

"Yeah, I reckon it is a little thick in here."

West studied her closely for several moments, his eyes narrowed.

"Doc Sargent wanted to marry you once, didn't he, Lola?"

"Something like that," she replied. "What about it?"

"He's still crazy about yuh, ain't he?"

Lola laughed softly as she rested her chin on her hands, paste-jewels glinting in the lamplight when she leaned her elbows on the green table-top.

"I'm afraid Doc is very fickle," she said, "just now he is crazy about that Harper girl, the daughter of the milliner."

West's eyes widened. "He is, eh? The Harper girl. I don't suppose you care, eh?"

"I'd hate to see him get her—for her sake."

"Lola," said West quietly, "I'm goin' to make you a proposition. Yo're the kind who can keep a shut mouth. A few days ago I lost a newspaper clippin'—lost it in the office, I'm sure. Doc was there when I lost it. I don't care how you do it—I want results—and I want to know if Doc has that clippin'. If he has, and I can get it, I'll give you five thousand dollars."

Lola looked curiously at Jack West.

"Doc is your boss gambler, and manager of this place; don't you trust him?"

"Lola, a man who has bucked the games that I've bucked don't trust neither man nor woman. Will yuh help me? You could use five thousand dollars, I reckon."

"I think I could," she replied thoughtfully. "I've never had that much money in my life, and never expect to have that much. It seems to me that if Doc has that clipping, he'd be willing to *find* it for five thousand dollars."

"There are things that you don't understand, Lola. If I *knew*

Doc had that clippin', I'd kill Doc. He knows it—and that's why he'll never find it."

Her brows lifted slightly as she said:

"At that rate, I'd be afraid to handle it myself."

"I don't ask you to handle it, Lola. All I'm askin' you to do is to find out if Doc has it—or had it. Use your own way to get this information—and you'll get the money—in good American gold."

"I see. I don't have to recover the clipping. All I have to do is to find out if Doc has it."

"That's all. If he's got it cached, I don't care whether I get it or not—as long as nobody else does."

West offered to buy Lola a drink, but she declined, because she never drank.

"You're a queer one," West told her. "But I'm glad you don't drink. Play the game with me, kid, and some day you may be runnin' this place."

THE EARLY morning activities of Tonto City had started when Josephine Swensen and Oscar Johnson, squeezed together in the rather small seat of a top buggy, drove into town. They were on their way back from the regular Friday night dance at Scorpion Bend.

Josephine was over six feet tall, and would weigh about a hundred and eighty. She was well past the thirty milestone of life. Her hair was a stringy blond, her face large, with prominent cheek-bones, little blue eyes and a large nose. Her small hat, with one huge rooster-feather sticking straight up the back, was poised over one eye as they drove up to the front of the Tonto Hotel.

Henry and Judge, on their way to the office, stopped to see the arrival of their jailer and his lady-love. Josephine got out, unassisted, turned, grasped the top of the front wheel of the buggy, and talked earnestly to Oscar, who sat there, looking straight ahead. Then she turned around and walked stiffly, haughtily, into the hotel.

Oscar merely turned his eyes and watched her enter the lobby. Then, without any warning, he emitted a shrill war-whoop, which could be heard all over Tonto City. The frightened horse leaped wildly, fairly jerking all four wheels of the buggy off the ground, and broke into a swift gallop down the street.

Less than two blocks beyond the hotel was the livery stable, with its broad plank incline which led up to the wide doorway. The equipage whirled past Judge and Henry, and Judge gasped:

"My God, he's only got one line!"

But apparently one line was sufficient, and luckily it was the right line. The running horse was yanked to the right, the buggy skidded sideways, almost overturning, and the runaway shot up that plank incline at top speed, the buggy rebounding so high at the top that the top of the buggy hit the cross timbers.

There was a heavy crash, the squeal of a frightened horse, followed by minor crashes and thumps.

"If he isn't killed—" gasped Judge.

But Oscar appeared at the doorway, as unconcerned as ever. He dusted the palms of his hands on his thighs, turned his head slightly as he spoke to someone in the stable.

"Yah, su-u-ure," he said. "Ay alvays have good time."

"Killed!" snorted Henry. "Judge, when Gabriel blows his horn, someone will have to shoot Oscar, in order to make it unani-mous."

"I can believe it, Henry. The man is impervious to harm."

THEY JOINED Oscar at the office door, and he grinned foolishly at them. Following them in, he sank down on his cot and proceeded to remove a pair of pointed-toe shoes, which were at least one size too small. Sighing with relief, he sank back and heaved a deep sigh, which seemed to come from the very depths of his soul.

"Yosephine and me have bruk oop," he stated.

"Again?" said Henry.

"Yah, su-u-ure. She say das is de end of everyt'ing, because she say Ay hu-meel-iated her too damn many times."

"It seems that you simply cannot be a gentleman," said Judge.

"Yentleman?"

"Yes, Oscar," interposed Henry. "You never treat Josephine as a gentleman should treat a lady. You are entirely lacking in the finer instincts. You are entirely too much of a swashbuckler."

"Ay am yust a Svede; and Ay am no swishbockler, Ay ta'l you. And Ay am yust as much of a yentleman as I ever vars."

"Granted," said Henry. "Just as much, Oscar. But what happened to humiliate Josephine?"

Oscar scratched his head violently for several moments.

"Ay am not yust sure. Ve had ha'al of a good time—Ay did. A big Svede from Silver City vants to dance oll de time with Yosephine, and Ay got mad as ha'al. He is oll dressed oop in a fancy suit. It got hot as ha'al in de dance hall, and de Svede took off his coat.

"Ay said to Yosephine, 'Don't forget who brought you ha'ar,' and she says, 'Ay am doing my best.'

"Va'l, Ay vent out and took a couple drinks, and come back. She is dancing with the Svede again; so Ay vent out on de floor, and Ay valk oop behind dem. Ay grab de Svede by de vaist of his fancy pants, and Ay says, 'Coom ha're to me!' and Ay storts for de stairs. Ay vars going to throw dis Svede down de stairs, and ven Ay got to de stairs, oll I've got is pair pants."

Henry leaned over his desk, choking violently, while Judge hammered him on the back with both hands, tears running down his cheeks.

"I suspect he had on red flannels, too," gasped Henry.

"Yah, su-u-ure," agreed Oscar, "but most of dem came off with dem pants. Oll he had left vars his shirt and his boots."

"And you don't know what humiliated Josephine," panted Henry.

"Ay am not sure. Ay guess it vars because Ay bruk up de dance."

"Well, did you give the pants back to their owner?" asked Judge.

"Yah, su-ure. Ay can't vare 'em. Anyvay Ay vant my pants all in one piece."

Oscar spat copiously and looked inquiringly at Henry.

"Is dere any of de prune yuice left?" he asked.

"Back there in one of the cells, Oscar," replied Henry hoarsely.

Oscar surged off the cot and went into the jail corridor, closing the door behind him.

"And so," said Henry, his eyes flooded with tears, "endeth the chapter entitled, 'The Love of Josephine and Oscar.'"

Judge nodded, being quite unable to talk for the moment. A step at the front door caused them to turn. It was Jack West, looking very severe.

"**WELCOME TO** the sheriff's office, Mr. West," greeted Judge huskily. "You have met Mr. Conroy, the sheriff, have you not?"

West's smile was slightly sarcastic, as he nodded briefly.

"I just dropped in to have a word with Mr. Conroy," he said.

Henry leaned forward in his chair, looking Jack West over, from boots to sombrero. West flushed slightly under the scrutiny.

"Somethin's wrong with my clothes?" he asked curiously.

"No," replied Henry, "I was merely wondering where you carry your brass knuckles, Mr. West."

"Just wonderin', eh?"

"Naturally. In my opinion they are about the lowest type of fighting weapons; and I would have you know, sir, that this office does not approve of their use in Tonto City."

Judge looked aghast at Henry Harrison Conroy. West shoved his hands in his pockets, and stood there, swaying on his feet, his lips closed tightly, as he looked at Henry.

"Yuh don't, eh?" he said harshly. "Well, it just happens that I don't care what you like, Conroy; and I didn't come here to listen to your likes and dislikes."

"I merely wanted you to understand our attitude in the matter," said Henry. "No offense, I hope."

"That don't interest me even a little bit. Right now I'm interested in buyin' some of the business places of Tonto City. Doc Sargent tells me that you're handlin' any deal that might be made for that female hat-shop."

"I made a price to Doc Sargent," nodded Henry.

"Yeah, I know. But what is the price?"

"Twenty-five thousand dollars."

"Twenty-five thousand, eh? Raisin' the ante, eh?"

"Yes."

"Conroy, what's yore game?"

"I haven't any; what is your game, West?"

"I told you that I'm buying in on Tonto City business. I've got a lot of faith in the future of the town."

"Mine, too, is unbounded, Mr. West. Observe the way in which prices are mounting. Twenty-five thousand today—thirty thousand tomorrow. As you gamblers say, the lid is off and the sky is the limit."

"Conroy, I've heard men say that you are a damn fool—but they didn't tell half of it."

"They very likely only knew half of it," smiled Henry.

Oscar came from the jail, closed the corridor door, and stood there, wiping his lips with the back of his hand. West glanced at him indifferently, and turned back to Henry.

"Let's drop all this damn foolishness, Conroy," he said. "Talk a little sense for once in yore life. I'll make you a decent offer."

Henry's eyes narrowed thoughtfully, as he replied:

"After what I have heard men say about you, Mr. West—I wonder if you could make a decent offer."

Jack West flamed quickly. His hands came from his pockets, clenched tightly, and he took a step closer to Henry's desk.

"Let me tell you somethin', you red-nosed, bug-headed—"

A SLITHER of heavy feet on the rough floor caused Jack West to turn his head quickly—but too late. Oscar's huge right hand, backed by every ounce of his big, muscular body, smacked against the right side of Jack West's head.

As big and powerful as he was, West was knocked completely off his feet by the force of that terrific blow, and the little office shook from the collapse of Jack West. With the grunt of a triumphant grizzly, Oscar wrapped his arms around West, swung him up, stepped to the doorway and flung him bodily into the street.

Not less than a dozen people saw West rolling over in the dirt. They came running from all directions, only to stop and stare at the man, who owned most of Wild Horse Valley, trying to sit up, his right ear cut and bleeding, and already swollen to the size and shape of a doughnut.

Some of West's men came from the Tonto Saloon and helped him across the street.

"Yust ta'al him," said Oscar calmly, "Ay do not need brass-knockles."

Oscar came back in the office, and Henry closed the door against the gawping crowd.

"Thank you, Oscar," said Henry simply.

"By gad, sir!" exclaimed Judge. "Do you condone such things, Henry?"

"Condone? By gad, sir, I applaud them. That punch will be heard all over Wild Horse Valley. It will serve notice on the rough element that brow-beating is taboo in this place, sir. I am only sorry that I was obliged to—er—sock him by proxy."

Jack West's men were very solicitous. They took him back to the private office, where they brushed him off and patched him up. Doc Sargent's face was solemn, but his eyes held a glint of amusement. West refused to call the doctor.

"I would, 'f I was you," advised one of the men. " 'F that ear swells up any more, it'll jist bust, thasall. Even a human skin can stand jist so much swellin', yuh know."

West ordered all the men out, except Doc, who waited patiently for his employer to do the talking.

"It was that damn Swede jailer," said West wearily. "I got a flash of him, just before he hit me."

"I suspected him," nodded Doc. "He's a powerful brute. The men said he threw you bodily into the street."

"Have one of the men get my rig at the stable," ordered West. "I'm goin' north right away."

Doc gave the order, and came back.

"What price did Conroy make you on that hat store?" he asked.

"That was what started the trouble. He asked twenty-five thousand dollars—the damn fool."

"Then I imagine the deal is off."

"Off! Yo're damn right it's off! I'll show them a thing or two. I'll put that sheriff out of business. I'll make all three of them wish they'd never crossed me. I'll be runnin' this town; and I'll be runnin' this damn county."

"That's the way to talk."

"I'm not just talkin', Doc; I mean it. I'll make Tonto City too damn hot for several people I know. I'll bring gunmen, and—well, you watch my smoke."

"It'll be interesting to watch," smiled Doc Sargent. "I guess your rig is ready."

"All right," grunted West. He started to get up from his chair, but hesitated. On the desk was another plain envelope, sealed.

WEST PICKED it up, swung around and looked sharply at Sargent.

"Did you write a letter? This one?" he asked.

"No, I haven't written any letter," replied Doc. "What is that?"

West ripped the envelope open. It was apparently empty, until West opened it from end to end, when he found a small clipping from a newspaper; smaller than the previous one. It was also yellow with age, and slightly faded. It read:

> Mrs. Jack West passed away last night at the local hospital, the victim of an alleged beating by her husband several weeks ago.
>
> The officers have redoubled their efforts to locate Jack West, for whom they have been searching on an assault charge, but which has been changed to murder, since this unfortunate ending of the affair.

West gripped the clipping in his right hand and lifted his head, looking straight at Doc Sargent. His face was as gray as the smoke trees along Wild Horse River, and his eyes seemed to burn deep into the mind of his boss gambler. Doc Sargent drew back.

"My God, I haven't done anything!" he breathed. "What is it?"

"The second one," whispered West. "By God!"

He got slowly to his feet, and Doc backed to the door.

"Get a grip on yourself, West," he begged. "I don't know—"

Slowly West opened his hand and looked down at the little piece of yellow paper. Then he slowly tore it to tiny bits in his palm, placed them on top of the desk, and lighted them with a match, ignoring the fact that he was ruining the polished wood.

The odor of burning varnish filled the room. With a quick motion of his hand, West brushed the ashes aside. Doc Sargent licked his lips, watching West closely. Doc had a derringer concealed in his right hand, ready for an emergency.

"Was that the one you lost?" he asked.

West shook his head slowly. There was color in his face again and his eyes were normal.

"I reckon my rig is ready," he said in a dull voice and walked out, going straight to the street.

Doc Sargent replaced the derringer in his pocket and drew a deep breath of relief. For once in his colorful life he had looked into the eyes of a killer.

"So he'll be running Tonto City—and the county, eh?" muttered Doc Sargent. "A big, big man. But there's somebody around Tonto who has got you whipped, West. I wish I knew him—and it's not the big Swede, either."

Doc went out into the saloon, where he stood at the bar, looking around the room. There was little activity in the Tonto at that time of the day. Doc was trying to puzzle out who had been in the office and left that envelope on his desk.

His searching eyes finally rested on Tom Silver, the swamper, who was putting a cover over a pool table at the rear of the room. Doc's eyes narrowed, as he studied the scar-faced man. It would have been easy for Tom to have left that letter when he cleaned out the office.

"So he forgot his last name," mused Doc to himself, as he remembered Tom Silver's reply at the time he was hired. "I wonder who he is. That scar would prevent anyone from recognizing him. Is he the man? It might pay me to find out—and, still, I've got to go easy."

CHAPTER VII

HOLD-UP

LITTLE REAL NEWS filtered out from the Yellow Warrior mine, where a dozen stamps ground out a yellow harvest. It was West's richest property, although it was said that the Gold Plate would be as rich a producer, when the mill was ready for production. A big crew was driving deep into the Lucky Stake, ignoring the low-grade stuff.

Armed men guarded the Yellow Warrior. No one knew when a shipment of bullion might be made, nor who would take it to the railroad at Scorpion Bend. Nick Borden had a crew of only six men at the Smoke Tree; six tight-lipped, hard-faced men, who had nothing to say about the property.

A shotgun guard rode regularly on the stage these days, although there had not been a stage robbery since the mines opened in Wild Horse Valley. There was no bank in Tonto City, but there were rumors that West might reopen the old Bank of Tonto, which had been closed for months.

West's boasted gunmen arrived in Tonto, one at a time, so as to not attract attention. Judge Van Treece, who was a walking encyclopedia of things Arizona, saw them, and mentioned the fact to Henry.

"There are five of them," stated Judge, "and I know the reputation of each one. They are unsavory."

"Do you suppose there is any significance in their being here?" asked Henry. "Naturally, they would gravitate to a new boom."

"They came too close together, Henry. No, I believe it is Mr. West's move to dominate things. He would hate us for what Oscar did to him, and West is famous for his hates."

"Is there any legal procedure?" queried Henry, a twinkle in his eyes.

"The law," replied Judge, "might prosecute them, in case we were murdered."

"As usual, Judge, the law does not prevent—it only punishes."

"It has its limitations, Henry. By gad! Here comes the long overdue Frijole Bill."

The little cook from the J Bar C tied his horse at the sheriff's hitch-rack, and came in, carrying a bundle inside a grain-sack.

"I brung yuh two gallons this crack," he grinned. "Them last prunes was great. Yuh see, I cut me some maguey plant, like the Mexicans use for tequila, and let her ferment a long time.

Then I cuts the prune whisky fifty-fifty with this here tequila, and if that ain't—well, you try it. She's shore a cross between chain-lightnin' and grizzly gizzard."

"Grizzlies have no gizzards," stated Judge soberly.

"Have you," queried Frijole, "ever dug into one t' find out, Judge?"

"No, I never have."

"Well, I have—and he had a gizzard. Take out that cork and git a whiff, Henry. She's shore nectar. I can allus tell how good it is by the way Bill Shakespeare, the rooster, acts, when he eats his fill of the mash. He's m' ther-mommy-ter—Bill is."

"**WHAT DID** he do this time?" asked Henry, sniffing carefully.

"Well, sir," Frijole sat down on Oscar's cot, his hands on his knees, "I'll tell yuh. Yuh know how it is with Bill Shakespeare, when he's full of mash—goes out to git hisself a wild-cat. He ginerally goes down in the dry-wash, finds the tracks of a old bob-cat, and trails him to his lair."

"Liar," said Judge.

"Lair," corrected Frijole. "Meanin' his hang-out."

"What a namesake for the Bard of Avon," sighed Henry.

"He's really the belligerentest rooster I ever knowed," declared Frijole. "Well, sir, I seen Bill headin' for the dry-wash; so I threw a saddle on the old buckskin, and made up m' mind I was goin' to witness the battle.

"Yuh see, Bill's in the habit of killin' wild-cats and hidin' of their skins—and I want a good pelt. Well, old Bill headed up the wash, with me close behind. The way that rooster can trail shore proves to me that his ma was scared by a bloodhound. We're way up in Smoke Tree Cañon when I lost track of Bill. It's so all broke up and narrer that I has to leave my bronc, and go on foot.

"I'm 'bout a quarter-mile beyond my horse, when all to once I hears a hell of a disturbance ahead. I knowed by the noise that

Bill has caught that wild-cat; so I puts on full steam ahead, jist to be there to save the hide.

"Well, sir, I comes around in a narrer place in the cañon, and m' hair shore stood on end. There's two mountain lions comin' down that narrer gut, jist as fast as they can run, and on the neck of the rear lion is old Bill Shakespeare, ridin' straight up, with the lion's left ear in his beak. And every time that lion hit the ground, Old Bill socks him in the right shoulder with his spur.

"Well, sir, I made m'self as thin as possible against the side of that cañon, and let 'em pass. It jist left me kinda weak in the knees, but I was able to git back to my horse, and go home. Bill wasn't back yet when I left, but them four hens of hisn was out on the corral fence, lookin' down the wash; so I reckon they seen him go past. He's shore some rooster, if I *have* raised him almost from a aig. How does that stuff smell, Henry?"

"After one whiff," replied Henry, "I can believe every word of your story, Frijole."

"Well," said Frijole, "I can take yuh right to the place where I stood when the lions went past."

"And show us the lion tracks, I suppose," said Judge.

"Tracks? Say, Judge, them lions was goin' so fast that they wasn't on the ground long enough to make a track. I jist wish you could have seen 'em."

"That," stated Henry, "is something that only happens once in a life-time. How is everything else at the ranch, Frijole?"

"Oh, purty good. Slim Pickins answered one of them mat-ree-mony ads in a little paper he got in Scorpion Bend. A female wrote to him, and Slim acted high-toned all that day. She asked him to send her his pitcher, but he didn't have none; so me and Danny found one of yours and sent it to her."

"My God!" exclaimed Henry.

"That's jist what Danny said she'd say," chuckled Frijole. "It was the pitcher of you in a plug-hat, holdin' a banjo."

"And that," sighed Henry, "will probably keep Slim from making an ass of himself."

"Oh, shore; she'll never write to him again."

"He'll be lucky if she doesn't sue him," declared Judge.

"I think," said Henry, "it is about time to sample this jug of chain-lightning. The discourse is getting personal."

NICK BORDEN and one of his men came to Tonto City that night. Borden smiled grimly as he noted the number of gunmen scattered about the establishment, and mentioned it to Doc Sargent.

"You must be expectin' trouble," he said to Doc.

"I don't know a thing about it, Nick," denied Sargent. "If West wants to pay for six-guns, I suppose it is up to him."

"Naturally," agreed Borden. "They say that plenty of bullion is bein' turned out at the Yellow Warrior these days."

"I can't say about that," evaded Doc Sargent. "My job is to run this place, Nick."

"Oh, I'm not pryin'," laughed Nick Borden. "I'll be turnin' out *mucho dinero* myself pretty soon. The Smoke Tree is gettin' to be a big thing."

"I've heard," said Doc, "that there isn't an ounce of gold in that whole hill."

"West told yuh that, didn't he? Tell him to come to see me, and I'll show him some stuff that'll make his eyes stick out."

Doc Sargent opened a draw-poker game, and Nick Borden took a hand in the game. Nick's man lounged around the saloon for a while, but finally went away. It was exactly midnight when Doc Sargent turned the game over to another gambler and went back to his office.

Nick Borden played with varying success until about two o'clock, when the game broke up. After a round of drinks, Nick Borden went home. He had not seen Doc Sargent since midnight, and mentioned the fact to the bartender.

"Well," grinned the bartender, "Doc's the boss; so he can do as he pleases about runnin' a game."

HENRY AND Judge occupied a room in the Tonto Hotel. They had partaken of plenty of Frijole's prune juice that night, and their awakening early next morning was not so pleasant. But somebody was using their door for a drum, it seemed.

Henry sat up, blinking sleepily, as the pounding continued. He shook Judge, who sat up quickly, like a jack-in-a-box.

"Somebody," said Henry, "has a grudge against our door."

And then he snuggled down in the blankets again, covering up his head. Judge yawned and looked critically at the door, which was vibrating from the blows without.

"One more assault like that," declared Judge, "and I shall most certainly shoot right through the door, sir, or madame."

"Yudge!" yelled Oscar's voice. "Is dat you, Yudge?"

"The Terrible Swede!" snorted Judge.

"Tell him to go chase a road-runner," advised Henry sleepily.

"Ay vant to coom in!"

"Walk in; the door isn't locked, you vitrified Viking."

Except for his hat and shirt, Oscar was fully dressed, his blond hair standing on end.

"Hasn't that prune juice stopped stinging you, or have you been at the jug again?" queried Judge severely.

"Ay am yust as sober as a hurse," panted Oscar. Henry sat up and looked critically at Oscar with one eye.

"A real novelty," he said.

"Ay coom yust as fast as I can," explained Oscar. "Das svamper in de Tonto Saloon coom and ya'l like ha'l at me. He vants me to coom and see something. Ay skal ta'l you, Ay saw it!"

"I know," sighed Henry. "Little green devils, with red hats on their heads, going helter-skelter, hither and yon. The most reasonable theory, I believe, is that the continued use of alcohol tends to disturb some optical nerve, which causes us to see strange and wonderful creatures. Now, I remember—"

"Yah, su-ure," interrupted Oscar. "But vat de ha'l has dis to do vit two men being oll tied oop in de Tonto Saloon?"

Henry blinked rapidly. "Tied up, did you say, Oscar?"

"Yah—su-u-ure—Ay ta'l you. Das ha'ar svamper—"

"Dead men?" asked Judge anxiously.

"Yust gagged."

"Gagged, eh?" said Judge. "Bound and gagged, Oscar?"

"Doc Sargent and anodder man."

"Dirty work at the cross-roads!" snorted Henry. "C'mon, Judge."

They piled out of bed and reached for their clothes. Henry was at the door when Judge grabbed him.

"Pants on, Henry," he stated.

"Oh, yes, certainly. I—I almost forgot."

A FEW moments later they went down the stairs and trotted across the street to the Tonto Saloon, where a curious crowd was already gathering. Oscar led the way back to the little office, where Doc Sargent, his mouth red and twisted from hours of trying to chew through a gag, was cursing Tom Silver for not turning him loose at once.

Pieces of the rope were scattered on the floor. Another man was sitting in a chair, massaging his wrists, a scowl on his face as he looked around the room. Doc Sargent caught sight of Henry and Judge.

"So there you are, eh?" he snarled. "Officers of the law!"

"What happened?" asked Henry.

"Plenty," replied Doc. "Thirty thousand dollars in bullion gone!"

"Gone where?" asked Judge.

Doc swore softly and turned to the doorway.

"Get out of here, the whole bunch of you; I want to talk with the sheriff and his gang. Close the door, Swede.

"Not that it will do a damn bit of good," said Doc, "but I've got to tell you about it. Everybody knows that the Yellow Warrior is producing a lot of gold. West was afraid of a hold-up. Yesterday a bed-roll was brought into this office, and inside was over thirty thousand dollars' worth of gold. At exactly twelve o'clock last night, a buggy was to stop at my back office door, and the bed-roll was to be dumped into the buggy. It looked like a safe way to take the gold to Scorpion Bend.

"I walked into my office at midnight, lighted a lamp, and got a gun stuck into my ribs. Two masked men were there, and they tied me up tight. Then they got the driver of the rig, gagged and tied him up, and drove away with the bed-roll full of gold. That scar-faced swamper found us this morning."

"Masked men," murmured Henry. "Two masked men, and apparently very efficient. Now, Mr. Sargent, just how many people knew about the way this gold was to be taken out of here?"

"Jack West and myself."

"What about this man—the driver?"

"I didn't know a damn thing," replied the man huskily. "I was to be there with a horse and buggy. I thought I was takin' somebody—not a bunch of gold."

"What about the man who brought the bed-roll from the mine?"

"It was brought here by the assayer at the Yellow Warrior. But not even the assayer knew when or how it was to be sent out. Anyway, he's perfectly honest."

"It is very unreasonable to suppose that someone else did not know about it, Mr. Sargent," said Henry.

"I tell you, they didn't," said Sargent. "They couldn't."

OSCAR WAS squatted on his heels, examining the pieces of rope which had been cut from Doc Sargent. He reached under a chair and picked up a rawhide hondo—the commercially-made loop for a lariat rope. Oscar looked at it quickly, stood up and slipped the hondo in his pocket.

"Wait a minute!" snapped Doc Sargent. "What did you pick up, Swede?"

"Not'ing—mooch," replied Oscar.

"I think you're a liar!" exclaimed Doc, and went up to Oscar. "Give me what you took off the floor, you dumb—"

Smack! Oscar slapped Doc Sargent across the face with his open palm, knocking him backwards across the room. It was like a blow from the paw of a grizzly. Doc Sargent crashed against the wall, then sat down heavily. Oscar stepped out, closed the door—and was gone.

"Heaven is my home!" exclaimed Judge.

"I have heard that it is a nice place," said Henry inanely.

Doc Sargent got to his feet, dazed but mad, and headed for the door.

"I'm going to kill that damn Swede," he swore huskily. "He's got something that will prove who pulled this job, I tell you. He can't hit me and get away with it. I'll fix him!"

As he started past, Henry reached out, hooked his left hand into Doc Sargent's collar and yanked him back. As mad as he was, Doc looked at Henry in amazement.

"You are not going to kill Oscar," declared Henry. "Another remark like that and I'll put you in jail for—for disturbing the peace and threatening to kill the jailer."

"Well, I'll be damned!" snorted Doc. "Getting tough, eh?"

"I swore to uphold the law of this county," said Henry firmly, "and I most certainly shall do it—even if it requires putting a gambler in the hospital. I hope, sir, that you catch my meaning."

"All right! If that's the way you feel—go and get whatever your damn jailer took off the floor. He got some evidence."

Henry released Doc and stepped back.

"Have you any idea what it was, Mr. Sargent?" he asked.

"I don't know what it was—but that big-headed Swede knows."

Henry and Judge walked through the saloon and halted on

the sidewalk, followed by several hearty laughs from those in the saloon.

"Derision," said Judge wearily.

"Derision—hell!" gasped Henry. "All along, I've felt—Look at us! Judge, you've got on my pants, and I've got on yours. But how—this waistband is closed and—"

"Closed? By gad, sir, you not only have my pants on, but you have them on backwards! Luckily, your coat is long, but even at that—well, it might be mistaken for a handkerchief, hanging from a hip pocket."

"Judge, I am mortified, sir; mortified, I tell you! And you! If that belt of yours slips one iota, you'll—Judge, let us go to the office."

"To the office," panted Judge. "Lean back as far as possible, Henry, and hold down on that coat."

"For once in an honest life," sighed Henry, "I have something to conceal. Cling to your belt, Judge; we shall not strike the set until the act is over."

CHAPTER VIII

"OUT!"

THEY REACHED THE office after what seemed an interminable journey, and closed the door. Oscar was sitting on the cot, the prune-juice jug between his knees, a six-shooter beside him.

"You—you—" spluttered Judge. "Oscar, will you ever have any sense?"

"Ay have yust been wondering," replied Oscar soberly.

"Stop chiding Oscar—and give me my pants," said Henry.

Oscar took a look at their pants, and doubled at the waist with unholy mirth. When the exchange had been effected, Henry looked upon Oscar severely.

"Now, just what was it you found over there, Oscar?" he asked.

Still chuckling, Oscar dug deep in a pocket and drew out a worn rawhide hondo, on one side of which had been burned in small letters the brand of the J Bar C ranch. Henry and Judge examined it closely.

"Das hondo belong to Danny Regan," said Oscar. "Ay burned de brand on it for him myself."

"I see," mused Henry. "The rope used to tie Doc Sargent belonged to Danny Regan."

"Rather a damning piece of evidence," said Judge.

"If it were in alien hands," nodded Henry.

"But you can't suppress evidence, Henry."

Henry looked at Judge in amazement.

"You—you would let this become evidence?" he queried.

"In this case, I believe it would become Exhibit A."

Henry glared at Judge for a moment, took a knife from his pocket and with a sharp blade deftly removed the lightly-burned brand.

"That will greatly lower the classification, I believe," he said.

"It undoubtedly destroys *all* evidence," sighed Judge. "However, the fact of its existence still remains in the minds of all three of us officers of the law."

Henry looked thoughtfully at Oscar.

"What was on that hondo, Oscar?" he asked.

"On it?" queried Oscar. "Ay never saw damn t'ing on it. Yust a plain hondo."

He took the hondo off the desk, rubbed the side of it violently on the none-too-clean floor and examined it critically before tossing it back on the desk.

"And now," sighed Henry, "I suppose the State of Arizona will expect us to find the robbers."

A horse and buggy stopped at the front of the jail, and they opened the door to see Danny Regan in the buggy. Slim Pickins was just in the act of tying two saddle horses to the hitch-rack near the Tonto Saloon.

"Anybody lose a horse and buggy?" asked Danny, laughing, as the three men crowded out against the hitch-rack.

"Did you find this one?" asked Henry.

"Shore did, Henry. It was about two hundred yards this side of the ranch house, away off the road, with the horse feedin' calm and peaceful."

"The horse was loose?" asked Judge.

"Jist as loose as a busted egg."

THE MAN from the livery stable was hurrying up to them, and he looked the equipage over closely. Several men, including Doc Sargent, were coming from the Tonto Saloon.

"That's the outfit that was stolen last night," declared the stableman. Doc Sargent looked sharply at Danny, who got out of the buggy.

"Where did you get it, Regan?" asked Doc.

"Oh, there you are!" exclaimed Danny. He looked around quickly, but turned back to Sargent and said:

"I just wanted to be sure that your boss wasn't around, ready to cave-in my ear again. Well, I'll tell yuh; we found it near the J Bar C, jist as loose as the morals of some folks around here; so we brought it to town. Any objections, Mr. Sargent?"

"What's that—in the back?" exclaimed Judge.

"It's the bed-roll!" exploded Doc Sargent. "Why—why, I'll be damned! It's still roped, too! I don't—"

"I dunno what the hell all this fuss is about, but I reckon it's all right," said Danny, and he swung the heavy roll of blankets and canvas to the sidewalk, where Henry proceeded to remove the rope. The men crowded in and watched Henry unroll the bed, disclosing what had made it so heavy.

"Drill-steel!" exclaimed a miner. "All short stuff, too. That's a hell of a thing to steal, ain't it?"

Henry stood up and squinted at Doc Sargent.

"Thirty thousand dollars, eh?" he said. "Steel must be high."

Doc Sargent's jaw had sagged perceptibly, but suddenly he began grinning with evident relief.

"It seems to amuse you, sir," observed Judge stiffly.

Doc nodded, and laughed aloud.

"I can see it now," he said. "Jack West was too smart for them. This was a dummy shipment."

"You mean—he tempted the robbers?" asked Henry.

"And I guess they fell for it, too," laughed Doc. "Well, I'm sure glad. It takes a load off my mind."

The assembled crowd laughed with him, and immediately accepted an invitation to have a drink on the Tonto Saloon. Doc had already sent a message to Jack West, telling him about the robbery, and he felt that West would get a good laugh out of the incident.

As the crowd trooped away, Henry took Danny into the office and told him about the branded hondo.

"That rope was stolen off my saddle over a week ago," declared Danny. "Some thief used it, tryin' to put the deadwood on me. I'll have to repay Oscar for gettin' away with it. Henry, did you see Werner, that new butcher?"

"Yes, I made it a point to go up to his shop. But he had already signed a contract with the LJ outfit, up near Scorpion Bend."

Danny nodded grimly. "I just wanted to tell yuh that me and Slim found where somebody had butchered two yearlin's. It was back in a cañon, this side of the ranch. They cut off the heads and legs. Mebbe happened three, four days ago."

"Do you think they were our yearlings, Danny?"

"Yuh can't tell, Henry; but I'm bettin' they were."

"Perhaps it was some prospector in need of some meat."

"A pretty big appetite, don'tcha think?" asked Danny.

"Yes, he *would* have quite an appetite, I suppose. But what can we do about it, Danny?"

"Well, it'll mean that we'll ride with a rifle handy. We can't stand for rustlers, yuh know. They got about eighty dollars' worth at that one spot—and that's money."

"That is very true. Danny, I wonder who pulled off that robbery last night?"

"Evidently some friends of mine," smiled Danny. "Or it might have been that they didn't know the ranch brand was on that hondo."

"That is possible. Well, you run along and talk with Leila. Don't worry about rustlers until we know definitely that it was not merely a hungry prospector. A—a yearling isn't very big, you know."

"Neither is eighty dollars in currency, Henry."

IT WAS late at night when Jack West came to Tonto in answer to Doc Sargent's message; and he was as savage as a grizzly. There had been no dummy shipment. That bed-roll had contained over thirty thousand dollars' worth of bullion. West knew nothing about the drill-steel, which was wrapped in the blankets. Doc mentioned the name of the assayer, and West flared quickly.

"Yuh can't put any deadwood on him. Anyway, two other men witnessed the packin' of that bullion. There wasn't any substitution at the mine. Doc," he glared savagely at the boss gambler, "are you tellin' me the truth about all this?"

"Do I look like a fool?" retorted Doc Sargent. "Why, they'd find out the substitution at the bank in Scorpion Bend. No, I tell you, it happened just like I said. They cut the ropes off me, and by that time that half-witted sheriff came along with his brainless help.

"While we were talking about it, that damn Swede got something from under that chair over there. I told him to give it to me, and then he—well, he slapped me so damn hard that I saw stars for five minutes—and in the meantime he pulled out."

"He did, eh? Yes, I reckon you would see stars. But what was it?"

"*Quien sabe?* I haven't seen the Swede since."

"And Regan brought the horse and buggy back, eh?"

Doc nodded gloomily.

"I wonder how much Regan knows about it," said West. "He holds no love for me, that's a cinch. Two men, eh? But what the hell's the use of askin' the sheriff to do anythin' about it? Regan is his foreman—and he'd back the damn kid. But I've started some wheels to movin', Doc. What's the use of havin' authority if yuh don't use it? I'm sick of that big-nosed sheriff."

"What have you done?" asked Doc Sargent.

"Wait and see. I'm goin' up to the Yellow Warrior to spend the night. Damn it, that robbery hits me hard. But keep still about it. Let 'em think it was a dummy shipment. It'll worry the thieves who got it."

"Just let her go as she lays, eh?"

"That's it, Doc."

IT WAS two days after the robbery at the Tonto Saloon, which, as far as Henry knew, was an unprofitable venture of the robbers. Just now Henry sat at his desk, while three other men occupied the available chairs. The men were Albert Rose, of Scorpion Bend; John Calvert and Edward Harris, of Silver City. These three men constituted the Board of Commissioners of the county, looking severe, but rather uncomfortable.

"You see, Mr. Conroy, we do not wish to publicly force the issue," said Albert Rose, their chairman. "It is very unfortunate, indeed; but there has been so much comment, and certain complaints against your office, that we have decided to ask you to resign."

"Complaints?" queried Henry. "I didn't know."

The three men nodded together, as though having rehearsed the act.

"You see," added John Calvert, a merchant of Silver City, "since this valley is getting prominent through the mining in-dustry, we really need a younger, more active sheriff. You are—

well, not exactly fitted to protect the peace of this country, Mr. Conroy."

"Mr. Harris, isn't that your cue to add to the indictment?" asked Henry.

"Oh, I allus vote with the majority," replied Harris quickly.

"Gentlemen," replied Henry ponderously, "I shall also vote with the majority. You please me mightily. In fact, I said to Jack West, 'Jack, I wish you would have a talk with the Commissioners. I am weary of this office, and I would like to have their opinion on accepting my resignation.'"

"Yuh did?" blurted Harris. "Well, gee, that ain't the way Mr. West told it to us, but—well, I reckon it was his way."

"Thank you," nodded Henry. "Now, gentlemen, just how soon can you appoint my successor?"

"That is all arranged," replied Calvert quickly. "Mr. West— that is, we have tentatively appointed Mr. Lou James, of Scorpion Bend."

"Good! Now, if you gentlemen will pardon me, I shall clean out the desk and pack up my personal belongings. Thank you very much for your consideration."

They filed quietly out, and Henry sat there for a long time, a queer expression in his eyes as he looked around the old office.

"So Mr. West had me kicked out, and Mr. West appointed his own sheriff to succeed me," murmured Henry. "Ah, well, perhaps they are right. It is a young man's work."

He looked up as Judge came in, and their eyes met. Judge understood.

"It will be nice out at the ranch, Henry," he said. "I guess the town is growing past us. But tell me, did they mention West?"

"Yes, Judge. West is a big man in Wild Horse Valley. He even told them who to appoint in my stead. A man name Lou James."

"I see. Mr. James. Limps slightly in his left leg. It was caused by a bullet from a deputy's gun fifteen years ago. Convicted of helping hold up a saloon down on the Rio. Two years sentence, I believe."

"You amaze me, Judge."

"Well, being a private citizen again, you must go in for more amazement. Turn about is fair play, you know."

"I hope Oscar stands up under the blow," said Henry.

"I don't believe he will ever notice the change, Henry."

"Except on pay day, Judge"

"I'll arrange with Frijole to have a jug of prune juice on that day. In that way, we can keep him in ignorance for years."

CHAPTER IX

THE MISSING GOLD

LOU JAMES LOST no time in taking over the sheriff's office. He was tall, raw-boned, hard-faced, and had a slight limp in his left leg. In appearance, he was the ideal type of Arizona sheriff.

Danny Regan made a trip to Scorpion Bend, and came back to the J Bar C full of information.

"Lou James owns the LJ spread at Scorpion Bend," he told Henry. "He bought out the Rafter A, a short time ago, and registered his own brand. It's a script brand, connected. Not a very big outfit, they told me. James has contracted to furnish Werner all his meat, and Werner has the contract to furnish all the meat to West's outfit. Henry, they've cut us out entirely."

"Not entirely, Danny," replied Henry gently. "They still use our beef."

"If those yearlin's was branded J Bar C—yes," admitted Danny. "Anyway, somebody had a taste of good veal. Slim and me are goin' to take a ride this afternoon, and see what we can see."

Armed with rifles, in addition to their six-shooters, the two cowboys went into the hills, first visiting the spot where the two yearlings had been slaughtered. There was no evidence of any further butchering in that cañon; so they rode north, cutting back through Smoke Tree Cañon, which they examined closely.

"Over there near Crazy Woman Springs might be a good place," suggested Slim Pickins. "That old corral is still pretty good, and it's kinda hidden away."

"I've been thinkin' about that," nodded Danny. "On account of the heat and flies, they'd butcher about sundown; so it may be that we're a little early."

"Mebbe we better kinda saunter," suggested Slim. "Man, wouldn't I like to notch a sight on a rustler."

"I hope to tell yuh," grinned Danny.

"Danny, how does Henry feel about bein' kicked out of office?"

"I don't reckon anybody will ever know, Slim. Henry covers it all with a laugh, even when it hurts. I used to laugh at him. No, I never laughed openly—but I laughed. He still don't know beans about the cow business—but he's square and white, Slim."

"He shore is," agreed Slim warmly. "Do yuh reckon he'll marry Mrs. Harper?"

"I hope he does. She's mighty glad he's out of office. I reckon we all are, as far as that goes. The only thing that worries me is the fact that West is goin' to boss this valley. Oh, yes, he is, Slim. In another year or two, he'll be tellin' us who to vote for. He'll be the dictator of Wild Horse Valley."

"Unless somebody shoots him, Danny."

"Well, that might happen, of course."

"You still owe him for that punch on the ear."

"I reckon Swede squared that up," laughed Danny. "He hurt West almost as much as West hurt me; and then he added to the score by slappin' Doc Sargent silly. Oscar Johnson may be a dumb Swede, but he sure can fight."

THEY CAME to the cañon below Crazy Woman Springs, and were riding along the brushy south side, when Danny

*The distant rider
fired one shot.*

suddenly drew rein. He lifted his head, sniffing the vagrant breeze from up the cañon.

"Wood smoke!" he exclaimed. "Hell's bells, I wonder if somebody started a fire in here! This stuff would burn—"

"Look!" grunted Slim, pointing across at the opposite rim, and a trifle to the west. "A rider on the rim, over there, Danny!"

The rider, clearly silhouetted against the sky, lifted a rifle and fired one shot. Danny and Slim instinctively ducked, but there was no sound from the bullet.

"A warnin' shot!" exploded Danny. "C'mon, Slim!"

They spurred along as swiftly as possible, but with the rocks and brush it was difficult to make speed. The rider was gone from the rim now. They broke out of the brush, galloped across a fairly open space, and came to the cañon rim just above the springs.

Two riders were far up the cañon, streaking away. Danny dropped off his horse and sent two bullets in their direction. But the distance was too great for accurate shooting, and a moment later they swept around a bend in the cañon, and out of sight.

"They had a lookout posted this time," grinned Danny as they crouched on the rim of the cañon. "Look! Over there by the corral. They've got a critter hog-tied. And there's their fire, too."

"Brand blotters, this time," said Slim. "They don't need a fire to do butcherin', Danny."

"It shore looks like brand-blottin'," agreed Danny. He looked all around, seeking a trail down into the cañon.

"There's a little trail over there," said Slim, pointing. "But don'tcha try to take a horse down there. I tried it, and we shore had a hell of a mixup. Yuh can go down on foot all right."

"All right, I'll go down. You stay here with the horses, and I'll have a look at that critter. Keep yore eyes open, feller; I don't want 'em sneakin' back on me."

"I hope they try it," laughed Slim. "Go ahead; I'll be watchin'."

He sat on the rim and saw Danny appear at the old corral, where he examined the animal, and then went over to the little fire. Then he went back and looked at the animal again, but made no move to release it. Finally he came slowly back toward the foot of the trail, and out of Slim's sight. He was so long in climbing back to the rim that Slim became worried.

Finally Slim left the horses and walked to the top of the trail, just as Danny came panting to the top.

"Didja git lost on yore way back?" queried Slim. "I thought you'd never git back."

"No, I didn't get lost," panted Danny. "But I found somethin'. C'mon, Slim; I'll show yuh why I was a long time comin'."

"But what about that critter?"

"Oh, yeah, I forgot. It's a J Bar C yearlin', with its throat cut."

"The hell it is! What was the fire for?"

"It's got me fightin' my hat, Slim. There's a runnin'-iron in the fire."

That trail was too narrow and steep for conversation. About halfway down it wound past some irregular shelves of rock, where a ledge of sandstone protruded from the hillside. Danny stepped off the trail onto one of these ledges.

"On the way up," explained Danny, "I happened to look over here and I seen somethin' glistenin' in the sunlight. Here it is."

HE TOOK a silver concha from his pocket and handed it to Slim. It was of Mexican manufacture, about two inches in diameter, and apparently of solid silver.

"Some puncher mourns his lost finery," said Slim. "Prob'ly dropped off the leg of his chaps. But what about it?"

"Yeah," agreed Danny. "But what would a puncher be doin' over here on that ledge of rocks?"

"Go ahead," grinned Slim, "I'll bite."

"C'mon."

For about thirty feet more Danny led the way over the broken ledges to a little cave, not over six feet in depth, and less than that in width. A slab of sandstone slanted down over the front of it, concealing it from anyone not on the ledge.

Danny dropped on his knees, reached into the cave and drew out a weighted gunny-sack. Again he sprawled forward and drew out another, while Slim stood there, wondering what it was all about. Reaching into one of the sacks, Danny drew out a small bar of pure gold.

"My Gawd!" croaked Slim. "What in the devil—"

"That's jist what I said," grinned Danny. "Look at the mark on that brick. That Y.W. means it's the missin' gold from the Yellow Warrior."

"But that was a dummy package, Danny."

"Well, I dunno about that. They said the shipment would weigh 'bout a hundred and twenty-five pounds; and there must be about sixty, seventy pounds in each sack."

"Great lovely dove! What'll we do with it?"

"Well," sighed Danny, "as much as I hate Jack West, we've got to take this gold to Tonto City. Mebbe he'll at least buy a drink."

"Gosh, it's a shame to have to take it back. I've allus bragged about my honesty—but I didn't realize what temptation meant. Don't you feel kinda sorry 'bout takin' it back, Danny?"

"I am gettin' me a few pangs," admitted Danny. "But imagine what them robbers will feel like when they don't find their loot."

"Or when they hear that it's been recovered," added Slim.

"Well, there's no use foolin'—they might come back. Grab a sack and head for the rim, feller. We're wealthy for a few minutes, anyway."

It was a hard climb back to the rim, and they went panting back to their horses, where they dropped the sacks on the ground and sat down on a rock to catch their breath.

"Been workin' hard, boys?" drawled a voice behind them, and they jerked around to see Lou James, the sheriff, and his new deputy.

The big sheriff had a revolver in his hand, while the deputy held a handy rifle.

"We was ridin' around, kinda lookin' things over," explained the sheriff, "and we heard a couple, three shots fired over this-away; so we moseyed over and found yore horses. I don't b'lieve

I've ever met either of you fellers. I'm Lou James, the new sheriff."

"Huh—howdy," gasped Danny. "My name's Regan. This is Pickins."

"Oh, yeah—Regan—Yo're foreman of the J Bar C, ain't yuh?"

DANNY NODDED. The deputy picked up a sack, spread the mouth and looked in on the gold bullion. He dropped the sack quickly and stepped back.

"I reckon it's that stolen gold, Lou!" he exclaimed.

"It shore is," agreed Danny. "We just found it—down there in a cave."

"Oh, yuh just found it, eh?" said the sheriff. "That's nice. In a cave, eh? Did somebody tell yuh where it was?"

"I can explain jist how I happened to find it," said Danny. "Yuh see, I—"

"It's gittin' late, Regan," interrupted the sheriff. "Anyway, yuh can tell that to a judge, I reckon. Mebbe we better put bracelets on 'em, Mike. Git their guns first; I've heard that Regan is kinda fast with a shootin'-iron."

"You don't need to put any bracelets on us," said Danny. "We never stole that gold. I can explain the whole thing, if you'll listen."

"Don't bother 'bout it," advised the sheriff. "Git the horses, Mike. We want to git back before it gits too dark."

"Wait a minute," begged Slim. "If yo're such a hell of a good sheriff, I'd like to tell you that down in that cañon is a J Bar C yearlin', with its throat cut."

"Well," drawled the sheriff, "I can't do much when they're in that sort of a fix. What didja cut its throat for?"

"Yuh might as well keep still, Slim," said Danny. "We should have left the damn stuff alone, and let Jack West recover his own gold. He's out to get us—and the sheriff is West's man— so we may as well call it a day."

"Yo're showin' some sense, Regan," grinned the sheriff. "I've got yuh where the hair is short; so yuh might as well smile and take yore medicine."

"I'll smile," replied Danny, "but you ain't the one that deals out the medicine—remember that."

The deputy brought their two horses, and started to fasten one of the sacks behind his saddle. Suddenly he dropped the sack, and his right hand flashed back to his gun; but before he could draw his gun, a rifle cracked wickedly, and the deputy was fairly flung against his frightened horse.

The three men turned quickly. Not twenty feet away were two masked men, who had stepped out from the brush, and two rifles were covering the startled sheriff. Slowly he lifted his hands above his head.

"Yo're smarter than yore deputy," said one of the men, as they came forward. The black masks were sack-like, entirely covering their heads, with only eye-holes.

One of them covered the sheriff, while the other went over and examined the deputy. He took his guns, and came over to the sheriff, also removing his guns.

"That deputy never knowed what hit him," said the man. He turned to the sheriff, and said:

"You've got the keys to them handcuffs, ain't yuh?"

"Well?" queried the sheriff.

"Unclock these two punchers."

Grudgingly the sheriff removed the handcuffs from Danny and Slim. The masked man laughed, and said to Danny:

"Pick out yore own guns, feller."

"We're shore much obliged," smiled Danny.

"Yo're welcome as hell, feller. Now, if yo're all through around here yuh might as well pull out—you two—unless you'd like to kick this tough sheriff in the pants."

"I'd rather do it when he's got a gun," replied Danny.

"Yeah, and I'd rather see yuh do it. He ain't bad—he's jist cheap."

"I'll git somebody for this deal," snarled the sheriff.

"Yea-a-ah?" drawled the masked man. "If you make too many cracks, we'll lay you out beside yore deputy. One more killin' don't mean a thing to us. All right, you two waddies might as well drift."

"Thank yuh kindly, pardner," said Danny. "If yuh ever need a favor, you know where to come."

DANNY AND Slim swung into their saddles, and with a wave of their arms, galloped away toward the J Bar C. Over a far ridge, they drew rein and rode side by side.

"Danny," said Slim seriously, "didja ever see such hair on a cat?"

"Never in my life. Listen, Slim. The sheriff is the only evidence against us. We're two to one, *sabe?* I mean, it's two of us against one of him, in case he tries to arrest us again. He's lost the gold, and his deputy is dead—but remember this—we never seen any gold and we never seen them men shoot that deputy. It's our only chance."

"I know what yuh mean, Danny. But who the devil are them two masked men?"

"Who knows? But I'll betcha this much; they're the fellers that butchered that yearlin'. They had that gold cached. Mebbe they got back on that opposite rim, where they could see us at that little cave. One of 'em had a pair of field-glasses tied to his saddle."

"Yeah, I seen them glasses," nodded Slim. "Mebbe yo're right. Well, I ain't sheddin' any tears over that deputy; he was a bad boy. And as far as the sheriff is concerned—I don't reckon he'll even try to put any deadwood on us—not now."

Henry and Judge listened in amazement to their tale. Both of them supposed that the robbers had only taken a dummy treasure; but this looked as though it had been the real thing.

"You two boys did not exactly act as law-abiding citizens," said Judge severely. "Why didn't you, after you had your guns, turn on the masked men, recover the gold and turn it over to the sheriff?"

"In the first place, Judge," replied Danny, "we don't *know* that the stuff was stolen gold. In the second place, them masked men had guns in their hands—and they proved to us that they'd shoot. And in the third place—we're not doin' any favors for that sheriff."

"In only one respect, Danny," said Henry, "did you two fail to act as normal human beings in this matter."

"When was that?" asked Danny.

"When you failed to kick the sheriff in the pants, as offered."

"I am very much afraid that you two are in for trouble," said Judge. "Even if you did not steal the gold and—"

"Wait a minute, Judge," interrupted Danny. "We were not even there. We don't know a thing. In fact, we don't know what they're talkin' about. Remember, Judge; the sheriff is the lone witness."

"The law might possibly accept his statement."

"After him serving two years for a hold-up, Judge?" asked Henry.

"Yes, that is true enough. Well, I wash my hands of the matter."

"You never had any hand in it," said Henry. "I shall be interested in knowing what became of the sheriff. Oscar went to Tonto City, possibly to see Josephine, and to get the mail. He may bring us some interesting news."

"Grub-pile!" yelled Fnijole. "Come and git it, before I throw it out!"

Henry seemed very thoughtful as he slowly ate supper. Finally he leaned across the table and said to Danny:

"Just what do you suppose the sheriff and deputy were doing out there, Danny?"

"He said he was just lookin' around."

"Looking around for what? That is part of the J Bar C range. Why would a new sheriff be riding around in the hills?"

"Well, lookin' at it thataway, it is kinda funny," admitted Danny.

"Rather queer," said Henry. "And to think that all six of you should gather at that same place. Your were on your own range. Then why did that sheriff and deputy draw their guns on you—before they could even suspect that you had gold in those sacks?"

"Yes, I realize now that it is strange. Could it be that they were coming to recover that gold?"

"And," added Slim, his mouth full of mulligan, "which couple cut that yearlin's throat?"

"Well, that's kinda hard to say," laughed Danny. "The only thing I'd swear to is that me and Slim didn't do it."

CHAPTER X

THE INQUEST

ABOUT AN HOUR later a buggy arrived at the ranch, and in it were Doctor Bogart, the coroner, and Edgar Nolan, the prosecuting attorney. Henry and Judge welcomed them warmly.

"We came to have a talk with Danny and Slim," stated the doctor.

"I will call them," said Judge. "I believe they are in the bunk-house, playing cards."

He brought the two boys in with him, and Doctor Bogart went straight into their reasons for being there.

"A short while ago Lou James, our sheriff, rode into Tonto City, seated behind his own saddle, his hands handcuffed to his saddle horn, while roped to his saddle was the dead body of Mike Haley, his deputy. Haley, had been shot down. It—"

"This is incredible!" exclaimed Henry. "Shocking!"

"It is true," replied the attorney stiffly.

"The sheriff told a queer tale," continued the doctor. "He says that he and Haley discovered Danny Regan and Slim Pickins with the missing gold from the Yellow Warrior, and arrested them. Then two masked men stepped into the scene, shot down the deputy, forced the sheriff to release his two prisoners, gave them their guns, and—"

"Wait a minute!" interrupted Danny seriously. "Is that new sheriff crazy?"

"Crazy?" parroted the doctor. "I—I don't—well, I haven't given that much thought, Danny."

"When he tells a story like that, he ought to be examined."

"Well, isn't it true?" queried the prosecutor.

"Why, I didn't know there *was* any missin' gold!"

"No one else did," admitted the lawyer, "until Doc Sargent admitted that there was."

"Well, he's sure tellin' a strange story," said Danny. "Don't it sound kinda queer to you fellers?"

"It does, to me," agreed the doctor.

"Then," said the lawyer, "you deny his story, Regan?"

"Would a man have to deny a crazy statement like that?"

"It kinda looks t' me," said Slim, "as though he mebbe knocked off his own deputy, and used that scheme to square himself. Anybody could pile a dead man on a saddle, climb up behind him and lock his own hands to a saddle-horn."

"But why try to implicate you two boys?" asked the lawyer.

"West hates this outfit," replied Danny. "He used his influence to get Henry out of office, and had his own man put in. Oscar Johnson knocked him down and threw him out of the office. West knocked me out with a pair of brass knuckles. Don'tcha suppose his hired man would try to put the deadwood on some of the J Bar C?"

THE LAWYER nodded solemnly and got to his feet.

"I suppose we may as well go back, Doctor. You try and have

a talk with the sheriff. The man may have a queer kink, you know."

"It wouldn't surprise me a bit," agreed the doctor.

"Just in case you don't know it," said Judge, "Lou James, the sheriff, served two years for a hold-up about twelve years ago. It was a deputy's bullet which gave him that permanent limp."

The lawyer looked keenly at Judge and drew a deep breath as he picked up his hat.

"In that event," he said, "I can't applaud Mr. West for his choice."

"In the parlance of the theater," said Henry, "none of Mr. West's acts have exactly been wowed at the J Bar C. We shall be interested in hearing further about the mental condition of the new sheriff."

"The inquest will be held at ten o'clock tomorrow morning," said the lawyer. "You might all attend."

"Delighted," smiled Henry. "But, as a word of caution, you really should have the sheriff watched—or disarmed—especially during the inquest. One never knows, does one?"

"I suppose that is true," agreed the doctor. "Well, good-night, gentlemen."

"Good-night, Doctor," replied Henry. "There is always a cordial welcome to either or both of you here, and at any time."

Henry bowed them out and watched them drive away.

"Danny," said Henry, "the world lost an actor when you became a cowboy."

"It gained a liar," said Judge dryly.

"Danny did not lie. He never denied being there, Judge. When that lawyer asked him if he denied it, Danny asked him if a man would have to deny such a charge. I really believe they think the sheriff is crazy."

"If he isn't," said Judge dryly, "he will be when he finds out that Danny and Slim deny being there."

AND JUDGE Van Treece was not far wrong. Next morning,

an hour before inquest time, Lou James sat in Doc Sargent's office at the Tonto Saloon, and Lou James was filled with impotent wrath. His flow of profanity had been weird and wonderful, but his vocabulary was nearly exhausted, when Doc said:

"All that is damned expressive, Lou; but it don't help matters. I've talked with Doc Bogart and Nolan, the prosecutor. They went out last night to talk with Regan and Pickins, who not only denied ever being out there with you, but suggested that you are as crazy as a sheepherder. Not only that, but both men believe Regan and Pickins."

"Them dirty liars!" wailed the sheriff. "Them dirty liars."

"Exactly," agreed Doc Sargent. "But, if you'll stop to think it over, Lou—your story does sound damned fishy."

"You, too?" queried the sheriff, almost crying with rage.

"Not me," denied the boss gambler. "I believe you."

"Well, what the hell!" wailed the sheriff. "If they don't believe me, what'll I do? I've got to tell the same story at the inquest."

"Can't you think of a better one?"

"And make myself out a liar on the first one?"

"Well, that's up to you. By the way, that prosecuting attorney asked me what penitentiary you lived in for two years, doing time for participating in a hold-up twelve years ago."

"Aw-w-w, hell!" snarled the sheriff, getting to his feet. "That ain't none of his damn business. They'll keep shootin' off their mouths until I get mad and lead up a few of 'em. Got any whisky in here, Doc? I shore need a shot right now."

Doc gave him a drink from his private bottle.

"You better be rather careful what you say at that inquest, Lou," said Doc. "They think you're a liar; so if you talk too much, maybe they'll know you are."

"But, Doc, I'm not lyin'."

"I guess you're not, Lou; but I'll bet that you and I are the only ones in Tonto City who believe you are telling the truth."

HENRY HAD a talk with the prosecuting attorney, before the inquest was opened, and the lawyer made a few notes to give to the coroner. The courtroom was filled to capacity when the sheriff was put on the stand to testify. He tried to be dignified and defiant, but was visibly nervous, as he began his rambling tale of what happened on the rim of Crazy Woman Cañon. He went into detail, and the crowd was silent, listening to the queer story.

When he finished, the coroner glanced at a piece of paper, cleared his throat, and said:

"Sheriff, you haven't told us why you and your deputy were out in those hills."

"I told yuh, we was jist ridin' around."

"For no reason whatever, Sheriff?"

"No!" snapped the sheriff.

"I see. You heard some shots, and searched for their origin?"

"That's what I said."

"You and your deputy were standing near the rim of the cañon, when you say you saw Danny Regan and Slim Pickins come over the rim of the cañon, each of them carrying a gunny-sack?"

"That's exactly what I told yuh."

"Yes, I believe you did. Then, you and your deputy covered them with your guns, took away their guns, and then looked at the sacks?"

"That's what I told yuh."

"Correct. Now, Sheriff, did you know that the gold was hidden in two gunny-sacks?"

"Of course I didn't."

"Did you suspect that the gold was put in gunny-sacks and hidden in a little cave on the cañon rim?"

"How the hell could I suspect such a thing?" flared the sheriff.

"Then why did you and your deputy cover these two men with your guns and take their guns, before examining the sacks or their contents? What right had you to do this?"

"I—I—well, damn it, they had that gold!"

"And you didn't even know it was in gunny-sacks?"

"Well—no. But it—"

"That is all, Sheriff. In my opinion, you are the only witness. There does not seem to be anything for the jury to do, except to bring in a usual verdict of death, caused by a party, or parties, unknown."

"Ain't you goin' to put them J Bar C fellers on the stand?" asked the sheriff.

"It would be only a waste of time for them to refute your testimony, Sheriff; you did it very well yourself."

"Yuh mean that I'm a liar?"

"Well," smiled the doctor, "I am not making any hair-trigger decisions regarding your veracity—but we did not quite believe your story. Has the jury arrived at a verdict? Thank you, gentlemen."

After the inquest was over, Henry remarked to Danny:

"I wish that you and Slim would ride over to Crazy Woman Cañon and see if that dead yearling is still there."

"Why, shore," agreed Danny heartily. "But I don't see—"

"Neither do I, Danny; it is merely a queer notion of mine."

The yearling was there, with a flock of hungry buzzards, and the running-iron was still there in that dead bed of coals. Henry smiled and rubbed his red nose when Danny reported.

IT WAS late that night when Jack West came to Tonto City. Doc Sargent told him all about the inquest.

"Lou James is plain dumb," declared Doc.

"Dumb enough," agreed West wearily.

"Do you believe his story?" queried Doc.

"Certainly. But Lou bumped into too many brains when he bucked up against that J Bar C. Van Treece used to be one of the smartest lawyers in the West. It was two-to-one, and they whip-sawed Lou James—and the gold is still missin'. All right, Doc; round up the men I sent down here, and bring 'em here.

I'm goin' to tell 'em to put that J Bar C outfit out of business—and I don't care how they do it."

"All right. I've been keepin' an eye on this office lately, watching for somebody to leave another plain envelope."

West's jaw tightened for a moment, his eyes searching the desk-top.

"I haven't seen any more," said Doc. "The only person I've ever seen come in here, when the office was empty, was that scar-faced swamper, who says his name is Tom."

"Yeah? I've noticed him. Where did yuh get him, Doc?"

"He drifted in here and asked for the job."

"How long has he been here?"

"Let me see. I think the first time I saw him was—why, it was the day Parke Neal died, if I'm not mistaken. Yes, I'm sure it was."

"The day Parke Neal died, eh?"

Doc nodded thoughtfully. "I've had an eye on him for quite a while. He's off shift at nine o'clock, and comes back at five in the morning. I don't even know where he sleeps."

"I'll have one of the boys trail him, Doc. That thousand dollar reward is still good. He'll have worse than a scarred face if he's mixed up in this deal."

Doc went out to find West's gunmen, and a shadowy figure moved away from the rear window of the little office. The figure circled the building and came around in front of the Tonto, where the illumination from the window disclosed the scar-faced Tom Silver.

He stood there for several minutes, smoking a cigarette, but finally crossed the street, went down past the sheriff's office, and struck off across the hills in the darkness.

CHAPTER XI

OPEN WARFARE

THINGS WERE QUIET in Tonto City next day. Doc Sargent spent most of his time keeping an eye on Tom Silver, and on the door of his office. West had detailed Lee Vane, a gunman, to watch Tom Silver, but Vane liked his liquor too well to be of much use a lookout.

When Doc went to supper, he locked the office door. Not only did he lock it, but he arranged papers on the floor in such a way that no one could enter in the dark without disturbing them. Doc was not exactly sure that someone did not have a key to either the front or rear door.

He came back from supper, unlocked the door and examined the papers, by the light of a match. Satisfied that no one had been in there, he was about to turn away, when the matchlight showed a plain envelope, almost in the center of the desk.

Doc lighted a lamp and sat down at the desk, where he picked up the envelope. No one could have entered the room—and still, there was the letter. And Doc could swear that it was not there when he locked the office. Doc had no compunction in opening the envelope. Inside was a single sheet of paper, on which had been printed with a pen:

YOU ARE IN THE SHADOW OF THE GALLOWS AND ONE OF THESE DAYS THE ROPE WILL BE READY. THE SCAR-FACED MAN KNOWS NOTH-ING OF THIS DEAL. IF YOU HARM HIM, THE BLOW WILL FALL SOONER.

There was no signature. Doc leaned back in his chair, trying to puzzle out how the writer of that warning knew that the scar-faced man had been suggested, and how on earth the letter had been left on that desk.

Doc shoved the note in his pocket, lighted a cigar, and sagged back, blowing rings toward the rough ceiling. He would not dare let Jack West know about this note. At least, not let West know he had opened and read it. West would kill him for doing that. Suddenly a disquieting thought caused him to blink violently. Suppose the writer of the note knew that Doc had opened this note—and might tell West, in another communication.

"But how could they?" Doc asked himself. "Both doors are closed, a curtain over the one window."

He inhaled deeply of the cigar-smoke and blew it ceiling-ward. For a moment or two he remained motionless. Then he swung out of his chair and went to the door. His eyes roved swiftly over the room, and he smiled slowly as he closed the door. The orchestra was practicing in the honkytonk, making a terrific din, as he sauntered over to the stairway. He went slowly upstairs to a narrow hallway. Turning to the left, he went down a short hall and stopped before a door. Without hesitation he opened the unlocked door, and stepped into the room.

Lola was standing in front of a dresser, clad in a dressing-gown arranging her hair. She turned in amazement to see Doc inside the doorway. He softly closed the door and came toward her.

"What are you doing in here?" she asked. "Walking in, without even knocking. You know well enough that—"

"Now, now," soothed Doc. "We won't argue about that, my dear."

"Well—sit down," she said and turned back to the mirror. With her left hand she patted one side of her hair, but her right hand dipped into a partly open drawer of the dresser.

"No, I don't believe I'll sit down," laughed Doc.

"Suit yourself."

"That's right, sister."

DOC MOVED quickly to the center of the room, and with a flick of his patent-shod foot, kicked aside a Navajo rug. Lola whirled, and her beautiful face went gray in the lamplight. Doc looked at her and laughed softly.

"I figured it all out, my dear," he said triumphantly. "Only the old flooring between here and my office—and the rug covered a crack big enough to let you drop a letter. And it gave you a great chance to listen, too."

Lola's eyes narrowed dangerously, but Doc did not heed.

"West promised me five thousand dollars to show him who put those clippings on the desk," he told her. "That is real money; but I'd rather play the game with you."

"Play the game with me?" she said dully.

"Yes—play the game with you. I've got you cinched, sweetheart. And you'll play the game the way I want it played, too. Why, you little fool, one word from me, and West would have your pretty throat slit. It might have been your game—once; but it's my game now."

"What right have you?" she asked slowly.

"Right? I caught you, didn't I?" Doc laughed harshly. "If I didn't think I could nick West for a thousand times that five thousand, I'd squeal on you—and take the five. Maybe I will—if you—if—"

Doc's voice broke. The lamplight flashed on a small, nickel-plated revolver in Lola's right hand, and it spat wickedly as she pulled the trigger. Doc Sargent went to his knees, and slowly slid forward on his face, without a word.

For fully a minute Lola stood there. Faintly she could hear the rattle and bang of the orchestra, and it suddenly occurred to her that the report of the gun might not have been heard downstairs. With a trembling hand she shoved the gun inside the waist of her gown.

She had no regrets over killing Doc Sargent. But how to get rid of the body, without incriminating herself? Forcing her nerves to do her bidding, she finished dressing and repaired her makeup.

Locking the door behind her, she went slowly down the hall.

Tom Silver, a bucket and mop in his hands, stood aside for her to pass, but she stopped.

"Come to my room," she whispered. Wonderingly he followed her into the room, where she lighted a lamp. He went quickly to the crumpled body on the floor, and turned it over.

"You got him?" asked Silver, looking up at Lola.

"I had to do it," she said grimly.

"That's all right," he said callously.

Tom Silver got to his feet and looked around.

"Can't have 'em find him in here," he muttered. "Wait! I just swamped out Doc's room. You go downstairs. Take it easy, don't hurry. Let me handle this. Wait a minute. What'd yuh shoot him with?"

Lola showed him the gun. He broke it open and took out the empty shell.

"Thirty-two, eh?" he grunted. "Gambler's gun! Go downstairs, and act natural; I'll fix this—if I'm lucky."

After Lola had gone down the stairs, Tom Silver picked up the body, took it outside and closed the door. Swiftly he carried it down the narrow hallway, and around to the left, where he opened the door of Doc Sargent's room. No one had seen him. The orchestra was busy again, and the drummer seemed to have a grudge against his bass, judging from the way he was beating it.

TOM SILVER placed the body near the bed, and went swiftly to a chest of drawers, where he took out a small Colt revolver. Quickly he removed a loaded cartridge and replaced it with the one from Lola's gun. He was going to try and make it look like suicide. It was the only thing he could do. He knelt beside the body, wondering just where to place the gun, when he heard the door creak open.

As quick as a flash he whirled around. Standing in the doorway was Lee Vane, West's gunman who had been ordered to keep an eye on the scar-faced man.

As quick as a flash Tom Silver lifted the gun and fired. The hired gunman was falling as Tom Silver sprang to his feet, and he saw a black dot appear in the center of the gunman's forehead. The man had hardly crashed to the floor when Silver dropped the gun beside Sargent's body, stepped over the other man, who had fallen inside the doorway, darted around the corner, and was in Lola's room, when an alarm was sounded downstairs.

That last shot had been plainly heard in the saloon, because, just at that moment, the orchestra had decided to take a rest. Several men ran up the stairs. Lee Vane's legs were extended into the hallway, so there was little difficulty in locating the scene of the tragedy. More men crowded into the narrow hallway, and Tom Silver came from Lola's room, mop and bucket in hand. Due to the crowd, he was unable to reach the main hallway, but talked with the bartender and one of the gamblers. His alibi was perfect.

They sent for the sheriff and the doctor, who had difficulty in getting through the crowd.

"Both of 'em killed with a thirty-two," said the sheriff, after a short examination had been made.

"Apparently both killed with this one gun," said the doctor. "You can see that it contains two empty shells."

"And Doc done all the shootin'," nodded the sheriff. "It looks t' me like he shot Lee Vane, when Vane walked in on him, and then turned the gun on himself."

Doctor Bogart nodded soberly. "That seems to be the solution. Was there anybody else on this floor when it happened?"

"Nobody, except the swamper, that scar-faced feller," said the bartender. "But he didn't see it. We was up here, right after the shot was fired, and he was down in Lola's room, cleanin' up. I know he was, 'cause we was crowded here in the hallway when he came from her room, with his mop and pail."

"I reckon we'll make it murder and suicide, Doctor," said the sheriff. Doctor Bogart nodded quickly.

"That is the way I see it," he replied.

There were plenty of willing helpers to take the two bodies down to Doctor Bogart's house. In making his official examination of the bodies, Doctor Bogart found the note. It puzzled him.

"And still," he told himself, "this might explain something about the tragedy. Perhaps this Lee Vane knew something about Doc Sargent, which might send Sargent to the gallows. Sargent suspects the scar-faced man of something, but this note says that the scar-faced man knows nothing about the deal. I shall turn this over to the sheriff."

When Lola went back to her room that night, she found that the floor had been carefully cleaned, and that there was a clean Navajo rug on the center of the floor.

TONTO CITY was shocked over the double tragedy, following so closely the murder of Mike Haley, the deputy sheriff. Lee Vane was almost an unknown in Tonto City. Jack West sat in the little office of his ex-boss-gambler and tried to puzzle the thing out. He was positive that Doc Sargent did not kill Lee Vane, and then kill himself. Sargent barely knew Vane.

The sheriff had given West the note that the doctor took from Doc Sargent's pocket, and this rather complicated things. West was sure it was another communication from the unknown person who had sent him those two clippings. Either Doc Sargent was the author, or he had opened a letter intended for West. The mention of the scar-faced man proved that somebody had overheard their conversation, or Doc Sargent had exonerated the man they knew as Tom.

West had detailed Lee Vane to watch the scar-faced swamper—and Vane was dead. The bartender had proved an iron-clad alibi for the scar-faced swamper; so West was obliged to eliminate him. He did not know which way to turn. Judge and Henry were having a drink at the bar when West left the office.

"It's plain to be seen that you're legal adviser at the J Bar C," said West to Judge, who bowed pleasantly.

"Thank you, Mr. West. We came in to extend our sympathy in your hour of bereavement. It must be quite a blow to lose a gambler and a gunman in the same evening. We sorrow with you, sir; do we not, Henry?"

"Yes, we do—not," agreed Henry solemnly.

"Still bein' funny, eh?" said West coldly.

"Back in private life, you know," smiled Henry. "And, by the way, I want to thank you for your political efforts in getting me out of the public eye, when I was more or less of a mote, I believe."

"I didn't have a damn thing to do with it."

"You did not? Well, well! I must note the names of the three commissioners, in order to add them to my list of bald-faced liars. Why, Mr. West, they told me you had me removed. In fact, they also told me that you selected Mr. James to succeed me."

"That's news to me," growled West. "Maybe you have information on who killed Doc Sargent and Lee Vane."

"No information," sighed Henry.

"But," said Judge, "it merely follows out the old adage—those who live by the sword—you know. The same thing covers six-guns. Vane was a gunman, pure and rather simple—and Doc Sargent was rather in the same category. As ye sow, so shall ye reap."

"I suppose you have an opinion on who killed Mike Haley, too."

"Too?" queried Judge. "No, I haven't, Mr. West. Haley? Haley? Wasn't he the same Haley who was arrested twice in New Mexico, on a rustling charge. The name was the same."

"I never heard of anythin' like that, Van Treece."

"I may be wrong, of course; but I don't believe it. Of course, we do not believe Lou James' story of the two masked men."

"Incredible," murmured Henry.

"Well, I believe it!" snapped West.

"Not so loud," cautioned Henry. "There is talk of sending James to the insane asylum—and you surely don't want to go along."

Jack West snorted in disgust and walked away.

"That, sir," declared Judge, "was a well-placed shot. Shall we drink again?"

HENRY LOOKED sharply at the poker-faced bartender, who had heard the conversation.

"Will you please open a sealed bottle of bourbon?" asked Henry.

"Sure," nodded the bartender. "But it's the same as you've been drinkin'."

"I realize that perfectly. But this saloon belongs to Jack West; and I'm taking no chances."

"You don't suppose I'd poison yuh, do yuh?" snapped the bartender.

"Guessing wrong has made a living for many a tombstone maker," replied Henry. "In this case, I like to see the seal unbroken."

The black-clad Nick Borden came sauntering in, spied West at a roulette layout, and went over there. West's greeting was a vicious scowl, but Borden smiled widely. From a side pocket of his coat he took a piece of ore, which he held out to West.

"Smoke Tree gold," he said. "Pretty good, eh?"

West looked sharply at the piece of rich ore.

"I've ordered a five-stamp mill," informed Borden. West gave him back the ore, and looked Borden over curiously.

"I had three of the best experts in the West look over that Smoke Tree property—and they reported that there wasn't two-bits worth of gold in the whole hill. I still believe 'em, Borden."

"Nothing strange about that," smiled Borden. "You believed what your sheriff told at the inquest, too, I understand."

"Suppose I did—what of it, Borden?"

"Oh, nothing. I understand that one of your gunmen and your boss-gambler shot it out between 'em. Or was it true that Doc shot the hired killer, and then bumped himself off?"

"What's yore interest in all this, Borden?" queried West.

"Oh, just natural curiosity, I suppose. I knew Doc pretty well, you see."

"Doc Sargent was a good man," said West.

"I suppose there is good in everybody, but I never found that quality in Doc Sargent. If you ask me, I think he was a snaky little gambler, and as crooked as the track of a sidewinder. He was your boss-gambler, and you trusted him, I suppose, but he'd have cut your throat too damn quick, if there was money in the job."

"I'm not askin' for yore opinion, Borden. Yore rep ain't none too good, as far as that's concerned."

"I'm not bragging," laughed Borden easily. "I understand you used your influence to knock Conroy out of office. Were you afraid of him, West?"

"He's a damn fool," growled West. "Sheriff! That—that specimen!"

"Speaking of specimens," grinned Borden, "you should have heard your sheriff testify at that inquest. You might, at least, have put in an intelligent sheriff—or don't you deal in brains?"

"Lou James has plenty brains, and don't forget it, Borden."

"I suppose they'd look like a lot, if they were spattered around a room. I don't mean head-filling—I mean thinking brains."

"I suppose you think yo're smart?" queried the exasperated West.

"Smarter than your three experts," agreed Borden, patting his pocket. "I wouldn't trade for your Yellow Warrior—even."

AND WHILE Henry and Judge visited Tonto City, Danny

and Slim were riding through the hills around Crazy Woman
Cañon, trying to find more evidence of rustling. They worked
carefully, now, keeping to the higher ground, and using an old
pair of field-glasses religiously.

Eventually they came out on the open rim above the old
springs, where they dismounted and searched the bottom of
the wide cañon with the glasses. Suddenly Danny swore viciously.

"Somethin' wrong down there, Slim!" he exclaimed. "Get
goin'!"

They rode swiftly down a dangerous trail to the wide bottom
of the cañon, where they raced down through the brush and
up past the corral where the yearling had been killed. Three
cows lay near the remains of the yearling, and more were scattered at intervals. Swiftly they searched the brush around the
spring.

"An even dozen—and mostly old cows," said Danny. "It's the
bunch that hangs close to water."

"But—but what killed 'em, Danny?"

"Some damn fiend has put poison in the spring. Mebbe
cyanide. Oh, the dirty cowards! Twelve cows! Slim, it's the first
move to put the J Bar C out of business. It means war, damn
'em. We've got to cover that water until we've got time to clean
out the spring. C'mon—we've got to work fast. By sundown
there'll be mebbe fifty head in here for water."

They tore down sections of the old corral fence, piling it on
top of the spring so that nothing could get to the water. Dead
crows along the muddy seepage below the spring attested to
the potency of the poison.

"Do yuh reckon they'll poison Antelope Springs and Moses
Well?" panted Slim, as they piled poles.

"Gawd, I hope not, Slim. We can't afford to keep a guard at
the three water-holes. Even if we could, they'd prob'ly shoot
the guards. There! I think that'll hold 'em. In the mornin' we'll
ride to Moses Well and have a look. We'll bring Oscar and

Frijole, and throw all these cows out of this range, down to
Moses—unless that's as bad. We'll bring shovels and dig 'em
all out clean—if we can."

"Do yuh reckon this is West's work, Danny?"

"If I knew it was, I'd go to Tonto City and shoot his gizzard
full of holes. C'mon, let's get back to the ranch. But don't stop
peelin' the old eye. A cow poisoner wouldn't hesitate to shoot
yuh in the back."

Henry and Judge received the news calmly, but Oscar flared
to a white heat.

"Ay skal ta'l you, Ay am going to kill somebody," he declared.

"Just who will you kill?" queried Henry.

"Ay don't give damn!"

"That is the worst feature of it, Oscar. Before any killing is
done, we must find who is guilty."

"Yust let me get my hands on 'em," growled Oscar. "Ay'll
choke de truth out of 'em."

"But you can't go and choke everybody in Wild Horse Valley."

"Va'l," admitted Oscar reluctantly, "Ay couldn't do it oll in
von day, of course."

"Fortunately. Danny, I suppose this is the first move to ruin
the J Bar C. It is a damnable way of doing it. However, we are
not quite ruined—yet. Judge and I will ride with you tomorrow.
If Moses Well is still pure, we will stay there, while the rest of
you drive the stock from Crazy Woman Springs. It is the least
we can do."

"Yah, su-u-ure," agreed Oscar. "You use de shotgon, Henry.
Ay loaded some shells vit bockshot."

"No, I believe I shall pin my faith on a rifle. Judge is much
better with the shotgun than I am. Or," grinned Henry, "would
you rather quote law to them, Judge?"

"Under the circumstances, sir, I believe the shotgun method
will get better results," replied Judge. "I hope and pray that I
may not need to fire a shot."

"I hope and pray that I do," said Henry soberly. "In my own pleasant way, I feel myself going berserk. Sort of a fee-fi-fo-fum complex, I suppose. You remember that old nursery rime, something about, I'll grind his bones to make my bread. Pleasant thought, of course. Make much better hash, I suppose.

"If someone will dig up the jug, I believe I could use a drink. Reckless youth, I suppose."

CHAPTER XII

THE LOST MINE

THE J BAR C men were away from the ranch before daylight next morning, heading straight for the water-hole known as Moses' Well. This was a sizeable trickle from between two huge rocks in a shallow arroyo. There was a small, mud-bank reservoir. Several head of cattle were drinking, and many more had finished by the time the six riders reached the spot, but there did not seem to be any fatalities.

"Well, it's a cinch they ain't poisoned this one—yet," said Danny. "Henry, and you, Judge, hide yore horses in the brush above the water, and then hide yoreselves in a spot where yuh can look things over. Stay there until we drift cattle in here; and if any stranger shows up, let 'em get up to the water. But at their first move to put anythin' into the water—blast hell out of 'em."

The four men rode away, and Henry and Judge proceeded to hide their horses, after which they sprawled in the brush behind rocks near the water. It would be hours before the four riders could possibly be able to move that bunch of cattle.

"Destiny is a queer thing," mused Henry. "Only a few months ago I had never been outside a city, never lived any place except in a hotel. My only impression of the West was gained from seeing a stage play, 'The Squaw Man.' Have you ever seen it, Judge?"

"No, I never have, Henry. But I have seen many squaw-men in real life."

"I suppose they all had the same experience. But what I meant to convey was the fact that here I am, hiding in the brush, far out in the wilderness, longing for an opportunity to slay a man. I suppose I should slink—and gnash my teeth. But I am too fat to slink, and I never was a successful gnasher. I wonder if it would help the illusion if I grew a fierce mustache."

"You would look like a walrus, Henry."

"Yes, I suppose—a desert walrus. Oh, well, I suppose there is no use. Even the horses protest. Did you note the actions of that buckskin horse of mine, Judge? He groaned dismally when I vaulted into the saddle—or was that a vault? And you'd have thought he had an anvil on each of his four feet. And would you believe it, in my callow youth, I actually dreamed of being a jockey. I suppose I had visions of winning by a nose."

"Sh-h-h-h!" hissed Judge. "Look! Two riders coming! Down that way, Henry. I saw them above the brush."

Henry started to get up, but Judge jerked him down.

"Oh, that is right; I forgot," grunted Henry, "you do the looking."

"They are watching the place," reported Judge. "Perhaps they suspect."

"Good!" sighed Henry. "Perhaps they will depart in peace."

Fully two minutes passed before Judge issued another verbal bulletin.

"They are coming on," he whispered. "They are very close, Henry. Now—they stop. Dismounting now. One of them has a package in his hands. Sit up easy, Henry, and have your gun ready."

Carefully Judge cocked both barrels of the shotgun.

KER-WHOOM! BOTH barrels of that shotgun went off,

*Henry started to get
away from that spot.*

sending buckshot skittering through the brush. The butt of the gun was against Judge's middle, as he was shifting it to a shooting position, and the recoil knocked the breath out of his lungs.

The two men darted for the brush, drawing their guns. The heavy, black-powder shotgun loads threw up a cloud of smoke.

Zee-e-e-e! A revolver bullet dug into the dirt, showering Henry with sand and gravel.

Sping! Another bullet ricocheted off Henry's rifle barrel, and he went crawling away from that spot.

Henry's objective was an outcropping of sandstone farther up the hill, where he believed he might be well above the two men. He had lost track of Judge, until he heard that shotgun roar again, and another putt of smoke eddied above the brush. Again those six-shooters cracked spitefully, sending bullets through that smoke-screen.

Now that Henry knew their attention was all upon Judge, he scuttled faster. He was so intent upon speed that he lost sight of that pile of sandstone. As a matter of fact, he came out above it. At his right was a rather deep arroyo, with precipitous banks. By standing erect Henry could see the two horses which the two strangers had abandoned, and the shooting had caused them to move farther away, dragging their reins. Henry looked around cautiously. By going straight ahead, along the ridge, he must surely get in above the two men. Stooping as low as possible, which lowered him fully six inches, he began moving slowly, his eyes very alert.

In fact, he was so alert to danger at his left that he did not notice that the bank on the right side was undercut. Suddenly the solid-appearing sandy silt broke loose, and Henry found himself falling into the arroyo.

He dropped straight down for a dozen feet, landed on a sandy shelf, which broke loose, and went rolling like a barrel to the bottom of the sandy arroyo, but still clinging to his rifle.

For several moments he sat there, dazed and winded, staring back at the top of the bank, where the sand and dirt were still sifting down the hill. A peculiar gurgling moan caused him to shift his eyes. Twenty feet away, under the overhang of the bank, was an old spotted cow, just surging to her feet, and beside her was a very young calf.

She was an old mossy-horn, scarred and skinny, who had probably had many a battle in defense of her off-spring. She twisted quickly, her rump against the bank, head down, a warning rumble in her lanky throat. Henry was on his feet, panting heavily, as he backed away in the sand.

Then he turned and began running up the arroyo, with the old cow bucking and twisting behind him, bawling angrily. Henry went through, or over the brush like a runaway tank. He went out of that arroyo, leaped over a Spanish-bayonet clump which was on the edge of an adjoining arroyo, landed on the seat of his pants, and went all the way to the bottom, where he landed in a cat-claw bush.

AND THAT was the end of the race, as far as Henry was concerned. All the belligerent mother-cows on the J Bar C could not get action out of Henry now. He had slid the seat out of his pants, and was sitting in a cat-claw, but he did not mind. He still had his rifle.

Slowly he crawled out of the bush and looked around. A

short distance down the arroyo was a rocky overhang, and under this were evidences that someone had camped there. Henry started for the spot, but he heard the sound of running hoofs, the crashing of brush.

A rider was racing around the upper end of the arroyo, partly concealed in the brush. Henry braced his legs far apart, flung up the rifle, and without even attempting to aim the weapon, pulled the trigger. The heavy weapon bucked wickedly, but Henry had the satisfaction of seeing the rider's sombrero flip off his head. An instant more and the rider swept on out of sight.

Cautiously Henry made his way up the arroyo and climbed out at the upper end. He knew that the rider did not stop to pick up his hat; and this hat might be evidence. Henry found it, snagged on a mesquite bush. Through the top of it was a jagged hole; and on the sweat-band were the two initials—D.R.

Henry quickly replaced the hat, and made his way through the brush. Someone was calling his name. It sounded like Oscar's voice.

"Yoo-hoo-o-o-o!" answered Henry. He reached the slope down to Moses' Well, and was tearing his way through the brush when they met him.

Danny, Frijole, Oscar and Slim—with Judge panting along, carrying the shotgun.

"They—they got away!" panted Judge. "The boys arrived too late. Are you unhurt, Henry? My God, look at your pants!"

"I can not turn around that far," replied Henry, soberly. "You let them get away, Judge?"

"I had little to do with it—they merely went. And, if I may ask, sir, what were you doing?"

"I?" Henry grounded his rifle. "Why, I—well, I attempted to flank them, Judge, when the bank broke away, and I was nearly deposited in the lap of a belligerent cow. I presume she thought I came to take her baby."

"And she took to yuh, eh?"

"Not quite *to* me," corrected Henry. "She lacked the necessary speed. Since then I have been—well, coming back."

"Anyway," said Danny, "you stopped 'em—and that's somethin'. One of 'em shot my hat off—but I was goin' too fast to even make a guess where the shot came from. But I shore heard that bullet."

"You should be more careful, Danny," said Henry soberly.

"Well, we heard the shootin', Henry; so we came back."

"I'm very glad you did. By the way, over there in an arroyo, I saw where someone had been camping. I did not examine it, but—"

"Campin'?" queried Danny. "Say, we'll jist look into that. Mebbe that bad bunch is livin' out here in the hills. Can yuh find it again?"

"I believe I can, Danny."

"How far over is it?"

"I believe," replied Henry soberly, "you go to the top of this slope. From there it is one fall, a cow-chase and a long slide."

"That's like a Kentucky distance," laughed Slim. "A look, two whoops and a brook."

DANNY FOUND his hat, and they examined the bullet hole in the crown.

"That's what I call damn good shootin'," said Danny. "Pickin' the hat off a man's head while his horse is buck-jumpin' this brush."

"A proficiency I hope to never attain," sighed Henry.

"You won't," consoled Slim. "You allus shut yore eyes and jerk the trigger."

"I know," nodded Henry. "Sorry, but that is my way."

They went into the arroyo, and Henry pointed out the spot. There were evidences of many small camp-fires, empty cans stacked neatly against the rocky wall. Two old rawhide pack-sacks were full of assorted foodstuffs, and a blackened coffee pot still contained coffee-grounds. A canvas covered roll of blankets, rolled up, gave them their clue to the owner. An old, empty envelope, on which were penciled figures, showed the address of Parke Neal, Tonto City.

"Parke Neal!" exclaimed Judge. "This was his camp. No wonder it hasn't been found!"

Danny quickly examined the bottom of the arroyo for tracks, and went striding down the soft sand, with the rest of the men following. Two hundred feet below the old camp, deep in a side arroyo, where the heavy brush almost concealed it, they found Parke Neal's prospect hole.

Here was an outcropping of brown quartz, into which Neal had driven a tunnel about six feet in depth. Judge knew something of mining. He examined the face of the little drift closely, picked up several pieces of the scattered rock, and turned, an expression of amazement on his long, lean face.

"My God!" he exclaimed softly. "A bonanza! Look at that stuff!"

"Yumpin' Yee-ru-u-u-salem!" exploded Oscar.

JUDGE SEARCHED his pockets and drew out an old envelope. With the stub of a pencil between his long fingers, he sat down and began writing swiftly.

"Is this just a sudden whim, or are you writing out your will?" queried Henry.

"I'm writing a location notice, sir. The six of us claim this as our legal property. Parke Neal never recorded this mine; so it is legal for us to take it. Now, what will we name it? Who has an appropriate name?"

"What color was that calf, Henry?" asked Danny.

"Sort of a yellow, I believe, Danny."

"That is it!" exclaimed Judge. "The Golden Calf. I shall locate six claims around this point of discovery, all under the one name. There! Oscar, go back and get me one of those empty cans. I shall put this notice in the can, and place it in a prominent position.

"Danny, you and Slim and Oscar go ahead and bring the cattle to this range, while Henry and I go to Tonto City and see that this is recorded at once. I believe we can find our way across the hills to Tonto City."

"You will pardon me, I am sure, Judge," said Henry, "but we will go first to the ranch."

"This, sir, is something that can not be delayed. Do you realize, sir, that this is worth a million dollars?"

"And, sir," retorted Henry, "do you realize that I have no seat in my pants? This gold may have blinded you—but I am sure it has not affected the optic nerves of the good folks of Tonto City."

"Go ahead," laughed Danny. "It's a cinch that them poison-ers won't make another attempt today. C'mon, you saddleslick-in' millionaires; let's go!"

Henry and Judge got on their gentle horses and started for the ranch.

"Do you really believe it is a bonanza?" asked Henry.

"Henry, it is another Mint."

As they rode through the hills, Judge scratched his head thoughtfully as he looked back several times.

"I can't quite figure it out," he admitted.

"What is the problem?" asked Henry.

"It is about those two men, Henry. I am very positive that they rode directly east. In fact, I saw them disappear in that direction."

"No one has disproved that, has he, Judge?"

"I haven't mentioned it to anyone, until now. But if they went east, how on earth could one of them shoot the hat off Danny Regan's head, when he came in from the north, almost di-rectly after I saw them disappear to the eastward?"

Henry shook his head slowly.

"It is rather remarkable," he admitted. "But as I have often said, Judge, anything might happen in Arizona."

CHAPTER XIII

CLAIM JUMPERS

JACK WEST LEANED against the counter in the recorder's office, chewing on a black cigar, as he thumbed the pages of the mining records. Only a clerk was working in the office at this time of the day; a tall, slatternly young man, with a narrow chin. West studied him as he stood at a high desk, copying with a pen.

"Yo're a new man around here, ain't yuh?" asked West.

The young man closed the book and came over to the counter.

"Yes, I've only been here a short time," he answered.

"Do yuh like it here?"

"Well, I ain't crazy about it."

"What does this job pay yuh?"

"Seventy-five a month. I'm on extra now. A feller must eat."

"That's right," nodded West, his eyes thoughtful. He glanced around the empty room, and lowered his voice.

"What would yuh do if yuh had a thousand dollars?"

The young man grinned lazily.

"A thousand dollars? Huh! I dunno, mister. That's a lot of money. Well, I wouldn't stay in this place, that's a sure thing"

"Nothin' to keep yuh here, eh? I mean, if yuh had a thousand."

"I should say there isn't—not me."

"Fine! You know who I am—Jack West. Come over to the Tonto Saloon tonight, about nine o'clock. I'll be lookin' for yuh—and we might make a deal that will pay yuh a thousand dollars."

"Yeah?" The young man looked keenly at West. "Wait a minute. I'm not going in on any deals that might put me behind the bars."

"I wouldn't ask you to, son. You merely do me a favor, get on the stage and pull out, one thousand dollars richer."

"I'll be over at nine o'clock," nodded the clerk, and Jack West smiled to himself as he went back to the saloon.

He was standing at the bar, enjoying a drink with the bartender, when a commotion outside caused him to go to the doorway. Lou James, the sheriff, was getting painfully off his horse. One eye was swollen completely shut, and the other nearly so. His nose was swollen, lips puffed, and one ear was swollen all out of shape.

"What on earth happened to you?" exclaimed West. James peered at him through his one usable eye, swore bitterly and leaned against a porch-post.

"Did somebody beat yuh up like that?" asked West. "Come back to the office where we can be alone. You need a drink, Lou."

TAKING THE sheriff away from the curious onlookers, West led him back to the office, where James sank down in a chair. West handed him the private bottle, and Lou drank noisily.

"That tastes good," he muttered. "I shore needed it."

"Now, what in the devil happened to you?"

"Yesterday afternoon," said the sheriff, "Conroy and Van Treece came to my office and told me that somebody was poisoning their water-holes. They swore that a dozen cows died around the one they call Crazy Woman Springs. I reckon they got mad because I didn't rush right down there.

"Anyway, I decided to go down there today. Let me have another shot of that stuff; I need it."

"Take a big one, Lou; and go on with yore story."

"Thanks. Well, I rode alone down there, and got off at the spring, when that damn Swede raised up from behind the brush, covered me with his gun, and came over to me. He took my gun and threw it in the brush, then threw his own along with it, and then he said:

" 'Ay vars ordered to shoot, but Ay radher fight.'

"Well, I done my best. God, that Swede hits like the kick of a mule!"

"Yeah, I realize that. Yo're big enough to handle him, Lou."

"That's all right. When he hits you on the chin, size don't mean a damn thing. I only remember gettin' hit once."

"Are you goin' to stand for 'em treatin' yuh like that, Lou?"

"I don't know what I'm goin' to do, except that I'm goin' down and see if Doctor Bogart can take some of the swellin' out."

"Was there really a dozen dead cows down there?"

"I reckon there is; I didn't count 'em."

"Well, don't forget that yo're the sheriff of this county."

"That don't save yuh from a crazy Swede who wants to fight."

"WITH CONDITIONS as they are, we should be at the ranch, my dear," said Henry, "but neither Judge nor myself could resist the temptation of dropping in near suppertime. You really have no idea how Frijole Bill can mistreat food."

"I am sure you are always welcome here, Henry," smiled Mrs. Harper. "Leila and I were anxious for more news, too. Someone said that Oscar nearly killed the sheriff yesterday."

"Yes, I'm afraid he did," sighed Henry. "What he will do next, no man knoweth. He elected himself to guard that water-hole, and the mere fact that the intruder happened to be the sheriff meant nothing to Oscar."

"Is Danny helping guard the water?" asked Leila anxiously.

"Danny and Slim went over to examine Moses' Well today," said Judge. "Oscar is still searching for cattle which might drift back to Crazy Woman Springs. They have dug out the water-hole, but still have it covered, because we have no way of testing it."

They sat down to supper, and Henry grew expansive, telling the woman about their Golden Calf mine.

"Is it really so rich?" asked Leila in amazement.

"The richest prospect in Arizona," declared Judge. "In fact, it is my opinion that it will prove richer than the Three Partners."

"It seems to me," said Henry, "that all prospects are compared to the Three Partners. Why not compare the Golden Calf with the mines of Solomon? Or was Solomon a miner?"

"As much of a miner as Jack West," laughed Judge.

"I saw Jack West today," said Leila. "That is the first time I have ever seen him. He owned the Three Partners, did he not?"

"Jack West, I believe, was the original discoverer," replied Judge. "That was over twenty years ago, when Maricopa was a small group of rough shacks. Life was hard in those days. Jack West had three partners, I believe. One was Parke Neal, and the other is rather a mystery man. I have heard that West beat Parke Neal out of his share of the mine. However, I have seen the record, and West's is the only name to appear. Neal swears that West had nothing to do with the discovery of the Three Partners. He intimated, I believe, that West got rid of their third partner. Perhaps he did. West is shrewd, and as unscrupulous as a wolverine.

"There is no doubt that the Three Partners was the richest gold property in the State. West sold it for a cold million dollars. But I firmly believe that the Golden Calf is as rich, if not richer. Just as soon as we can have an expert—"

Someone was rattling the door of the millinery shop, and Leila hurried from the room. It was Danny and Slim, two very excited young cowboys.

"They're tryin' to jump our claim!" blurted Danny.

"Jump it?" queried Judge. "Impossible! Our property is duly recorded. Sit down, boys; you seem all upset."

"I hope yo're right," said Danny. "Me and Slim was over at Moses' Well, lookin' things over, when we heard several blasts. They didn't seem far away so we went over and looked at our mine. Nothin' had been touched; so we sat down, wonderin' where the blastin' was bein' done. We was there about half an hour, when two more went off. They was so close that we could feel the earth shake.

"Not over four or five hundred feet away, over in a gulch, north of our claim, we found three men workin' on a mine. We rode in on 'em and asked what they were doin' there. One feller, he said his name was Jim Short, claimed to have located the mine a couple of weeks ago, and told us to go and look at the records. Their property covers all our Golden Calf."

"Why, that is incredible!" exclaimed Judge.

"That ain't the word I used," said Danny, "but I reckon it means the same thing. Me and Slim came here as fast as we could."

Judge got slowly to his feet, looking at his watch.

"The records must show," he muttered. "We still have fifteen minutes before the office closes. Let us have a look at the records."

A FEW minutes later the four men clattered into the recorder's office, and demanded to see the book of mining records. Only the gray-haired recorder was in the office. Judge swiftly turned the pages to the recorded notice of the Golden Calf. On the preceding page was the recorded notice of the Lucky Hunch Mining Co., dated ten days ahead of the Golden Calf. It recorded five full claims, headed by the name of Jim Short. The other four were out-of-state addresses.

Their dreams of wealth vanished as they leaned against the counter and looked dumbly at each other. Henry turned the book around and looked at it keenly.

"Judge," he said huskily, "where is the returned notice of the Golden Calf?"

"Here," replied Judge, and took it from his inside pocket. On the front fold of the notice was the pen-written notation of book and page: Book 2—Page 200. Henry glanced at it, and called the recorder.

"Where is the young man who was here when we had this recorded?"

"Why," smiled the recorder, "he decided to quit. Yesterday he took the stage for Scorpion Bend. I believe he was going to California. Is there anything wrong, gentlemen?"

"This location record," replied Henry, "shows that it was recorded on page two hundred; *and there is no page two hundred in this book.*"

He turned the book around, and the recorder looked at it closely.

"Well, isn't that queer? No, there isn't. I suppose the young man made a mistake."

"I am very much afraid that there was no mistake, sir," said Henry coldly. "If you will examine it closely, you will see where the page has been removed with a sharp knife."

Deep in the binding was the evidence.

"But I don't understand it," protested the recorder, puzzled.

"I do, sir," said Henry. "But the man who did it has gone to California—and California is a mighty big State."

They left the old courthouse and stood on the sidewalk together.

"Plain highway robbery," said Judge bitterly. "The clerk was bribed to remove the page, after which he recorded that Lucky Hunch, setting the date back ten days, and finally recorded our mine again, and on the next page."

"What can be done about it?" queried Henry.

"The law," replied Judge, "would decide against us."

"Law be damned!" gritted Danny. "Let me and Slim and Oscar settle this deal."

"Let us be sensible," said Henry. "I suggest that we go home. Unless I am mistaken, Frijole finished a fresh batch of prune juice yesterday. This is the first million I have ever lost—and I need something to cushion the shock."

That night, while Henry, Judge, Frijole and Oscar mourned their loss in prune whisky, Danny and Slim slipped out to the stable, saddled their horses and rode back quietly to Tonto City.

"There's an old sayin', Slim," said Danny. "Somethin' about fightin' the devil with fire. Anyway, it's worth tryin'."

"I'll do anythin' once, except eat tripe," replied Slim.

That night Jim Short sold the Lucky Hunch to Jack West for enough money to take him to California, too. West made out the bill-of-sale, which Short signed. The other five owners did not count in the deal, because they did not exist.

THE NEXT morning three of West's men, with several pack-horses loaded with provisions, powder and tools, left for the Lucky Hunch.

There were no roads; so they were obliged to use pack animals.

They knew the location of Parke Neal's discovery, and that was their destination.

Everything went well until they drew up at Parke Neal's camping place, where they met Danny, Slim, Frijole and Oscar, all armed with rifles.

"What's this all about?" asked the man in charge of the expedition.

"Was you figurin' on jumpin' this claim?" queried Danny.

"We ain't jumpin' anythin', cowboy. This property was bought from Jim Short last night; and we're workin' the claim for Jack West."

"Jim Short? How'd he come to own this—when we located and recorded it. We don't know Jim Short."

"You better find out 'bout him then," said the man. "This claim belongs to Jack West. Let's unload the animals, boys."

Danny's rifle clicked softly.

"Now, listen to me, young feller—" said their spokesman.

"I'm through listenin'," gritted Danny. "In this country, we shoot claim jumpers. I'm givin' yuh jist ten seconds to start yore caravan out of this country. Git ready, boys. One, two, three, four, five—"

"All right, we're goin'. But we'll be comin' back, with the law behind us; and don'tcha forget that."

"Six, seven, eight—"

"They're goin'," chuckled Frijole. "How 'bout throwin' a little gravel into their boots, Danny?"

"Not unless they slow up a little, Frijole."

"Das is a good yoke," chuckled Oscar. "Ay'd like to ponch das smart faller in de yaw."

"Well, what's the next move?" asked Slim, grinning widely.

"Oh, I suppose we might as well visit the water-holes and see how things are goin' along. It's up to West to make the next move."

CHAPTER XIV

THE FARO DEALER

THE THREE MEN and their pack-horses went straight back to Tonto City. Jack West was up at the Yellow Warrior, but a messenger soon brought him to town, where he learned from the men what had happened to them. West immediately sent for the sheriff, and told him.

"I want you to deputize several men," stated West. "Arm them well, accompany these three men back to that property, and see that they are safely started on their work."

"All right," replied the sheriff. "I don't reckon there's any question of ownership, Jack."

"No question at all."

"Yuh don't suppose them damn fools will start shootin', do yuh?"

"Are you afraid, Lou?" sneered West.

"No, I ain't scared. But I'd rather do it alone. If I take a lot of gunmen along, it'll prob'ly mean a battle. 'F I can show 'em where they're all wrong—"

"Give 'em a battle, damn 'em," snarled West. "I put you on

this job, didn't I? Take enough men along to wipe 'em off the earth if they try to stop yuh."

"All right, Jack; I'll be ready in a little while."

But Lou James was not satisfied. His experiences with the J Bar C outfit had not been at all beneficial to his health. His eyes were still discolored from contact with Oscar Johnson's fists. Just to be sure of his legal rights, he went up to the recorder's office.

"I'd like to see the book yuh record mines in," he said.

The man gave him the book, and he made a search, after which he went down on the street, where several of his men had gathered with their horses. West crossed the street, and the sheriff met him.

"That Lucky Hunch mine ain't never been recorded, has it?" asked the sheriff cautiously.

"Recorded? Of course it has. You don't need to worry about that."

"When was it recorded?"

"Oh, I don't know the exact date," West rubbed his chin thoughtfully. "I believe it is next to the last record in the book."

"No," said the sheriff, "it ain't, Jack. The last one is the Golden Calf, and the next one to it is a group of claims up near Silver City."

"Yo're crazy, Lou! Why, I looked at it yesterday."

"Mebbe I am," agreed the sheriff, "but I don't think so. You better be sure about it before we declare war on the J Bar C."

"Come on, and I'll show yuh."

They went back to the office, and West examined the book. Cursing softly to himself, he sprung the book open wide, feeling deep into the binding. Then he closed the book with a bang and walked out of the office, with the mystified sheriff behind him. On the street, he went to the three men who had been at the prospect.

"Take that stuff back to the Yellow Warrior," he ordered. "The rest of you fellers can put up yore horses."

"But what does it mean, Jack?" asked the sheriff.

"Mean? Damn it! It means that I'm out two thousand cold dollars and them J Bar C crooks still own that property."

"Did yuh forgit to record it?"

"Yeah, I suppose that's as good a reason as any." And Jack West strode away, muttering to himself.

The sheriff turned back toward the courthouse, where he met the recorder, who said:

"I wanted to tell you something, but you went out so quick. Last night somebody broke the lock on my office door. But as far as I can discover, they haven't touched a thing."

"Nothin' in there to steal, is there?" asked the sheriff.

"Well, there isn't anything that could be used. We don't keep any money in there, of course."

"Well, I don't reckon there's anythin' to be done about it."

"**IT IS** absolutely incredible and unlawful," declared Judge, as he and Henry sat on the ranch house porch. "I hold no brief for the crook who destroyed our original record. It was damnable, sir. But for one of our—our own outfit to deliberately break a lock on the door of a public office, enter therein and feloniously remove one whole page from a book of records, I—well, sir, I haven't words to express my feelings on the matter."

Henry squinted through a glass of Frijole's Delight, cleared his throat softly and replied:

"With your limited vocabulary, Judge, I believe you have done very well with the subject. In fact, your legal outlook on life causes you, at times, to become more or less of an unmitigated ass. No doubt you have heard of fighting the devil with fire. That is what happened, and in this case the devil got singed to the extent of one gold mine."

"True enough, we retain ownership, Henry; but in such a way. We put ourselves on a par with sneak thieves."

"Really, Judge, you can not consider this as petty larceny. In fact, it was not a criminal act, except the breaking of the lock. We merely undid a crooked deal—and won back a million."

Judge lifted his glass, toying with it in his long fingers.

"At least," he said softly, "our consciences are clear, Henry. The guilt was neither mine nor yours, sir. It was done without our knowledge or sanction. I offer a toast to our purity of thought and deed."

"Then you will have to drink alone, Judge."

"Alone? Why, if I may ask, sir?"

"Because," smiled Henry, "it was I who suggested the scheme to Danny Regan."

"You?" Judge's eyes opened wide. "You suggested—"

"Ordered—if you like the word better, Judge."

"You—I—well, it—well, Henry, to you, sir; I didn't think you had that much sense."

"Drink hearty, Judge—to you, also, sir—and to the Golden Calf."

Danny and Slim rode in and unsaddled their horses. Both men carried shovels, which they stood against the corral fence, and came wearily to the house.

"They doped Moses' Well last night," said Danny, sinking down on the steps. "Two steers died before we got there, and another one was pretty sick. But we dug the whole thing out. The bottom was white with somethin'—arsenic, I reckon."

"Where is Oscar?" asked Henry.

"He insisted on goin' down to Antelope Springs. We took some lunch along, but didn't eat it; so he took it for his supper. Said he was goin' to stay there all night, and try and kill somebody early in the mornin'."

"Oscar," smiled Henry, "has the nocturnal habits of a duck hunter. He will be there, trying to get a shot at the early flight of poisoners. Danny, you and Slim get some glasses; this stuff is better than usual."

"Not me," replied Danny. "I'm crazy enough without drinkin' Frijole's prune whisky."

"I'll take a chance," said Slim. "The Pickins family has allus been noted for their ability to take punishment."

FRIJOLE CAME back from Tonto, where he had gone for provisions and the mail.

"I noticed that the parts of the stamp mill for the Smoke Tree mine has got as far as town," he told them. "Six big six-horse trucks, loaded down. They've got a well-drillin' rig, too."

"Nick Borden must mean business," said Judge. "I suppose we shall have to figure on a mill one of these days, Henry."

"The mills of the gods," sighed Henry. "They grind slowly, but they grind exceedingly small."

"I was not speaking of that kind of mill, Henry."

"That kind of a mill speaks for itself, Judge. I have been thinking of the cost of installing machinery and all that, in order to operate a mine. I believe our best move would be to sell it out, Judge."

"That's it," said Slim, wiping his lips. "A million apiece, Judge."

"Slim, can you conceive of a million dollars? Have you even the most remote idea of what it means?"

"Hell, no! But I could shore use it. I'd git me a new Stetson and a damn good ropin'-saddle and—"

"And wear clean socks every day—that belong to yuh," added Danny. "I don't mind yuh wearin' mine, Slim; but I wish you'd wash 'em before yuh put 'em back in my war-sack."

"A million," sighed Slim, "would shore be well treated by me."

"What would you do with a million, Frijole?" asked Henry.

"Daw-gone! Well, I'll tell yuh somethin'," replied Frijole. "I'd git me a boiled shirt, so damn slick that a fly couldn't git a foot-hold onto it, and I'd walk m'self into some saloons I know, and I'd say:

" 'Feller, give me a short champagne.' "

"High-toned stuff, eh?" grinned Danny.

"Yo're danged right! And I'd throw a fourbit piece on the bar, and tell the barkeep to keep the change."

"I wonder what Oscar would do with a million," said Henry.

"That Swede!" snorted Slim. "Why, he'd hire the Army and Navy, and lick 'em, one at a time. What would you do with yore million, Henry?"

Henry smiled thoughtfully.

"Why, I hadn't given it a thought, until you gave me an idea. I believe I would back Oscar in his fights against the Army and the Navy. It would be as safe as any investment I know."

THERE WERE no customers at the faro game. Lola looked up as Jack West came in, with his foreman from the Yellow Warrior. They went straight back to the office. Several miners argued at the bar, but business in general was slow. Anyway, it was too early in the evening.

Lola got out of her chair and went slowly upstairs. Walking quietly down the hallway, she paused at her door. Opening the door slowly she stepped inside. She always kept a lamp burning on the table, turned low; but even in the faint rays from the lamp she saw a man sprawled on the floor in the center of the room.

Closing the door easily, she advanced toward the middle of the room. Suddenly the man twisted with the speed of a snake, and Lola was looking into the muzzle of a six-shooter. It was Tom Silver, his scarred face twisted with anger. Neither of them spoke. Slowly Tom Silver came to his feet, and a scuff of his foot swung the Navajo rug back into place.

"What's your game?" asked Lola.

"Why do yuh think I have any game?" he retorted, coming close.

Lola reached over and turned up the lamp.

"You knew about the crack in the floor, I see," she said.

"I found it when I cleaned up the blood of the man you killcd," said Tom Silver. "I've been wonderin' why yuh killed him."

"I am very grateful for what you did that night," she said slowly. "I can never repay you for that."

"Did Doc Sargent catch you listenin'?" asked Silver.

"That is something we will not discuss."

"All right."

Tom Silver slowly pocketed his gun and came over beside the table.

"How well did you know Parke Neal?" he asked.

"Parke Neal?"

"Yes. How long have yuh known him?"

"Possibly six weeks before he was killed. I felt sorry for the poor devil, and grubstaked him."

Tom Silver nodded. "What is yore last name, Lola?"

"What is your name, Tom?" she countered, smiling.

"I reckon that leaves us right where we was. Would yuh mind tellin' me how old yuh are?"

"What is your guess?"

"Twenty."

Lola laughed, but her lips tightened for a moment.

"It reminds me of a poem I heard once, something like this:

> *"She was old, so old, yet her years, all told,*
> *Numbered a score and three,*
> *But she knew by heart,*
> *From finish to start,*
> *The Book of Iniquity."*

"Twenty-three, eh?" mused Silver. "The Book of Iniquity. But you don't know it, Lola; not at twenty-three. I've watched yuh. Men don't mean a thing to you. That's why men come to yore table. You treat 'em all alike. But look out for Jack West. He's crazy about you. Oh, he ain't the kind to make a fuss over a girl."

Lola laughed harshly. "You know a lot about Jack West, Tom. How long have you known him?"

Tom Silver shut his lips tightly, his eyes narrowed.

"I've only been here a short time," he replied.

"And yet you know Jack West so well. Perhaps you got all that information through a crack in the floor of this room."

"What I know, or don't know, is my business," he said coldly. "I helped you out of a nasty mess—remember that. I had to murder a man to save yore neck—and mine, too. We've got to be friends. What I do is my business, and the same with you. Sort of a silent partnership, Lola."

She held out her hand and they shook solemnly.

"You are the first man I have ever trusted, Tom," she said.

"A partnership of Cain," he said bitterly. "Mebbe I better go out first?"

"No," replied Lola. "I'll go down now. Put the rug back when you finish with it, Tom."

LOLA WAS back at the faro table when West and his mine foreman came from the office. They had a drink at the bar and West sauntered over to Lola's game, where he sat down.

"I ain't had much chance to talk with you since Doc got killed," he told her. "Things have kept me on the jump. Yuh didn't find out anythin' from Doc—about those clippin's, did yuh?"

Lola shook her pretty head. West's hard eyes glinted with admiration as he looked at his biggest gambling attraction.

"Doc usually kept his mouth shut," said Lola.

"He was paid to keep it shut. Everybody who works for me gets paid for the same thing, Lola. I brought you something kinda nice, just to show my appreciation."

He fumbled awkwardly in his pocket and drew out a jeweler's plush-covered ring-box. Opening it carefully, he tumbled out a three-carat diamond solitaire, set in platinum.

"I didn't know the exact size," he said, "but we can have it made to fit."

Lola picked it up from the faro table and handed it back to him.

"I can't accept it," she said simply.

"Yuh can't? Why, I don't see—why can't yuh?"

"Why do you want to give me that valuable ring?" she asked.

"Well, I'll tell yuh, Lola—I—I appreciate yore work here."

"I am paid a good salary."

"Oh, damn the salary! I mean by that—well, listen, Lola. Inside a year, I'll own all this valley. I'll be the biggest man in this State. There's nothin' yuh can't have. I'll buy yuh anythin'. What do I care if you've been a dance-hall singer, faro-dealer—damn it, yo're the prettiest woman in this country. What do yuh say?"

Lola looked straight at him, and her eyes were as hard as the sparkling bauble in his open hand.

"Your proposition doesn't interest me in the least," she replied.

"It don't, eh? Well, I'll—"

"Is the bank running this evening?" asked a voice behind them, and they turned to see the black-clad Nick Borden, his white teeth flashing in a wide smile. He saw the diamond ring in West's hand, and he chuckled softly.

"Tryin' to sell the family jewels, eh?" he said. "Nothing left, except honor. Too bad, too bad. Well, you're not the first man to bite off more than he could chew, West."

West got to his feet, flaming with wrath.

"Let me tell you somethin', Borden," he gritted.

"Please don't," replied Borden. "I never follow any man's advice; I only play hunches—my own."

Lola was laughing. West looked at her steadily for several moments, turned on his heel and went back to his office. Borden looked at Lola seriously.

"I saw the play," he told her. "Wasn't West tryin' to give you a diamond ring—or was it a proposal?"

"Is that any of your business?" she asked coldly.

Borden shrugged his shoulders and smiled at her.

"I was just a little curious," he explained, "because I've almost made up my mind to marry you myself."

"I suppose your mind is the only mind to make up."

"I was just fooling, my dear. I didn't want to play faro. Why, I wouldn't bet against one of Jack West's games if he'd let me deal the cards myself. I—well, I thought you was in an embarrassing position; so I horned in and busted it up. But you should have taken the diamond."

"I can handle my own affairs," she said stiffly.

"Yeah, I'll bet you can, Lola. But I wish you'd go in there and sing. I like you a lot better when you are singing. I like your eyes better, when they look less like a pair of smoky topazes."

"My eyes have nothing to do with you, Mr. Borden," she said.

"That is all you know about it," he retorted, and walked away.

JACK WEST was in a murderous mood when he went back to his office. He flung himself in his chair and took a big drink from his private bottle. Everything seemed to be breaking wrong for him. With all his wealth and his organization, he was being balked in the things he wanted to do. His foot scuffed a piece of paper on the floor and he glanced down.

It was a piece of ruled tablet paper, folded twice. He picked it up and unfolded it. On one side were penciled figures, as though someone had made out a bill. He held it closer to the lamp. The figures read:

To ⅓ of $1,000,000.00 . . . . $333,333.00
Interest for 20 years at 7 per cent $466,660.00
                                              _____

            Total. $799,993.00

"One-third of a million dollars," muttered West, puzzled

over the large amount. "Interest for twenty years—twenty years—"

He lowered the paper to the desk, staring at the blank wall of the office. A million dollars! Twenty years' interest. West's face twisted bitterly. Parke Neal was dead—rotting in his grave on the side of the hill above town. There was only one answer. Slowly he tore the paper to bits and threw them in a cuspidor.

"They'll never collect a damn cent," he told himself. "But who put that paper on this office floor? Was that note, which was found in Doc Sargent's pocket, only an alibi for the scar-faced swamper?"

West got to his feet and walked to the door, but stopped, his right hand gripping tightly on the butt of the revolver in his pocket. Slowly he released the gun and went back to his desk, where he took another drink.

"I almost made a fool of myself," he muttered, "I've got to *know* things first."

He walked out into the saloon and went up to the bar. The scar-faced swamper was through for the night, and as he walked past the bar West spoke to him.

The man stopped.

"Is anybody usin' Doc Sargent's room now?" he asked.

"Not since Doc used it, Mr. West."

"All right; I'll sleep there tonight."

"It's all swamped up fine. I put clean beddin' on the next day."

West nodded, looking with narrow-lidded eyes at the back of the scar-faced man as he walked out.

"He's a queer lookin' jigger, Mr. West," observed the bartender. "But he minds his own business, and he shore does his work good."

"That's all yuh can ask of either a man or a horse," said West dryly.

CHAPTER XV

A WILD NIGHT

THE FOLLOWING AFTERNOON, while Danny and Slim were inspecting the water-holes, Oscar and Frijole went to work on building a new corral. Oscar had failed to kill anybody at Antelope Springs; and was quite disappointed, after spending a chilly night, sans blankets.

"Ay don't like das ha'ar yob," he told Frijole, as he piled poles into a wagon-box. "Ay van't to be a detacktive."

"Yea-a-ah?" queried Frijole.

"Yah, su-u-ure. Ay had a ha'al of a good yob, as a yailer. Ay hope to be de sheriff of dis county, Free-holey."

"Yeah, that'd be fine. I ain't easy to tickle, but I'd shore laugh myself plumb to death."

"Su-u-ure. Ay would make you de onder-sheriff."

"That breaks m' laugh right off in the middle, and sends me into hy-stericks," remarked Frijole. "I reckon that's enough poles for this trip. Say, do yuh know it, we've gotta take this wagon to a blacksmith-shop pretty soon, and have a couple tires set. Them two front ones is almighty loose."

"Yah, su-u-ure," agreed Oscar. "Das a good idea, Free-holey. Ay vould like to go to town, too."

"Yeah. I'll betcha them girls in the Tonto shore miss you."

"Su-u-ure," grinned Oscar sheepishly. "Yosephine miss me, too."

"Huh! The only time Josephine ever missed you was when you ducked that chair and she crowned the drummer. She's a fighter."

"Yosephine," declared Oscar, "is de heavyweight champion of Minnesota."

*A gun cracked and
the horse went down.*

"She is, eh? How do yuh figure that?"

"V'al, she licked das Lars Svensen, Norvegian champion of Minnesota."

"Yeah, that's right. But that makes her the Norwegian champion."

"V'al—Ay suppose so, Free-holey."

"Well, we better git home with this load of poles, so I can cook supper."

As Frijole explained it to Henry:

"I've got to have flour and beans and a lot of other stuff from town, and that wagon won't stand another day of pole haulin'. Me and Oscar will take it in this evenin', and have the blacksmith shrink on them tires, and I'll load up the stuff I need. We ort to be back here by—oh, ten o'clock."

"You should," nodded Henry. "Keep Oscar sober, and both of you keep out of trouble. You know how belligerent Oscar gets after a drink or two."

"I shore do. Well, I'll keep him as sober as an angel."

"Are you sure that angels keep sober, Frijole?"

"Well, I reckon they have to keep sober."

"I see. Perhaps, when the poet said, 'Oh, Death, where is thy sting?' he didn't think of sobriety among the angels. Or was it a poet, Frijole? I'm just a little vague."

"That's the way I look at it, too," agreed Frijole.

"We both need to brush up a little," said Henry.

"Yeah, I reckon so," nodded Frijole, "but I ain't goin' t' town to do any struttin'."

"In my opinion," said Judge, as the two men rode away on the wagon, driving a half-broken team, "no good can come of those two going to town in the evening. You should have insisted on Danny and Slim making the trip."

"Danny and Slim have been in the saddle all day, Judge. Frijole needs flour, beans and a lot of stuff."

"Indeed? I happen to know that there are two sacks of flour and one large sack of beans in the store-room."

"I know there is, Judge. But," Henry smiled slowly, "that may not be enough. Those two men are of legal age. Who am I to tell them to stay here? I am merely their employer—not their keeper."

FRIJOLE CHUCKLED on the way to town.

"That's the advantage of workin' for a feller like Henry, Oscar. I told him what I needed, and he said to go and git it. He never checks up on the stuff in the store-room."

"Hanry is a good yigger," declared Oscar.

"They jist made *him*, and then busted the mold," stated Frijole. "And lemme tell yuh somethin'; he's smarter 'n he looks."

"Yah, su-u-ure," agreed Oscar heartily. "Sometimes Ay almost believe Hanry has Svedish blood in his body. Das feller is smort as ha'al."

"Well, if he has," grinned Frijole, "it's a hell of a long ways back, and he's outgrowed the handicap."

They arrived at Tonto City and took the wagon to a blacksmith shop just off the main street. The smith was ready to close his shop, but Frijole pointed out the urgency of the job.

"All right," said the smith. "Tie the outfit around at the back, and when I'm through I'll drive it around and tie up in front of the general store. They'll be open until nine o'clock."

That was quite all right with Frijole and Oscar, who went to the Tonto Saloon, where they absorbed several drinks apiece, before looking around.

"I heard you was having trouble with somebody poisoning your water-holes," said the bartender.

"We ain't had the trouble yet," replied Frijole. "That's still comin' to 'em. Yuh heard about them gallinippers tryin' to jump our Golden Calf mine, didn't yuh?"

"I heard a little talk about it. Have you really struck gold?"

"Ay skal ta'al you!" exclaimed Oscar expansively.

"Have you got a lot of it?"

"We figure," stated Frijole, "that the vein is about sixty feet wide, sixty feet tall, and runs plumb to China. And," Frijole grew very confidential, "she runs over a million dollars a ton."

"That's a pretty fair prospect," admitted the bartender.

"Well, we can tell more about it after a little diggin'. It may be bigger than we think."

At nine o'clock, when the general store was due to close for the day, Frijole had forgotten the flour and beans. He and Oscar were trying to dance with the girls in the honkytonk, but with little success. Later, Frijole missed Oscar for a while, but finally found him at a table in the honkytonk, weeping briny tears.

"Whazzamatter?" asked Frijole.

"Ay am hort-sick," declared Oscar. "Ha'r Ay am, vasting my time vit scorlet vimmin, and poor Yosephine—"

Oscar broke down again.

"Of all the cock-eyed Swedes, yo're the worsht," declared Frijole. "What about Josephine?"

Oscar waved a huge paw in the general direction of the wall

behind him, where there was a huge lithograph, advertising a certain brand of whisky. It depicted a very beautiful young lady, caressing a huge Percheron horse, bedecked in full harness.

"Das reminded me of Yosephine," sobbed Oscar.

Frijole braced himself against the table and managed to focus his eyes on the picture. He squinted at Oscar, blinked his eyes, shook his head violently, and looked at the picture again.

"Oshcar, you shore got 'magination," he stated.

"Looks yust like Yosephine," sobbed Oscar.

"Yeah, there's a shertain reshemblance," agreed Frijole, "but you'd have t' take that bridle off, t' be sure 'bout it."

OSCAR'S PERIOD of mourning was short, but his memory was long. He saw Jack West in the gambling room, and decided to make an example of him. But in making a drunken stalk, he neglected to observe a poker game, between him and West. No one ever knew who owned which poker-chips, because Oscar, tank-like, went over the table, lost track of Jack West, and stumbled out of the place, during the confusion.

Frijole found him out in front, clinging to a porch-post, and talking Swedish to the post.

"Leggo the posht," ordered Frijole. "The sheriff's lookin' for yuh, Oshcar. Anyway, 's time t' go home."

It was nearly one o'clock in the morning, and the town was in darkness, except for the Tonto Saloon. Arm in arm they stumbled across the street to the team and wagon, where Oscar, after several futile efforts, managed to get up on the seat. Frijole untied the team, but was unable to climb up to the seat. There was no end-gate in the wagon; so he was able to enter from the rear.

"Let'r go!" he yelled at Oscar, who emitted a raucous war-whoop.

A moment later the team twisted wildly, cramping the wagon so badly that it narrowly missed turning over. Then, with a lurch of the frightened team, a bang and rattle as the wagon-box

settled back on the running-gears, the equipage went out of
Tonto City, with both horses on the run. Frijole was bouncing
around in the wagon-box, several times in imminent danger of
being thrown from the rear.

"Hol' 'em, Oshcar!" he yelped, "Hol' 'em down, you crazy
Swede!"

"Yee-e-e-minee-e-e-e!" shrilled Oscar. "Who de ha'l's got
de lines, Free-holey?"

"Ain't you got 'em?"

"Ay have not!"

Frijole Bill managed to get to his feet, clinging to the back
of the seat. The team was running full-speed, and the wagon
was swaying and bouncing over the rutty roads. The truck-loads
of machinery for the Smoke Tree Mine had cut up the road
badly, and at every chuck-hole the wagon went completely off
the ground.

The seat came off the side-boards, and Oscar landed in the
bottom of the box, along with Frijole.

"Ve better yump!" yelled Oscar. "Das ha'ar t'ing is going to
ha'al in a minute."

But Oscar's time-limit was too generous. He had no more
than declared the destination of the equipage when there came
a terrific crash, a general upheaval, and both men landed in the
brush beside the road. For several moments the air was full of
sand and dust, which blew away on the night breeze. Oscar's
voice piped weakly:

"Ay bet ten dollar Ay am deader'n ha'al."

A bush adjacent to the voice of Oscar jerked violently for a
moment, and then Frijole said weakly:

"If yuh lose—will yuh come over and help me? I come down
here upside down, and I've got a mesquite snag up inside my
boot."

"Ay am badly hort," wailed Oscar. "Everytime Ay move, Ay
squeak."

"Well, take yore time," said Frijole resignedly. "I'm still hangin' upside down from one boot. Are yuh still squeakin'?"

"Ay guess Ay am oll right, Free-holey."

After much grunting and groaning they were both out of the brush. The team had swung off the road a short distance beyond and was tangled up in the brush, but the wagon seemed intact. The runaway and accident had sobered them sufficiently to allow them to climb to the seat. But this time they held the lines.

Oscar had a quart of rye in his coat pocket, which had escaped injury; so they each had a big drink before going on to the ranch, where they left the wagon beside the stable, unharnessed the team and put the horses in the corral.

In the bunk-house Danny Regan opened one eye and looked them over. As long as they were sober enough to undress, they must be all right, he decided.

"Nothin' happened to you fellers, eh?"

"What could happen to yuh in a dead town like Tonto?" countered Frijole.

"Das right," agreed Oscar. "Das town is yust like graveyord."

"Well, it took yuh a long time to find it out."

"We ain't the kinda fellers that pass snap-judgment on any man's town," replied Frijole.

BREAKFAST WAS ready at the J Bar C, and Frijole Bill, red-eyed and sleepy, was about to hammer the suspended triangle of steel at the kitchen doorway, when two horsemen rode in through the main gate, and went slowly down to the stable.

Danny Regan and Slim Pickins were coming from the bunk-house.

"That's the sheriff and Lem Schuyler," said Danny. Schuyler owned a small ranch several miles north of Tonto City.

Frijole turned from the triangle and watched the two riders. Henry came through the kitchen and stood in the doorway.

"Who is it?" he asked. Danny came over to him.

"That's the sheriff and Lem Schuyler," he replied.

The sheriff and the rancher were looking into the wagon-box. After a few moments, the sheriff climbed into the wagon and leaned over, looking closely at something. Frijole spat dryly, and looked toward the bunk-house, where Oscar had put in an appearance.

"Seem to be lookin' at somethin' in the wagon," said Slim.

The sheriff got out of the wagon and both men came up to the kitchen porch, leading their horses. Both men looked very grim.

"How are yuh, Lem?" called Danny. "Long time I no see yuh."

"Hyah, Regan," replied the rancher.

They stopped, and the sheriff eyed them coldly.

"What's on yore mind, James?" asked Danny.

Lou James ignored the question, as he looked keenly at Oscar Johnson, and said:

"Would yuh mind tellin' us about it, Johnson?" he asked.

"Yust what in ha'al do you vant to know?"

"What time did you git back here last night?"

"It was right close to two o'clock," interposed Danny. "They woke me up and I looked at the clock."

"That bunk-house clock is five minutes fast," said Frijole.

"What time did you leave town, Johnson?"

Oscar looked helplessly at Frijole. Neither of them knew what time. Henry came out to the edge of the little porch.

"What is this all about?" he asked.

"In case yuh don't know," replied the sheriff, "I'll tell yuh. Last night, somewhere between midnight and one o'clock, some men drove a team up to the Gold Plate mine. They're buildin' a new mill up there, but they's got a one-shift crew takin' out high-grade ore.

"There's a night guard on duty up to twelve o'clock, when he's relieved by another man, who stays until mornin'. This first guard went to find out who was comin' in the wagon, and he got popped on the head. The other guard comes along a little later, and they jumped him, but he shot a couple times.

"This mornin' they found both guards tied up tight, and sixty sacks of high-grade ore missin'. Yuh know, they put it in them small, canvas sacks—but each sack is worth a hell of a lot."

"Interesting—so far," agreed Henry. "But where do we figure in it?"

"You figure in it like this," replied the sheriff. "Them sixty sacks of ore are down there in yore wagon."

"That—that is incredible, sir!"

"Yea-a-ah? And more than that, there's a dead man in there with them sacks."

Judge came out in time to hear the last remark. Frijole took a deep breath and looked at Oscar, who was wide-eyed in amazement.

"Well, bless my soul!" exclaimed Henry. He looked accusingly at Oscar and Frijole.

"You—you—well, do not gawp! What happened?"

"Let us see the evidence," suggested Judge.

THEY CROWDED around the wagon in silence. The sacks of ore were there, and the dead man, staring at the sky with lifeless eyes, was there, too.

"Who is he?" asked Judge.

"His name's Hardy, I think," replied the sheriff. "He was shift-boss at the Gold Plate."

Oscar leaned dejectedly against a wagon-wheel, trying to puzzle things out in his own mind, which was more or less of a blank.

"Are you the new deputy, Lem?" asked Danny.

"Hell, no!" exclaimed the rancher. "I'm lookin' for a team and wagon."

"Didja lose one?"

"Somethin' happened to it. I left that team tied in front of the general store last night, while I played me a little poker; and when I came out, the team was gone."

"Huh—how late was it there?" asked Frijole anxiously.

"I don't know. I come out about two o'clock, and it was gone."

"Wait a minute!" exploded Frijole. "The blacksmith was to leave our team there, too! Somebody stole our team and wagon—and me and Oscar got the wrong team. That's it, by golly!"

"Well, what the hell didja do with my outfit?" roared Schuyler.

"That—that's a question. I—I remember—yeah, that was it! Oscar didn't have the lines, and the team ran away. Why, by golly, I'll betcha we busted up right where the road forks to the Gold Plate. Take a look at the side of that wagon and the wheels. Yuh can see where somethin' hit it."

"What hit it?" asked the sheriff.

"The wagon we was in. The team ran away, and when we hit this wagon, me and Oscar was throwed out. Then we found this team and wagon, and came home with it, thinkin' it was the same one."

"Yuh mean," said Schuyler, "that my team kept on goin'?"

"They vars going like ha'al, yust before we hit, Ay know that," said Oscar.

"I reckon that's the answer," growled the sheriff. "Yuh see, about the time this robbery was takin' place, that big Swede was fallin' over a poker-table in the Tonto; so they couldn't have had any hand in it. Would yuh mind hitchin' up a team, so we can take this wagon-load back to Tonto City?"

"I've got a damn good notion to have both of you pelicans arrested for stealin' my team and wagon," growled Schuyler.

"It would furnish plenty of laughs for a jury, sir," said Judge.

"Oh, I ain't exactly a damn fool," said Schuyler, grinning. "Yuh see, I was in that poker game last night, when the Swede done his high-dive. I was seven dollars loser, when he went over the table, and when I got back on my feet, I had thirty-seven dollars worth of blue chips. I quit the game a hundred and sixty dollars to the good."

DANNY AND Slim hitched up the team and turned it over to the sheriff. Then they all filed back to breakfast.

"The town," said Danny, "vars yust like a graveyord."

Oscar smiled foolishly.

"You gallinippers dang near got yourselves in jail, don'tcha know it?"

"Yah, su-u-ure," admitted Oscar.

"Draggin' in here at two o'clock in the mornin', with sixty sacks of stolen ore and a dead man in the wagon. Not only that, but yuh prob'ly busted up Schuyler's wagon and killed his team. Well, ain't yuh got anythin' to say for yourselves?"

"Yah, su-u-ure," replied Oscar blandly. "Ve had a ha'al of a good time, Danny."

"Of course," smiled Henry, "that settles the argument."

"Henry, you never understand the gravity of things," said Judge. "You are too lenient. Why, I believe you could excuse the devil for tormenting lost souls."

"Hardly that, Judge. You see, I do not believe in the devil—and it has never been proved that a soul ever gets lost."

"I'm jist a wonderin'," said Frijole, bringing a fresh platter of bacon and eggs, "what became of the driver of that wagon. He must have lit a-runnin', when we hit him."

Henry placed his knife and fork on the table, a puzzled expression in his eyes.

"Did anyone examine the dead man?" he asked. "I mean—to determine how he was killed?"

"I didn't see any blood on him," said Danny. "The sheriff didn't say what killed him."

"Judge," said Henry, "I believe we will ride to Tonto City this morning."

"The sheriff took the only team we've got caught up," said Danny.

"We shall ride on our trusty steeds, Daniel."

Judge groaned audibly.

"Was that an expression of anticipation?" queried Henry.

"It was advance sympathy for your horse, sir," replied Judge.

CHAPTER XVI

THE THREAT

DOCTOR BOGART'S EXAMINATION of the dead shift-boss showed that the man died from a broken neck. The sheriff explained to Jack West about Oscar and Frijole, and the extra team and wagon. West listened grimly.

"Hardy got what was comin' to him, Lou," he said. "He must have been drivin' that team when the crash came. They tried to steal that load of high-grade ore. My own men—stealin' from me."

"I thought for a few minutes that I had the deadwood on that J Bar C outfit," said the sheriff. "Damn 'em, they seem to wiggle out of everythin'."

"Don't worry about that layout; I'll handle them, Lou. One of these days I'll have this whole damn county right under my thumb. I'll own everythin' worth ownin', elect my own officers, and tell 'em all what I want done."

"I'm with yuh, West," said the sheriff. "Anythin' yuh want done—jist yell."

"Mebbe I'll call yuh on that one, Lou—some of these days."

"Anythin'," repeated the sheriff.

"That's fine."

"I was talkin' with a bartender last night," offered the sheriff, "and he was tellin' me what the J Bar C cook told him about that mine they've got out there. He said their gold vein was sixty feet wide, and sixty feet high."

"Yea-a-ah? That's quite a vein of gold, don'tcha think?"

"I reckon so. How wide is the vein in the Yellow Warrior?"

"The richest vein is about twelve inches, Lou."

"My God, they must have the world by the tail out there!"

"Yeah, I reckon they have. They'll probably flood the world with gold."

"Well, why don'tcha buy it, West? He told the bartender that it assayed a million dollars a ton."

"Lou," smiled West, "do you know anythin' about gold mines?"

"Only what I've heard."

"Well, you better stick to wearin' a sheriff's badge, and forget what drunken cowpunchers and ignorant bartenders tell yuh."

"I guess prob'ly that's the best thing to do."

WEST WALKED to the doorway with the sheriff, and they saw Henry and Judge arrive in town; two queer-looking riders on two old horses which were about ready for the glue-factory.

They dismounted heavily in front of the Harper millinery store, and walked stiffly inside the place. West smiled grimly, his hands shoved deep in his pockets.

"I heard," said the sheriff, "that Henry Conroy was goin' to marry the Widder Harper."

"Yuh did, eh?" smiled West.

"Uh-huh. Her daughter is engaged to Danny Regan, too."

"I heard about that one."

"I'd shore like to git the deadwood on that J Bar C outfit," said the sheriff. "I had two of 'em—once—for a few minutes."

"Well, keep tryin', Lou; yuh never know when yore luck might change."

"That's right; yuh never do. But it might git worse."

"Yeah, that might happen. Well, how about ridin' up to the Lucky Stake with me, Lou? I'm goin' to pull all the men off that job and put 'em on the Gold Plate. I reckon I'll suspend operations on the Lucky Stake until I get the Gold Plate producin'."

"Shore, I'll ride up there with yuh," agreed the sheriff.

"Lou, yuh don't happen to know where that Golden Calf mine is, do yuh? I mean, would yuh be able to ride to their point of discovery?"

"No, I couldn't; I've never seen it."

"All right. I believe there's a man at the Lucky Stake who can take us there. I'd like to take a look at the thing."

"I'd like to see it, too. After what I heard about it."

"Who wouldn't?" smiled West. "After what *you* heard."

They found a man who could guide them out to the Golden Calf, and Jack West was amazed at the prospect.

"Except for the size, you wasn't so far wrong, Lou," he told the sheriff as they rode back. "I wonder what kind of a deal I could make with the outfit."

"Take it away from 'em," suggested the sheriff callously.

West looked thoughtfully at the sheriff.

"How far would you go in backin' my play, Lou?" he asked.

"Jist as far as yuh need me. Hell, I don't like that J Bar C no better than you do. I'd like to punch lead into every damn one of 'em."

They stabled their horses in Tonto City and had a drink at the saloon bar. There were two of West's gunmen in there, and they joined in the drink.

"C'mon back to the office—I want to talk to you fellers," West said.

Lola was at the foot of the stairs, talking with one of the girls, but she went quickly upstairs, entered her room and locked the door.

IT WAS siesta time at the J Bar C, next day; but Henry was the only one to enjoy it. The cowboys were all working, and Judge had gone to town; so Henry stretched out in an easy chair on the old porch and took a nap. He dreamed that someone had exploded a dynamite load in the Golden Calf, and blown all the gold away. He was still shaking from the force of the explosion when he awoke to find Leila Harper shaking him.

He looked up at her, blinking foolishly, wondering at the sudden turn in his dream, when he suddenly realized that he was not dreaming.

"Where is Danny?" panted Leila. "Where is he, Henry?"

"My gracious!" exclaimed Henry. "You seem agitated, Leila. Where on earth did you come from? I must have been asleep."

"I must find Danny," she replied. "Judge stayed with mother, and I rode his horse. Read this; it came in the mail today."

She handed him a small sheet of paper, on which was written:

Your life and your daughter's life in danger. Would advise that you leave Tonto City at once. Do not delay.

"Why—why, this is ridiculous!" exclaimed Henry. "An anonymous note, anyway. I don't see—well, what does it mean?"

"Who knows?" replied Leila. "Mother is worried sick. She doesn't know what it is all about. We don't know what to do."

Henry studied the note again.

"Leila, I wonder if this is a bluff. You remember they tried to buy out your hat shop. It might be—and still, as you say, who knows? What did Judge say about it?"

"He is worried, too. Can't we find Danny?"

"I believe they went to Crazy Woman Springs. Yes, we might find them. At any rate, we can try."

"Let's hurry."

Henry looked with sad eyes at the only two horses in the corral. His ancient steed had been accidentally turned out, and the two in the corral were not Henry's type of saddle-animal. He had heard Slim speak of that blaze-face sorrel as a jug-head that tried to bite his own tail. The other one, a tall bay, was, according to Danny, fifteen years old and had never felt a rope since the day he was branded.

"Please hurry," begged Leila.

Henry took a lariat from the fence, opened the gate and entered the corral. He had seen Slim and Danny rope their own horses every morning—and it looked simple. The two horses crowded into a corner, twisting and turning, only to suddenly whirl and dash past him along the fence. His loop was so big that it got both horses around the neck, but the bay sagged back and tore loose from the loop, leaving Henry with the blaze-face sorrel.

"You certainly are improving," said Leila.

Henry managed to tie the rope to the fence, while the blaze-face eyed him malevolently. Henry did not bother to put on a blanket, but cinched on the bare saddle. Strangely enough, the horse did not fight away from the bridle. Henry led the horse out of the corral and closed the gate.

"That isn't the horse you ride to town, is it?" asked Leila.

Henry sighed and looked at Leila.

"You are worried, too," said Leila.

"I—I feel a complete physical let-down," said Henry grimly.

HE HELD the reins tightly, managed to set his left foot in the stirrup, grasped the horn with both hands—and started up. The blaze-face started going sideways, away from Henry, who was clinging with both hands, one foot in the stirrup, and the other foot half-over the saddle.

They crashed into the corral fence, and the jerk threw Henry into the saddle. The sorrel bounced away from the fence, but Henry's sharp jerk on the bit drew the animal up quickly. Fumbling with both boots, Henry managed to find the stirrups.

"I didn't realize that you could ride that well," said Leila.

"Needs must, when the devil drives," he quoted, and much to his surprise the sorrel moved in beside Leila's mount, and they rode out through the main gate.

"Leila," he said, "can you or your mother think of any earthly reason why anyone should harm either of you?"

"Why, no, we can't. There isn't any reason."

"Is there anyone who would want to prevent you from marrying Danny?"

"Not a soul—that I know about, Henry."

"Leila," he said gently, "there is something I haven't told you yet. You see—well—"

"About you marrying mother?"

"Did she tell you?"

"Would I have to be told? I am not blind."

Henry rubbed his nose and looked at the bobbing ears of the sorrel.

"It will be the happiest day of my life," he said. "You see, I don't want anything to interfere with that—not anything."

"I hope we can find Danny," said Leila anxiously.

They came into the old trail to Crazy Woman Springs, and Henry took the lead, bobbing along under his huge sombrero, and wondering how long the sorrel would wait, before "trying to bite his own tail." Being in single-file there was little chance for conversation.

It was six miles from the ranch to Crazy Woman Springs. Henry was merely guessing that the boys were at the springs. As far as he knew, they might be over at Antelope Springs, miles east, or at Moses Well.

They were about three miles from home, traveling slowly along the brushy trail, when several head of young cattle drifted across the trail ahead of them. As they reached the spot where the cattle had crossed, a yearling steer trotted parallel to the trail, and Henry noticed that a rope dragged from the animal's neck. Its knees were skinned, too, and a patch of hide was off its left hip.

Apparently this yearling had been roped and thrown, but in some way had escaped with the rope. The J Bar C mark was plain on its left side. Henry merely noted these things, but gave them no serious consideration.

A SHORT distance farther on, the trail swung sharply to the right, around the head of a brushy cañon. As they came out in the open, Henry saw a rider, far off to the left, silhouetted against the sky for several moments as he drove several head of cattle over a sharp ridge.

Henry knew that all the cattle had been taken off the Crazy Woman range and thrown on the ranges farther east; but it meant nothing to him that these cattle were heading west, and going away from Crazy Woman Springs. He drew up and called back to Leila:

"We will turn and go back a ways, Leila. I saw one of the boys over that way."

They retraced their way around the head of the cañon, where Henry took the lead, going toward the spot where he had seen the rider.

"I only saw one of them," he told her. "But I am sure they are working together."

There was no trail now, and Henry was obliged to steer by dead reckoning. A heavy mesquite growth made it impossible for them to follow a direct route until they struck an old cattle trail, which seemed to lead where they wanted to go.

Henry was scanning the country for another glimpse of riders, when the sorrel stopped short at the edge of an arroyo, which was at least twenty feet deep. As Henry jerked around to see what had stopped his horse, he got a kaleidoscopic view of four men, going into swift action. He saw a little fire, a bound and struggling animal, and the four men, scattering like quail.

A gun cracked wickedly, and the sorrel went down, as though something had jerked its legs from under it, pitching Henry aside and into a thick bush. He was dazed and stunned for the moment. Dimly he heard more shots, but they meant nothing to him just now. He squirmed loose from the bush, but in the wrong direction, and pitched head-first into the arroyo. He made a half-turn and landed, sitting down in the soft sand, and with hardly a sound.

"Circus stuff," he muttered foolishly, and got to his feet. His gun had fallen from his holster, but he gave it no thought. There was the little fire, and the struggling yearling. There was not a sound now. Henry stumbled over and looked at the yearling. It was lying on its right side, and there, in bold script on its left side were the combined initials "LJ." A runnin-iron had been cast aside, and Henry picked it up, only to drop it quickly.

"That's hot!" he announced to the world.

His big hat was at the foot of the sharp bank; so he went back, picked it up and went hunting for a place to climb back to the top. Fifty feet down the arroyo he found the cattle trail, and went up to the top. He stopped and scanned the country.

"Leila!" he exclaimed sharply. "Where on earth is Leila? She was with me."

He took off his hat and mopped his brow. As he dropped his hand to his side, his head jerked from a blow, and he went flat on his back, while from across the arroyo came the whip-like snap of a rifle.

HENRY HAD no idea of time or space. Only his sense of hearing remained. He could hear voices, above the buzzing in his ears. They seemed far away, but very distinct.

"I told yuh I got him cold—right between the eyes."

"Yuh shore did; damn good shootin', too, if yuh ask me. Well, he's out of the way. There's his horse over there, too. Didn't I tell yuh I seen that horse go down? That's why I wanted to Injun back here and git that fat pelican."

"I reckon you was right. We better cut that yearlin' loose and high-tail it out of here, before somebody comes to investigate them shots. I'll be damned if that fat jigger didn't almost ride off that bluff, right into us. It shore scared me."

"Scared all of us," chuckled the other. "Well, let's git goin'."

Henry had not moved a muscle, for the simple reason that he was incapable of any movement. The statement of his demise registered on his brain as a cold, hard fact. He had heard them walk away. Suddenly his head began to ache. His muscles twitched back to life, and he opened his eyes. That is, he opened one. The other seemed heavy with something.

"Dead men do not ache," he told himself, and then chuckled aloud.

After some effort he managed to get to a sitting position, where he felt himself over and looked around.

"They say that souls have no substance," he muttered. "If that is true, I am not dead—because I am most certainly substance."

His exploring fingers found that the bullet had glanced off his forehead, digging considerable of a hole, which had spewed blood all over his face, and especially into his left eye. He mopped some of it out with a handkerchief, and got drunkenly to his feet.

His sorrel was sprawled on the edge of the arroyo, drilled through the head, killed instantly. It was after he looked at the horse that he remembered Leila again. The roped yearling was gone, the ashes of the fire had been kicked into the sand.

"Maybe she went for help," he said hopefully as he picked up his hat, but found his head too sore to bear its weight.

The outlook was not bright. It was about six miles back to the ranch, and those high-heel boots were not made for walking. He left his spurs on the saddle and started out, hoping to strike the old trail back.

"Henry," he said aloud, "you, sir, are a hell of a rancher. You were a disgrace as a sheriff, a failure as a cattle raiser, and—and—damn it, you can not even die gracefully. Your head is so hard that it turns bullets. You should join a carnival and get a job, putting your head through a hole in the canvas, and let the yokels heave baseballs at you, at five cents a heave. I am, sir, so thoroughly disgusted with you, that I could even enjoy watching you drink yourself to death."

CHAPTER XVII

NO SALE

JACK WEST SPENT much of the afternoon in his office, conferring with the foreman of the Gold Plate mine. West had suspended operations at the Lucky Stake, and sent the men all over the Gold Plate in order to speed up the work on the mill.

After the foreman left the office, West sat at his desk, deep in thought for several minutes. Suddenly his eyes focused sharply on a tiny shower of dust, which sifted down to the polished top of his desk. Lazily he got to his feet and stepped over to a cabinet in the corner of the office, where he took a drink from a bottle, his eyes keenly searching the ceiling.

He walked back to his desk, glanced over a few papers, and walked to the door, which he opened, held it for a moment or two, and then closed it. There was a soft, rustling noise at the ceiling, and an envelope dropped like a plummet to the top of his desk.

For fully a minute he stood there. Then he opened and closed the door again, after which he walked over to the desk. It was some kind of plain envelope, sealed; and inside was the funeral notice of Mrs. Jack West, clipped from a newspaper. West merely glanced at it, shoved it in his pocket and stepped back to the door, which he opened quickly.

Lola was standing, half-way down the stairway, talking with two of the girls from the honkytonk, while Tom Silver, mop and bucket in hand, came down the stairs past them, and went into the gambling room.

"Lola's room," said West to himself. "That swamper goes there every day to clean up the room. Which one dropped that envelope?"

His teeth gripped his cigar tightly, his agate-hard eyes watch-

ing Lola, laughing at some joke. He cursed her under his breath.
The scar-faced man came from the rear of the gambling-room,
and walked past West, intent only on his duties.

"One of 'em," West told himself, "but which one? There's just
one safe move—get 'em both—cold."

He left the door of his office and walked out to the street.
Judge Van Treece was standing in front of Harper's store,
looking down the street. West looked at him and smiled grimly.
He crossed the street to the front of the general store, and Judge
came up there.

"HOW'S THE gold mine?" asked West.

"My opinion may not be worth a cent, sir," replied Judge,
"but I believe it is a bonanza."

"You've got six claims out there?"

"Yes, sir."

"I'll give yuh ten thousand dollars for the mine, sight unseen."

"You must have seen it," replied Judge, "because you would
not pay that amount of money for the Mother Lode—without
inspection."

West laughed and shook his head.

"Just another of my foolish deals," he said.

"Like the Three Partners Mine?"

West's eyes hardened quickly.

"What do yuh mean?" he asked sharply.

"Merely a remark to show you that I know just how foolish
you are."

"Oh, I see. Well, how much do you want for that prospect,
Van Treece?"

"We haven't decided on a selling price, because we haven't
considered a sale, Mr. West. Offhand, I would say that we might
consider one hundred thousand dollars. I say, we might."

"Hell!" snorted West. "Why, it's only a prospect!"

"So was the Three Partners when you sold it."

"What do you know about the Three Partners?"

"The selling price was no secret—or was it?"

"Exaggerated a little, I'd say."

"But still—only a prospect, if my memory does not fail me."

"It was worth all they paid for it."

"I feel the same about the Golden Calf, Mr. West. It appears so rich that we would have no trouble in interesting capital, in case we wish to develop it. By the way, wasn't it some of your men who tried to jump it? I heard they were in your employ."

"You know damn well what happened!" snarled West. "One of your gang stole a page out of the records. Yeah, that's what I said—stole it. The J Bar C took that page out, and nullified my location of the Lucky Hunch."

"As Mason to Mason," smiled Judge, "what did it cost you to get page two hundred removed from that same book?"

"I don't know what yuh mean, Van Treece."

"Think it over," smiled Judge. "It may come back to you."

JUDGE TURNED on his heels and went back to the millinery shop, where Mrs. Harper was waiting anxiously.

"I don't see what can be keeping Leila," she said. "She said she would be right back. Judge, you don't suppose anything has happened to her, do you?"

"My dear Mrs. Harper," soothed Judge, "nothing would happen. She is a good rider, and that horse is perfectly reliable. In fact, even a gallop is as foreign to that horse as—as wheels on a goose."

"But that warning note, Judge."

"Yes, yes. But it merely warns both of you to leave Tonto City. Oh, I am very sure that she will be home soon. You must not worry."

But Leila did not come home, nor did anyone come in from the J Bar C until well after dark. By that time Mrs. Harper was frantic from worry. Judge was standing outside the shop when Danny, Slim and Oscar rode in. Judge called to them, and they dismounted in front of the shop.

"Where is Leila?" blurted Judge anxiously.

"Leila?" queried Danny. "What about Leila, Judge?"

"Where is Henry?"

"Ain't he here?" gasped Danny. Mrs. Harper came out, but Judge took her arm and they all went into the house, where they listened to Judge telling all he knew about it.

"But she wasn't at the ranch," said Danny, white-faced now in spite of his copper-like coat of tan. "Henry wasn't there either."

"I thought something was funny," said Slim. "I accidentally turned Henry's horse out this morning. I meant to pick it up again, but forgot it. Before supper I noticed that Henry's saddle was gone, and so was that blaze-face sorrel."

"He couldn't ride that sorrel," said Danny quickly. "Why, he couldn't even saddle that jug-head."

"Don't fool yourself," said Oscar gravely. "Das Hanry is smort yigger."

"I know, Oscar," nodded Danny wearily. "But that horse is as wild as a wolf. Slim can tell yuh that."

"He stuck my nose in the dirt twice, hand-runnin'," said Slim. "He's *mucho malo caballo*, that feller."

"But where on earth could they be?" wondered Judge. "They must be together—and Henry riding a wolf."

"Yah su-u-ure," agreed Oscar. "Ay bet tan dollar they are oll right. Hanry is smort yigger."

"But what about that note?" asked Danny. "What did it mean?"

"Nobody knows," replied Judge. "Leila took the note. She wanted to see Henry and Danny."

"Do yuh reckon they got lost in the hills?" queried Slim.

"That old knot-head that Leila was ridin' would come home, if she'd let him," said Danny. "God knows what happened, if Henry was ridin' that sorrel. Oh, I can't believe he'd ever be able to rope him. Henry can't use a rope."

"Don't fool yourself," stated Oscar again. "Hanry is smort yigger, you bet."

"Can't you think of anythin' else to say?" asked Slim testily.

"Aw, let him talk," said Danny. "We're all more or less crazy, I reckon."

"Das oll right," agreed Oscar. "Ay am smort, too."

"Listen, Oscar," said Danny. "Do you realize that Leila and her mother got a note in the mail today, which told them that their lives were in danger? Leila came out to find me—and where is she?"

"Ay don't know," replied Oscar blankly.

"Yuh might as well try to talk sense to a wooden Injun," said Slim.

"V'al," said Oscar, "Ay never went to school a ha'al of a lot, but it seems to me we could do more by honting den by yust talking."

"I reckon, at that, you've got more brains than we have," said Danny. "Let's go back to the ranch. If they ain't there, we'll head into the hills. God knows what good that will do—in the dark—but we'll be doin' somethin'. You stay here, Judge; we'll bring yuh word just as soon as we have anythin' to report."

FRIJOLE BILL had washed the supper dishes, and was sitting in a corner of the kitchen, reading a year-old magazine, when Henry came up to the doorway. Frijole took one look at him in the lamplight, dropped the magazine and gasped:

"What the hell's this?"

And well he might remark. Henry's shirt and pants were nearly torn off his body, his feet were bare and bleeding, and in addition to the dried blood on his face, his forehead was swollen badly. He was at the point of collapse when Frijole grabbed him and eased him into a chair.

Then the cook ran for the prune whisky jug, filled a cup and held it for Henry to drink. When it was empty he filled it again, but Henry motioned it away. The potent liquor brought renewed life to Henry. Frijole looked at Henry's feet, drank the cup of whisky himself, and started a fire under the teakettle.

"I am rather a mess, Frijole," mumbled Henry.

"You set there and take it easy, Henry. I'll need a lotta hot water for you. But how in hell didja lose yore boots?"

"Couldn't walk—had to take them off."

"Gawd, yore feet are full of cactus! I don't see how yuh walked at all. Hell, you must be tougher'n I thought."

"Yes, I am rather remarkable," admitted Henry. "I was killed today."

Frijole looked queerly at him.

"Where is Leila?" queried Henry. "She came back all right?"

"I ain't seen her, Henry. Here—drink another cup of this chain-lightnin'."

"You—you say she hasn't been here?"

"No, she ain't."

"She was with me, when they shot my horse," he said slowly. "That was before they killed me—I believe. Yes, I'm sure it was."

"Now, that's all right," assured Frijole. "You have a drink, and it will be all right."

"Locoed as a sheepherder," he told himself. "Got to humor him."

He poked more wood into the stove and tested the water with his finger. Henry drank the second cup of that liquor.

"Where is Danny?" he asked.

"Danny and Slim and Oscar went to town, Henry. Where's yore hat and gun?"

"I don't remember losing the hat, Frijole. I believe I lost the gun when I fell into the arroyo. They killed my horse on the edge of the arroyo, and I fell all the way to the bottom."

Frijole came from the stove, looking keenly at Henry.

"They shot yore horse? What horse?"

"That blaze-face sorrel. The one Slim said tried to eat his tail."

"You was a-ridin' that sorrel, Henry?"

"Yes, I rode him today."

"Worse'n I thought," sighed Frijole, and turned back to the stove.

"Who shot yore horse—the sorrel?" asked Frijole.

"Cattle rustlers."

"Cattle rustlers, eh? How'd yuh happen to select that sorrel?"

"He was the only available horse," replied Henry slowly. "Leila came on Judge's horse. She—she wanted to find Danny; so I—I had to saddle that sorrel."

FRIJOLE LOOKED thoughtfully at Henry. Something terrible must have happened to put him in this condition. Perhaps he wasn't crazy after all.

"Why did Leila want to find Danny?" asked Frijole.

Henry felt gingerly of his sore forehead.

"Something about a note," he said dully. "It was some—" and Henry toppled off the chair.

Frijole half-dragged, half-carried him to his room, where he put him on the bed.

"Your string kinda frazzled out, Old Timer," said Frijole. "I'll git me some hot water and a towel, and kinda fix yuh up. Dawgoned, if that don't look like a bullet scrape on yore forehead! Kinda deep, too. Huh! I wonder what about Leila? I don't *sabe* what this is all about."

The house reeked of carbolic acid and horse-liniment when the three cowboys came back to the ranch. Frijole was seated on the foot of the bed, pulling cactus thorns from Henry's feet, when the boys came bursting into the bedroom. They stopped short, staring at Henry, who struggled to sit up. That last thorn was very deep, it seemed.

"What in the devil happened to him?" gasped Danny.

"He walked home in his bare feet," replied Frijole. "How are yuh, Henry?"

Henry blinked at the light, turned his head and looked all around.

"It looks very much like a wake," he said huskily.

"Henry, where is Leila?" asked Danny anxiously.

"Leila? I don't know, Danny."

"She was with you, wasn't she?"

"That is right—I forgot. Danny, I don't know where she is. I tried to find her."

Danny sat down on the edge of the bed.

"Take it easy, Henry," he said patiently. "You've been hurt pretty bad. Don't try to talk fast. But for God's sake, tell us what happened."

"It is like a queer dream, Danny; but I believe I can tell you all I know."

He told them about Leila coming, and how he saddled the sorrel, in spite of the fact that he knew that the animal was an outlaw. Slowly, and in detail, he explained their trip. He even told about seeing the young steer with the lariat around its horns. He remembered where they turned back, after seeing the rider on the sky-line.

His description of the four men was vague. He could not identify the voices, which had proclaimed him dead, and he could tell them little about his return journey, except that he was unable to find the old trail, and was obliged to discard his boots in order to walk at all.

"Six miles through mesquite thickets and cactus," said Frijole.

"He's a tough yigger," declared Oscar.

Danny got to his feet and leaned against the bed.

"You boys go to bed and get some sleep," he said. "You can't do anythin' in the dark."

"What are you goin' to do?" asked Slim.

"I'm goin' out there," said Danny dully. "I've got to look."

"There'll be two cowboys with yuh, feller," said Slim.

"Three," corrected Frijole.

"You've got to stay with Henry," ordered Danny. "You've got to be here—if she does show up, Frijole."

"Yeah, I reckon I have," nodded the little cook.

ALL NIGHT long the three riders combed the hills in the dark. At daybreak they found Henry's dead sorrel and removed the saddle and bridle. A hundred yards away Slim found the horse Leila had ridden. It had been shot twice through the neck, one of the bullets killing it instantly. At the bottom of the arroyo Oscar found Henry's revolver.

Wearily they went back to the ranch house. Henry, his head bandaged, his feet encased in an old pair of moccasins, was sitting on the porch with Frijole. Oscar gave Henry his gun, and Henry thanked him gravely. Frijole prepared a breakfast for the three cowboys.

"We found Leila's horse," said Danny miserably. "It wasn't but a little ways from your horse."

"Dead?" asked Henry huskily.

"Shot twice through the neck. But where is Leila?"

"I'm afraid, Danny. Maybe she recognized them. That—that would be fatal. They couldn't let her tell."

"Yuh better come in an eat somethin', Danny," called Frijole. "I've done poured yuh out a cup of prune whisky."

"It will do you a world of good, Danny," advised Henry, "I drank two last night, and passed out entirely."

After breakfast the boys decided to go to town and tell Mrs. Harper that they had failed to find Leila.

Henry insisted on going; so Frijole hitched a horse to the old ranch buggy and went with Henry.

Danny, Slim and Oscar arrived in Tonto City far in advance of Henry and Frijole. All three of them went into the Harper shop, but the place was empty. Danny led the way to the living quarters, but there was no one in sight.

"Well, that's shore peculiar!" exclaimed Danny. He opened the door to the kitchen and gasped audibly.

In the middle of the kitchen floor, bound and gagged, was Judge Van Treece. Swiftly they cut away the ropes and the gag, which had been made from an old towel. Judge's muscles were cramped, and his jaw was nearly paralyzed. He tried to talk, but it was only a mumble.

Slim gave him a drink of water while Oscar rubbed his wrists to restore circulation. Henry and Frijole arrived before Judge was able to give a coherent account of what happened.

"It was about midnight," he told them painfully. "Mrs. Harper was too worried to go to bed. I had been out on the street a dozen times, looking and wondering. The last time I went out two men stepped from the alley. One grabbed me, while another put a gun in my face. They made me back into the shop, which was unlighted, and then they gagged and bound me on the floor. A little later they dragged me back to the kitchen, where they left me alone in the dark. That is all I know."

"You—you don't know what happened to Laura?" asked Henry hoarsely.

"No, Henry," replied Judge miserably. "I never saw her again after I was captured by those two men."

"Masked?" asked Danny.

"I suppose they were—it was too dark for me to see."

They all walked out to the street. The three commissioners had been to breakfast, and were coming past the shop, going back to the courthouse. Henry and Oscar were crossing the street, going toward the Tonto Saloon. Henry was limping badly in his ill-fitting moccasins. John Calvert, one of the commissioners, looked at the four men, and the disheveled appearance of Judge caused him to stop.

"Is something wrong, Van Treece?" he asked.

"I could choke the three of you," replied Judge savagely. "Since you turned control of this valley over to Jack West hell has broken loose. Robbery, murder—and now, damn your narrow souls, two women have disappeared. Henry Conroy was shot down yesterday on his own range, and Leila Harper either killed or stolen. Last night masked men gagged and bound me, while they took Mrs. Harper away."

The three commissioners stared blankly at their accuser.

"Why—why, that isn't possible!" exclaimed Albert Rose.

"Does the sheriff know about this?" asked Edward Harris.

"I was released fifteen minutes ago," replied Judge.

"This is terrible!" snorted Calvert. "I can't believe—"

"We don't care what yuh believe," said Danny. *"We know."*

Frijole spoke softly to Danny:

"I'm goin' across the street. Henry's got a six-gun inside the waist of his pants, and he looked as crazy as a sheepherder when he left us."

CHAPTER XVIII

HENRY KILLS A MAN

HERE WAS A merry crowd at the Tonto bar as Henry limped in behind Oscar. Lou James, the sheriff, one of West's gunmen, several miners, and a bevy of honkytonk girls. They were all laughing and talking, paying no attention to Oscar, who walked past them and stopped at the bar. One of the girls saw Henry, and laughed huskily.

Henry had stopped short of the bar, looking rather grotesque with his bandaged head and queerly-clad feet. Lou James turned his head, his jaw sagging, as he saw Henry. Slowly he turned, facing him.

Henry's face was almost as white as the bandage, his eyes mere squinted slits, almost invisible.

"You cattle thief," he said huskily, "tell me where you took her."

The sheriff stared at him, unable to reply, it seemed. The tip of his dry tongue barely parted his dry lips, his eyes staring.

The sheriff jerked sideways; his gun fell.

"Tell me the truth, James," Henry said. "If you do not tell the truth now, I shall kill you."

James laughed harshly, his right hand dropping to his side. Henry's right hand tugged at his waist-line.

"You drunken fool!" shouted James. "Drop that gun, or I'll—"

James' draw was swift—but not swift enough. Henry had fired that big forty-five Colt from against his waist. James jerked sideways, his gun falling to the door; and then he went to his knees, his back to Henry.

"You old fool!" snapped the gunman, who was next to James.

He jerked out his gun, but before he could use it, a raging tornado in the shape of Oscar Johnson crashed into him, knocking him against the bar, which rocked under the impact. Oscar's powerful left hand was locked around the gunman's right wrist, which snapped like a pipestem when the big Swede twisted sharply.

The gunman screamed wildly as Oscar picked him up in his powerful arms, and with a mighty swing threw the luckless gunman over the top of the bar and against the back-bar mirror, splintering the huge glass and sending bottles and glassware in a crashing shower. And the victim rolled over limply and fell behind the bar, knocked unconscious.

Henry had not moved; he still stood there, slightly unsteady on his sore feet, but with the cocked Colt gripped in his right hand. Oscar dusted off his hands and walked over to Henry.

"Thank you," said Henry simply.

"*Valkommen,*" replied Oscar calmly.

They backed to the doorway together. Danny, Judge, Slim and Frijole, together with the three commissioners, were at the doorway. Oscar shifted his eyes to the splintered back-bar mirror, and his hearty laugh roared out as he pointed at it.

"Seven years hord-luck for das place," he declared.

"My God, what happened in there?" asked Commissioner John Calvert.

"I killed Lou James, your sheriff," replied Henry calmly.

"In the name of God, why did you kill him?"

"I killed him, sir, when he tried to draw his gun. I accused him of being a cattle rustler, and of stealing Leila Harper."

One of the miners had been sent for Dr. Bogart. Others took the injured gunman from among the débris behind the bar.

"Conroy came here to kill Lou James," said one of the men. "It's murder, jist as sure as hell."

"James went for his gun," said the bartender. "I seen him."

"Keep that to yourself," warned a gambler. "One of you fellers better go to the Yellow Warrior and tell Jack West."

THE MEN from the J Bar C went across the street. The three commissioners had summoned the prosecuting attorney, and the four of them were going to the Tonto Saloon.

"We better go home," said Danny. "They'll try to frame up on yuh, Henry. Between West and the commissioners, they'll try to make it murder. Frijole, you get the horse and buggy, while I go over to the store and get some cartridges. How are we fixed for thirty-thirty shells, Slim?"

"Yuh might get a couple boxes, Danny."

"Are you preparing for war?" queried Judge, visibly shaken.

"Plenty guns and plenty ammunition is a hell of a good argument in favor of peace, Judge," replied Danny. "You better go with Frijole and Henry—there's room in the buggy, if yuh set familiar."

The three of them crowded into the buggy, and drove away from Tonto City.

"I can hardly believe this is all true," declared Judge. "It is so damnably incredible for you to have done such a thing, Henry. It—it is—well, like a jackrabbit whipping a wildcat. A thousand-to-one chance. By all rights, you should have been killed, sir. James is a finished gunman."

"He most certainly is—finished," replied Henry grimly.

"Levity—in the face of present circumstances!" exploded Judge. "I am afraid we shall have quite a job keeping you from jail."

"Aw, hell!" drawled Frijole. "Where could yuh find a Arizona jury which would convict Henry of murder, when James was facin' him, with a gun in his holster, and Henry promisin' to shoot him? Lou James was knowed as a gunman. Henry jist beat him, thasall."

"If it had only happened some other place," sighed Judge. "Our job now is to prove that it was self-defense."

"Our job right now," declared Henry, "is to find Laura and Leila; the rest can wait."

"Henry," said Frijole, "would yuh mind tellin' me how yuh ever figured that Lou James was stealin' our cows?"

"Wait until we get to the ranch," replied Henry. "I'll explain it to all of you."

Back at the ranch they gathered in the main room, where Henry took pencil and paper.

"You boys wondered why you found a dead yearling and a branding-iron," he said. "I gave that a lot of thought. Yesterday I found the answer—only in a different way, There was an LJ yearling, still roped, a fire and a hot iron. Do you see what I mean, Danny?"

"Not yet, Henry."

"The LJ brands on the left side. So does the J Bar C, Here is our brand."

Henry drew out the J Bar C brand. Then he put his pencil at the top of the J, made a loop to the right and back to the left, which included the short bar between the two letters. From the loop of the J, he continued it to form a script L. Using the C for part of the script J, he completed the LJ connected brand.

"I'll be a dirty name!" exploded Danny. "It's perfect!"

"I believe it is," agreed Henry. "They altered the brand on the yearlings they butchered, before killing them, because of brand inspection. I suppose the LJ outfit had an idea of stealing every calf or yearling on that range."

"Henry," said Danny seriously, "I take off my hat to you. You have uncovered the slickest piece of brand alterin' I ever seen."

"Yah, su-ure," agreed Oscar heartily. "And das Hanry is yust one fightin' yigger, Ay ta'al you."

"But we haven't one scintilla of proof," sighed Judge.

"We don't need proof, Judge," said Danny grimly. "This case won't never go to court. It's a case of J Bar C versus Jack West and the Tonto Saloon."

"I have a feeling," said Henry quietly, "that the devil is laughing."

THE TONTO was still buzzing with excitement when Jack West came. The body of Lou James had been laid out on a pool table, and Dr. Bogart had finished setting the broken arm of Abe Cort. West knew all about things before he arrived. Tom Silver, the scar-faced swamper, was busy with his mop and pail, cleaning up the floor in front of the bar. All three commissioners and the prosecuting attorney were there. West beckoned them back to his office and closed the door.

"Where's Conroy and his gang?" asked West.

"They went home right after it was all over," replied Calvert.

"All right! Swear in a new sheriff and arrest Conroy for murder."

"But was it murder?"

"It wasn't anything else. Conroy came here to kill James."

"It seems that the evidence of eye-witnesses is conflicting, Mr. West. There was one man, a miner, I believe, who gave me his impressions of the trouble, and in his opinion Conroy gave James an even break. In fact, he says that James reached for his gun. We were here a moment after the shot was fired. James was down, and his gun was on the floor, several feet away from his body."

"Who is that miner?" queried West.

"I believe I could find him—but I don't believe I shall."

"You don't, eh? I'll remember that—next election."

"By that time I hope there will be enough honest voters in Wild Horse Valley to elect an honest prosecutor, Mr. West."

"It doesn't seem to me," said Calvert, "that James was much of a success as an officer of the law. In fact, Conroy accused him of being a cattle rustler. There must be a strong reason for a man like Conroy to make such an accusation. And there is the fact that two women are missing. I—I don't quite understand what it all means."

"Cattle rustler!" snorted West. "That damned old fool of a Conroy wouldn't know anythin' about cattle rustlin'. Well, what are yuh goin' to do—drop it? Are yuh goin' to let the J Bar C murder public officers? If yuh are—I'm not."

"I believe," replied the prosecutor coldly, "that our actions in this case will be governed by further investigation. Henry Conroy is not going to run away, Mr. West. And if you have any personal thoughts of revenge, I would advise you to forget them. The law is perfectly able to cope with the situation."

"It is, eh? Then go and find those two women yo're talkin' about. Find out who is rustlin' J Bar C cattle—if anybody is. And while yo're at it, yuh might find out who robbed me of thirty thousand dollars' worth of gold. If yuh have any luck in that, yuh might find out how Doc Sargent and Lee Vane got killed—and who killed Hardy, my shift-boss, and threw him into that wagon-load of stolen high-grade ore."

"Quite a calendar of crime," nodded the prosecutor. "I believe it is high time that Wild Horse Valley had a sheriff."

"I believe," stated Albert Rose stiffly, "that we will try and make our own selection this time."

The four men filed out of the office, leaving West at his desk glaring after them.

"Four more ready for the discard," swore West to himself. "I'll show 'em who's boss before this is finished."

OUT IN the saloon, Nick Borden stood with his back to the bar, a glass of whisky in his hand, and a smile on his face. Abe Cort, three-fourths drunk, his right arm in splints and bandages, was sitting at a card table. The body of Lou James had been removed, but there was little noise and no loud talking.

"A good, old-fashioned killing sure cools off this place," observed Borden. "Jack West ought to instruct his sheriffs to quit stealin' cows when they take office. He should hang crape on the front door and close up this place."

Several of the gamblers looked malevolently at Borden, but made no reply. The four men came from West's office, and Borden laughed as they walked past him.

"Don't look so sad," he told them. "We all make mistakes. You gents ought to dump West overboard, and run yore own offices."

Unable to insult anyone in the saloon, Borden finished his drink and walked to the doorway. Just outside, leaning against the wall, was Tom Silver. Without turning his head, Silver said quietly:

"Lola's gone. She didn't sleep in her room last night. None of the girls have seen her since she went off shift."

Borden's jaw tightened. "Maybe she went out on the stage."

"No," said Silver, "she didn't; I saw the stage leave here."

Nick Borden hitched up his belt and walked across the street, where he mounted his horse.

Jack West had a drink.

"Borden was in here, shootin' off his mouth," said the bartender.

"What about?" queried West quietly.

"Said yuh ought to put crape on the door and close up this place. Then he told them four men that they ought to dump you overboard and run their own jobs."

"He did, eh?"

"Uh-huh. He went to the door and stood there a while. I may he wrong, but I think he talked with that scar-faced swamper. Anyway, after he left, I seen the swamper pass the window. He must have been near the doorway when Borden stood there."

"Thanks," replied West dryly, and walked away.

CHAPTER XIX

THE DOPED DRINK

NO ONE AT the J Bar C had figured out just what to do. There was nothing definite to work on, it seemed. They were all sitting in the main room when Nick Borden rode in. It was his first visit to the ranch. Judge met him on the porch and they looked gravely at each other. Henry and the boys came out, and Borden nodded coldly.

"Why not sit down, Mr. Borden?"

"I rode in from Tonto," replied Borden, "where they told me all the news. I congratulate you, Conroy."

"Thank you, sir," replied Henry simply.

"I'm not much of a hand to make speeches," said Borden.

"I'm not what you'd call a good liar; and I'm not in the habit of takin' sides in a battle. A man usually has plenty to do if he minds his own business."

"Why not sit down, Mr. Borden?" suggested Henry.

"Thank yuh very much—but I can talk better this way. Van Treece can testify that I'm no angel; so I ain't comin' here under any false colors. Five years ago I blocked Jack West on a minin' swindle, which would have paid him a cold million; and West never forgets.

"I had a fine job as boss gambler in a big place, and was makin' the biggest money I ever made. West tried in every way to get me fired, and when it wouldn't work, he bought out the place, just to fire me. I went to Colorado, where I wasn't known, and got a job in a mine, where I was doin' fine. There was a girl, too.

"Not the kind of a girl you'd think would care for me.

"Mebbe I was wrong, but I let sleepin' dogs lie. I was straight as a string. Jack West found it out—and told that girl and her folks all about me. He told things that wasn't true, too. Damn him, he came hundreds of miles to ruin things for me. Since then, I've been on West's trail. Damn him, I want to see him broke, down and out—like he made me. That's my story. I've got six good men at the Smoke Tree—and I'm the seventh. If yuh need me, we'll come."

Nick Borden turned, walked back to his horse and rode away.

"That makes thirteen of us," said Henry slowly.

"Are we to ally ourselves with gunmen?" asked Judge.

"Perhaps," said Henry, "I had better move over with Borden."

"Thirteen!" snorted Frijole, "That's bad luck."

"Thorteen," declared Oscar, "is yust von better den twelve."

"I wonder why in hell Borden didn't shoot West," said Slim.

"Shooting is too good for him," declared Oscar. "Ay'd yust like to kick him in de pants."

"I believe that is what Borden thinks," said Henry. "Perhaps he hasn't any desire to kick West in the pants. Hate is a queer thing. I do not believe I have ever hated. It is so useless. I suppose I should hate somebody—now. But I just feel so damned helpless. If we could only think of something to do."

"I don't know who to hate," said Danny wearily.

"Yust vait a minute!" said Oscar. "By Yimminy, Ay have idea! Das Lou Yames had some hired men. If Ay could get my hands—"

"That's it!" exclaimed Danny. "My God, we had to wait for the Swede to get the idea. We'll get them dirty thieves and make 'em tell where Leila is. They might know where her mother is, too! Of all the dumb fools, we're the worst."

"Without a doubt," agreed Henry. "Frijole, bring me my old boots; I shall wear them if it is the last thing I ever do."

"Ride with the moccasins on your feet," advised Judge.

"And ruin the traditions of Arizona gunmen?" queried Henry.

"What tradition, Henry?"

"Did you ever hear of a gunman dying with his *moccasins* on?"

"But there's only one gentle horse in the corral," said Danny. "The others are a plumb salty bunch. Why don't you—"

"Give Judge the gentle-one, Danny; you apparently have forgotten that blaze-faced sorrel."

"I take off my hat to yuh, Henry; you've got guts."

"Forceful, but inelegant, my boy—and thank you kindly."

"I have no desire for the appellation, myself," said Judge stiffly.

"Few lawyers need them, Judge," replied Henry. "They have the law behind them, you know."

THE HORSES were swiftly saddled. Slim held Henry's horse until Henry was in the saddle, and Henry led the cavalcade from the ranch, for the simple reason that the animal ran away with him. But after a mile race, carrying Henry's load, the animal decided to take things easy.

They went straight into Tonto City and up to Werner's market, where the fat butcher looked upon them with alarm.

He told them he had not seen any of James' men that day. Yes, there were three of them, who worked cattle for James; and they lived in a shack down on the flat below town.

But there was no one at the shack. The absence of bed-rolls and war-bags attested to the fact that the three men had flown. They went over the place carefully, and in an old pair of overalls, hanging on a nail, Danny found the note Leila had brought to Henry.

"They got her," whispered Danny. "This proves it."

"That is the note she showed me," said Henry. "They must have taken it from her, Danny. Perhaps they wanted to know who wrote it."

"It kinda looks like a woman's writin'," said Slim.

"Some men write small thataway," remarked Frijole. "This is a hell of a fix we're in. James is dead and his men are gone. Now, how in the devil are we ever goin' to find out anythin'?"

They rode back to Tonto City, where Danny dismounted and went into Werner's market.

"Did you find anybody at home?" he asked Danny.

"You know we didn't, Werner. And listen to this: Lou James stole J Bar C cattle, and you peddled 'em to the mines. Mebbe yo're innocent—mebbe not. But if we can prove that you had any hand in it, I'll shoot you so full of lead that even a taxidermist couldn't make yuh look natural."

Without waiting for any reply, Danny went back to the men.

"I'm not going back to the ranch yet," he told them. "I can't do it; I'd go crazy. The rest of yuh go home. I'll poke around here and see what I can hear. My God, there must be an answer somewhere."

"Let me stay with yuh, kid," begged Slim. "Yuh might need a hand."

"No, Slim, I'd rather be alone."

"Yuh won't start any trouble—alone?"

"No, Slim; I promise to behave. I'll be back tonight—some-time."

They rode away, and Danny tied his horse to the hitch-rack near the Tonto Saloon, where he stood for a long time, arms folded on top of the rack, staring into the street. One of the dance-hall girls, going around to the rear entrance, spoke to him. He looked at her, and she ran the rest of the way.

"He just looked at me, and I ran like hell," she told the piano player.

"Why?" he asked curiously.

"Because I've got legs, I suppose," she retorted, and walked away, but he called to her and she came back.

"Where's Lola?" he asked.

"I'm not Lola's keeper," she replied. "You ain't stuck on her, too, are you?"

"Listen, kid, this is business with me. She's got some new songs; and I heard she quit the joint."

"Suits me," replied the girl. "She's too damn stuck up. I heard that West was going to make her the boss-gambler. If he does, we couldn't touch her with a ten-foot pole."

"I'm not worryin'; I just asked."

"And I answered you, didn't I?"

"Yeah—as intelligently as you could, I suppose."

DANNY REGAN spent the rest of the day and the evening watching the street, hoping against hope that one of the LJ riders would come back to Tonto City. He talked with the stage driver from Scorpion Bend, asking about LJ cowboys.

"I don't know that outfit," said the driver. "That feller James ain't owned it very long. No, I didn't meet a single rider on the way down here."

Danny forgot to eat supper. He went into the Tonto and sat down in the gambling room, apparently indifferent to every-thing, but watching for strange cowboys. West still had three of his five gunmen left, and they kept an eye on Danny Regan.

Word had been passed to watch the young foreman of the J Bar C.

Hours passed, but Danny still sat there, hunched against the wall, his hat pulled low over his eyes. Finally he got to his feet, walked into the saloon and stopped at the bar.

"Whisky," he ordered huskily.

There were other men at the bar, laughing and talking. The bartender lifted a bottle to the bar, and sent a glass spinning over to Danny. He filled the glass, drank it at a single gulp, and flung some silver on the bar.

Danny walked slowly from the saloon, halted for a moment on the sidewalk, but turned and walked toward the hitch-rack. Except for the Tonto Saloon, the town seemed in darkness. He halted at the hitch-rack and fumbled at the tie rope on his horse.

"What's wrong with me?" he muttered. The world seemed to be going around like a top. He grasped for the hitch-rack, but missed it, and fell on his knees in the dirt. A moment later he sprawled on his face, almost under the hoofs of his horse.

SLIM AND Oscar were in Tonto City at daybreak, looking for Danny. They questioned everyone they met, but no one knew where he had gone. A man told them he had seen Danny in the Tonto Saloon about midnight, sitting alone in the gambling room.

"It would be jist like the danged fool to head for Scorpion Bend, lookin' for some of that LJ outfit," said Slim. "But Danny gave me his word that he wouldn't do anythin'—and I still believe him."

"Yah, su-ure," agreed Oscar.

"Somethin' has happened to him."

"Yah, su-ure."

"Oscar, can't you say anythin' but 'Yah, su-ure'?"

"Yah," replied Oscar.

"That's better. There's the stage, ready to pull out. Let's go up there a minute."

Werner, the fat butcher, was inside the old stage, hunched back in a corner, but the two cowboys did not see him. As far as Werner was concerned, Tonto City could butcher its own beef. He did not want any taxidermist to try and make him look natural.

Slim and Oscar went back to the ranch.

"I believe we are unduly worried about Danny," stated Judge. "He is perfectly able to take care of himself. I only hope he has some vital information when be returns."

"I only hope he returns," sighed Henry.

Late that afternoon the three commissioners, the prosecuting attorney and Jack West sat in the commissioners office. West chewed grimly on his cigar as he studied the four men.

"That is the situation, Mr. West," said Calvert. "We absolutely refuse to appoint either of the two men you have recommended."

"All right," nodded West coldly. "Appoint anybody you please. I can tell you this much—I'm about through with Tonto City and Wild Horse Valley. I am the biggest investor in this country! If I take my pay roll away from Tonto City, what remains? Damn it, I can close all my properties indefinitely—and I'll do it."

"If you can't boss the country?" queried the lawyer.

"Put it any way you want to," snarled West, and walked out, banging the door behind him.

"Well, I don't know what comes next," sighed Albert Rose. "We have turned down West's men—and our choices have turned us down. It don't seem to me that any honest man wants the job as sheriff of Wild Horse Valley. Gentlemen, the job has gone begging."

"But we must have a sheriff," said Calvert.

"And right away, too," added Rose. "But who can we get?"

The lawyer laughed shortly. "There still remains—Henry Harrison Conroy."

"Yes," replied Calvert, after a long silence, "there still remains Henry Harrison Conroy."

"We forced him to resign," reminded Rose. "He wouldn't take it again. He's honest, even if he is inefficient."

"Well," smiled the lawyer, "if we don't appoint someone very soon, one of you commissioners will have to become sheriff."

"I think," said Calvert seriously, "that we should ride out and see Henry Harrison Conroy. Will you go along?"

"Yes," replied the lawyer, "I'll go along—if only to hear the three of you politely insulted by a man who is perfectly entitled to say just what he thinks of all of you."

CHAPTER XX

COLD MURDER

DANNY REGAN'S RETURN to consciousness was painful and bewildering. His head ached and he was terribly nauseated. He was bound, hand and foot, and was lying on loose rubble, while to his ears came the soft *drip, drip, drip* of water. The air was damp and mouldy, and the darkness was impenetrable. At first it was like a nightmare to the young cowboy; then he gradually realized that it was not a dream, but a painful reality. He had a hazy recollection of that drink of whisky, and its effects.

"Doped," he told himself bitterly. "Knock-out drops of some kind. What a fool I was to take a drink in that place. The bartender had that bottle all fixed for me."

After what seemed years, he saw a flickering, bobbing light, and heard the hollow boom of footsteps. It was a masked man, carrying a lighted candle, and in the faint illumination Danny could see that he was in a tunnel or stope.

The man came up and held the candle close to Danny's face. "Still alive, eh?" he said.

"What is this all about?" queried Danny. "What happened?"

The man laughed. "Yore horns growed too long, feller."

He yanked Danny around and examined the knots.

"Why am I kept tied up like this?" queried Danny.

" 'Cause we ain't had no orders yet to knock yuh on the head. Don't worry—we'll get 'em."

"What place am I in?"

"Keep askin' questions, if yuh enjoy it," laughed the man. "I'm damn shore I'll never answer any of 'em."

"Where is Leila Harper and her mother?"

"Jist like I said—there ain't no answers in this book."

The man took his candle and went away, hunched over, the candle-light throwing grotesque shadows along the walls of the tunnel. Danny twisted and pulled, trying to loosen the ropes, but the wet lariat only pulled tighter. The booming of the foot-steps died away, and there was only the dripping of water to break the stillness.

IT WAS after dark when the three commissioners and the lawyer arrived at the J Bar C. Oscar Johnson, armed with a shotgun, challenged them from beside the porch, but allowed them to go into the house. Henry, Judge, Frijole and Slim were there.

"Judging from our reception at the doorway," smiled Calvert, "you gentlemen are not taking any chances."

"Apparently it doesn't pay to take chances," replied Henry gravely. "Danny Regan, my foreman, has been missing since last night."

"Missing?" queried the lawyer. "My God, Conroy, it seems to be an epidemic! What in the world could have happened to him?"

"I wish I could answer that question. What brings you gentlemen out here tonight?"

The four men looked at each other, waiting for someone to act as spokesman. Finally the lawyer cleared his throat and replied:

"Conroy, since the—er—demise of Lou James, this county has been without the services of a peace officer. You see—"

"Just a moment," interrupted Henry gently. "Why any emphasis on the word since? It seems to me that the county was without a peace officer ever since he was appointed."

"I believe the commissioners will join me in granting that point, Conroy. They admit making a great mistake."

"And would like to apologize," added Calvert.

"What is wrong here?" queried Judge. "Have you gentlemen had a falling out with Jack West?"

"Mr. West proposed two of his own gunmen as eligible for the office," smiled the lawyer. "They were not acceptable."

"In other words," stated Henry, "you refuse to accept West's selections—and have none of your own."

"We had three," admitted Calvert. "They all refused."

"So we are offering it back to you," added Rose.

"So you are offering it back to me," said Henry. "When no one else wants it—you ask me to take it back. Thank you kindly."

"Then you will accept?" asked Calvert eagerly.

"Gentlemen," replied Henry gravely, "before I would do such a thing, I would see you all in hell, dressed as Eskimos, and shoveling flames with iron-handled shovels."

"And that's what I call bein' warm!" exclaimed Slim.

"At least," sighed Calvert, "you will accept our apology for ever asking for your resignation?"

"Gladly, gentlemen," nodded Henry, "In fact, I feel—"

From in front of the house came a sharp cry, something thudded against the porch, and there was a mixture of yelps and curses, followed by heavy footsteps on the porch. Before Slim could reach the door, it was flung violently open, and Oscar stumbled in, dragging a man by one arm and the collar.

Slim shut the door when Oscar flung the man down in the middle of the room, where he sat, goggling around vacantly.

"Yust a damn peeper!" roared Oscar. "Ay saw him coom around de hoose and try to listen."

THE MAN was undersized, with a thin face and a broken nose. He wore cowboy clothes, and looked as though he had not suffered a bath for weeks. His thin lips drew back in a snarl as he looked around the room.

"Who sent you here, young man?" asked Judge severely.

"Go to hell, will yuh?" snarled the man.

Oscar pounced on him, twisting him like a child might twist a rag doll, and then threw him into a chair. The snarl was gone now. The cowboy's face was contorted with pain, and he sucked deeply, trying to pump air into his tortured lungs.

"He's one of Lou James' punchers!" exclaimed Slim. "I've seen this whippoorwill around Werner's butcher shop."

"I don't know what the hell yo're talking about," declared the captive.

"You will—before we finish with yuh, feller," declared Slim.

"Yah, su-ure," agreed Oscar. "Das ha'ar yigger is going to talk plenty. Ay know how to make him talk."

"Keep yore paws off me, you damn grizzly," wailed the cowboy.

"Ya-a-ah!" snorted Oscar. He grabbed the man by the collar and one wrist.

"Who vants a ving off de chicken?" asked Oscar.

"Leggo!" screamed the cowboy. "Yo're breakin' my arm!"

"Yust stort talkin', and Ay quit twisting."

"I'll talk! My God, I'll talk!"

The cowboy sank back in his chair, his thin face beaded with perspiration, lips quivering.

"What do yuh want to know?" he panted. "Keep that damn Swede off me, will yuh?"

Henry turned to Judge. "You ask him the questions, Judge."

Judge nodded and drew up his chair in front of the captive.

"You worked for Lou James' LJ outfit?"

"Yeah, I worked for him."

"You helped alter brands on J Bar C cattle for Lou James?"

"I helped him—yeah."

"You were one of the four men who were branding a yearling, and who shot down Henry Conroy, I believe. What became of that girl?"

The cowboy shut his lips tightly and his face was white as he looked around at the circle of faces.

"The—the girl—" he mumbled.

From a side window of the room glass tinkled sharply. They whirled to see a rifle muzzle protruding into the room, and before anyone could move, the room shook from the heavy report.

Their captive still sat upright in his chair, but just above his left temple was a round black hole. Slowly he toppled over, sprawling across the floor. The gun muzzle was gone before the man fell. Slim stepped over quickly and drew down the blind. There was no use running out there in the dark, searching for the killer.

"God!" breathed the prosecutor. "This is terrible!"

"If they had only waited another minute," sighed Judge. "He was about to tell us what we want so badly to know."

"There must have been two of 'em," said Slim. "This other feller couldn't afford to let our man tell what he knew."

The three commissioners looked as though they wanted to stampede. In fact, Henry Harrison Conroy seemed to be the only cool person in the room. He got slowly to his feet and faced the commissioners.

"Gentlemen," he said calmly, "I have decided to become sheriff of Wild Horse Valley, subject to your approval and appointment."

"You—you—after this?" queried Calvert in amazement.

"This," replied Henry, "is only a preliminary. All I ask is that you appoint me—and then step aside."

"Gladly!" exclaimed Rose. "I—I really feel sick."

"The law will be solidly behind you, Conroy," promised the lawyer.

"So damn far behind," said Henry, "that it won't interfere, I hope."

NICK BORDEN and his six men haunted the Tonto Saloon that night, but took no part in the drinking and gambling. There was a man running the faro bank, and a new swamper. West mixed with the crowd, buying drinks and making himself generally agreeable, but he knew that Borden and his men were watching him all the time. Not until daylight did they relax their vigilance, and one man watched while the others went to breakfast.

After breakfast Borden noticed activity around the sheriff's office; so he walked past there, and was surprised to find Henry and Judge. He stood in the doorway and looked curiously at them.

"Well, this is kinda funny," he observed. "Did they appoint you, Conroy?"

"I believe that was their intention, Mr. Borden," replied Henry.

"Well, they could have done a damn sight worse. I wonder what our mutual friend, Mr. West, thinks about it."

"I doubt that he knows it yet."

Oscar came down the sidewalk, and Borden moved aside to let him in.

"Ay yust got dis at the post office," stated Oscar, handing a letter to Henry.

It was for Danny Regan, and post-marked at Scorpion Bend. Henry looked at it critically.

"A letter from Scorpion Bend for Danny, Judge," explained Henry. "Do you think we should open it?"

"That would hardly be ethical, Henry."

"In that event, I shall open it," declared Henry, which he proceeded to do. The color drained from his face, as he read the few written lines on the single sheet of paper.

"From Leila!" he exclaimed. "My God, Judge; listen to this:

"DEAR DANNY:

"Mother and I are leaving the country, and by the time you receive this we will be far away. You have been as good as gold to both of us, dear, and someday, if we are lucky, we may be together again. I can say no more.
                    "Lovingly,
                              "LEILA.

"P. S. We are both all right."

Henry groped for his chair and sat down heavily, the letter clutched in his hand. Borden's eyes narrowed as he looked at Henry.

"I'm sorry," he said slowly. "I know what it means, Conroy. I know you were goin' to marry Mrs. Harper. Why, in the name of God, they ever took her—I don't know. Lola's gone, too."

"Lola?" queried Judge.

"The girl who ran the faro bank, Van Treece."

"She—she's gone, too?"

Borden nodded shortly. "Since night before last."

"A beautiful creature," said Judge. "I have seen her."

"I—I hoped to marry her—some day," said Borden.

Henry aroused from his lethargy and read the note again.

"Why should they go away?" queried Judge. "That note sounds as though they were going of their own accord, Henry."

Suddenly Henry lifted his head and laughed harshly.

"Well," he said briskly, getting to his feet, "I suppose we may as well prepare for the inquest over the latest casualty, Judge."

THE CHANGE in Henry was so abrupt that Judge stepped over to the desk and read that letter again. Henry was actually humming a little tune as he opened the corridor door and went to inspect the cells of the jail.

"Gone crazy, Van Treece?" whispered Borden.

"I am afraid that is exactly what has happened, Borden. The man has suffered greatly, both mentally and physically. There is a breaking point, you must remember."

Borden nodded and walked out to the street.

"Ay don't understand," said Oscar blankly.

"Listen, Oscar," whispered Judge, "I'm afraid Henry has lost his mind—crazy, you understand? We'll have to watch him closely all the time."

"Yah, su-ure," sighed Oscar gloomily.

Nick Borden rode slowly back to his mine that morning. Somehow, he did not believe that Henry had lost his mind.

"I'll have the boys keep a watch on that sheriff's office, too," he told himself. "You never can tell what that fat comedian's got under his hat."

Slim and Frijole came in, and to them Judge confided his fears regarding Henry's mental state. They observed Henry closely, and were obliged to agree with Judge.

"Somethin' inside his head jist snapped—like that," declared Frijole, snapping his fingers.

"You didn't hear it snap, didja, Judge?" asked Slim seriously.

"No, I must confess that it was not audible, Slim."

"Anyway," said Frijole, "I brung in a jug of prune whisky. Poor old Bill Shakespeare, the rooster—"

"No," interrupted Judge, "don't lie about that rooster eating the mash and fighting a wild-cat."

"Not this time, Judge. Bill ain't come back from chasin' them two lions. Prob'ly won't, until he's done et 'em to the bones."

"You don't think Henry's liable to git vi'lent, do yuh, Judge?" asked Slim anxiously.

"I am not qualified to pass on mental disorders, Slim.

However, I wish you two would stay around town today. I confess I am worried."

Henry Harrison Conroy did not seem worried. His nose was a bit more red, and his step was more brisk.

"I talked with Doctor Bogart," he told Judge, "and we have postponed the inquest over that unfortunate cowboy until to-morrow. It is merely a matter of form, anyway."

CHAPTER XXI

AT THE MINE

IT WAS JUST at dusk when one of West's gunmen took a horse and buggy from the livery stable and drove up to the Tonto Saloon, where Jack West tossed a valise into the back of the buggy and climbed in with his driver. Henry watched them drive out of town, going toward Scorpion Bend.

It was Oscar Johnson, standing in the rear doorway of the jail, who saw Henry ride away from their little stable, near the rear of the jail. Oscar hurried to tell Judge. Slim and Frijole were in the office, and they all made a hurried exit to get their horses.

"I cannot imagine where that old fool is going alone," panted Judge, trying to fit a saddle on backwards. Slim took it away from him and put it on properly.

"Frijole scooted along ahead," Slim told Judge. "He'll trail Henry and then pick us up later."

Another vigilant rider, one of Borden's men, also rode out of Tonto City, not far behind Frijole. But Henry did not know he was being followed. He was no longer riding a sway-backed vintage of 1886, but a real he-man's horse. A forty-five swung in his holster, while another, the gun he had used on Lou James, reposed inside the waist-band of his tightly-fitting overalls.

Where the road forked to the Gold Plate mine, he halted

briefly. He had never been to the Gold Plate. Swinging the big
bay horse to the left, he went up the deeply-rutted road for
about a mile, where the road forked again. There were no sign-
posts, but without hesitation he took the right-hand road. There
was no moon, but the starlight was sufficient to guide him.

Heavy loads had torn deep ruts in the road, where it climbed
up through the hills. About two miles from the forks, silhouetted against the sky, he could see the buildings of the Lucky
Star mine.

He turned off the road and stopped behind a mesquite
thicket, where he climbed stiffly from his saddle. As far as he
could see, there were no lights at the Lucky Stake. He knew
that West had taken his crew from there to the Gold Plate,
possibly leaving a watchman.

Far back in the hills a coyote chorus started. Henry smiled
grimly, wondering what he would have thought about those
coyotes a few months ago. Now, they were part of his life. The
bright lights of the city meant nothing to him now. Arizona
had claimed him, body and soul.

A deer came down through the mesquite, moving like a
shadow, until a down-wind caused it to go thumping away,
snorting softly. An owl, flying on noiseless wings, passed very
close to Henry. Then he heard the soft thudding of hoofs, as
two riders passed on the road; their horses at a swift walk.

They passed quickly, blending into the night, going toward
the Lucky Stake. He waited about five minutes, then followed
them, leading his horse and walking ankle-deep in the yellow
dust. Within a hundred yards of the buildings he turned off the
road and selected a place to leave his horse.

He had no definite plans, as he went slowly up through the
brush, and find himself close to the dump of one of the Lucky
Stake tunnels. Going carefully, he climbed to the top of the
rumble and stopped near the portal of the tunnel. Slightly below
him, and to the right, was the huddle of new shacks.

He heard a door close, and a few moments later he heard

the scuff of footsteps as a man came up the trail toward the tunnel. There was a half-ton ore-car on the wooden track, and Henry crouched behind it.

The man halted at the portal of the tunnel and lighted a candle. He was rather short, but heavy-set. Then he disappeared into the tunnel.

Henry crept over to the portal. It was not a big tunnel. On the right side of the timbered entrance the loose rock had slid away, leaving a few feet of space between the timbers and the rock wall. Henry leaned back in this space, partly concealed by the upright timber, and waited for the man to return. Henry had no idea who the man might be, nor why he went into the tunnel.

From his concealment he saw the flash of a light in one of the buildings.

"If they ever offer a prize for the biggest fool in Arizona, I know who will get it," he told himself.

Then he heard the hollow booming of footsteps from inside the tunnel. They seemed to be coming, very slowly. Someone was talking, too. They were closer now, and he heard:

"...none of my business. I was told to tie yuh at the knees, and keep yore hands tied behind yuh. 'F I'd had my way, you'd be playin' a harp by this time. Here we are."

The lighted candle flashed almost against Henry as the man drove the point of the candle-stick into the timber. He blew out the candle, leaned out past the timber, and Henry slashed him over the head with the barrel of his forty-five, held in both hands. Without a sound the man went flat in the dirt.

THE MAIN building at the Lucky Stake was of rough lumber, unpainted and unfinished. It was to be used as an office and sleeping quarters for the executives. The main room was twenty by thirty feet in size. The windows were covered with blankets. Two saw-horses and some lengths of planks constituted a table, on which was an oil lamp.

Seated against the wall, their hands bound behind them,

were Leila and her mother, Lola, the faro-dealer, and Tom
Silver, the scar-faced swamper. Four masked men were stationed
around the room. From an adjoining room came the low
murmur of voices. Not a word was spoken in the main room.
Then a door creaked open, and Jack West stepped into the room.
Behind him came another man, masked in black, as were the
four guards.

The prisoners looked dumbly at West, who stopped at the
table, looking at them, a scowl on his face.

"Sorry I had to keep yuh waitin' all this time," he said, "but
this is the first time I had a chance to be with you. And when
it comes to this sort of a deal; I like to handle it myself."

"I didn't suppose you'd have the nerve to do this without a
mask," said Tom Silver.

West grinned slowly. "It don't require nerve—when I know
you'll never tell anybody what happened. You scar-faced fool,
do yuh realize that you'll never see the sun rise again? Think
that over."

Mrs. Harper was staring at West, a puzzled frown between
her eyes. It was the first time she had ever seen him, except at
a distance.

"I—I didn't know," she faltered. "You are *that* Jack West."

"Oh, no, yuh don't!" West laughed at her and shook his head.
"You got wise—and now you'd deny it. Damn yuh all!" He drove
his fist against the top of the table. "You've tried to trip me
up—but I've got yuh all. You thought you'd strip me of my
money. Well, all you'll get is a swift trip to hell. I'll—"

One of the guards opened the door cautiously, and Danny
Regan stumbled into the room, his hands behind him, a rope
around his knees. Behind him came the short, heavy-set guard,
black-masked.

"Set him down with the rest," ordered West harshly.

"Danny!" exclaimed Leila. "Danny, they got you, too?"

"Yeah, we got him, too," laughed West. "It don't pay to cross
Jack West."

"I'm all right, Leila," said Danny, his eyes on West.

WEST LAUGHED and turned to one of the guards.

"Better take a look around outside," he said, and the man walked out. West turned back to his prisoners.

"We're goin' to make this short and sweet," he said harshly. "Lola, your case comes first. You worked with Nick Borden. You listened at the crack in my ceiling and heard about that shipment of gold in the bed-roll. You told Borden, and Borden got it."

"That's a lie!" snapped Tom Silver. "I listened at the window of yore office."

"Yuh did, eh? And you told Nick Borden, eh?"

"All I'm sayin' is that I was the one that told. Lola didn't have a damn thing to do with it. You made a mistake when you took her, West."

"I did, eh? Who dropped those clippings on my desk—you?"

Tom Silver was stumped. West laughed.

"So that was Lola. A dirty little blackmailer, eh?"

"No one blackmailed you, you dirty killer!" flared Lola.

"In God's name, who are you?" asked West.

"I would be ashamed to tell you—ashamed that I didn't kill you weeks ago. I became a dance-hall singer, faro-dealer, and I worked my way into your employ—just to put the fear of a just God into your merciless heart before I drove a bullet through it."

Jack West's face was white, as he looked at her flaming eyes.

"You—you... were... my... wife's kid?" he said slowly.

"I saw you kill my mother," she replied simply.

"So that's—well, what the hell!" he snarled. "It sure had me puzzled. Going to scare me to death before you shot me, eh? I wonder if you shot Doc Sargent. Yeah, I reckon yuh did. Mebbe he caught yuh. But you didn't kill Lee Vane, too. You ain't that clever with a gun. Well, I know all I need from you."

West turned from Lola and looked at Mrs. Harper.

"So yuh recognize me, do yuh?" he sneered. "When I gave yuh two hundred dollars over twenty years ago, to send yuh back East to yore folks, I thought I was through with you forever. Yeah, I was sure the big-hearted gambler. You said so yourself. And when that crazy husband of yours disappeared, I outsmarted Parke Neal, and got that gold mine all for my own.

"Mebbe you thought you was smart when you sent me a bill for yore third of a million dollars, plus interest for twenty years. Why, I recognized you right away. That's why I tried to buy out yore shop. I wanted yuh out of the way before yuh knew I was the same Jack West. They called me 'Handsome' when you knew me.

"Oh, I've got yuh all rounded up. I'm sorry about yore daughter, but she got caught—and knew too much."

"What are yuh goin' to do with us?" asked Tom Silver.

West laughed softly. "Oh, that is all prepared, Scarface. We are abandoning our first tunnel because it's too dangerous—and useless. Why, one good blast would cave the whole damn two hundred feet. The folks of Tonto City saw me start for Scorpion Bend this evening. We had a couple horses cached out along the road. Later, we'll ride back there and go on to Scorpion Bend."

"Yo're a cheerful murderer, West!" observed Danny Regan.

"Why not? Survival of the fittest, Regan. I set out to ruin the J Bar C, and I'll do it. I'll run Conroy and Van Treece out of the country—or kill 'em. Yo're the first one to be removed."

West turned and looked at Tom Silver.

"This case is about closed," he said. "Scarface, who in hell are you, and what was yore game?"

"You'll never know, you crooked snake. You can't get away with all this. Yore money won't help yuh, West. Some of yore men will talk, and they'll hang you to the highest tree in the state."

West laughed harshly. "Not as long as I've got the money to buy men. And you won't care, anyway, because yore bones will be under two hundred feet of rock. That's all, boys—the case is—"

THE DOOR was jerked open and a masked man sprang inside, closing the door swiftly.

"Hell!" he almost screamed. "Look out! I found Dan Evans at the tunnel mouth, his head caved in! And there's men all over the damn place, Jack!"

"Evans?" gasped West. "Why, I—I—"

"Do yuh want to git trapped?" yelped the man. "I tell yuh—"

"Trapped!" West's face was white. "We can't let 'em find—"

He whirled with a gun in his hand and fired point-blank at Tom Silver. His shot was echoed by the revolver in the hands of the heavy-set guard near the door; and West twisted on his heel, his gun swung high. Swiftly Danny Regan's right hand swung from behind his hack, flame spouting from a forty-five Colt. The heavy-set guard was shooting methodically, the gun held in both hands, and the other guards were caught in a murderous cross-fire.

A bullet smashed the lamp, and the only light in the room was the lightning-like flashes of the guns. Then they were all stilled. Men were running all around the outside of the house, and Oscar Johnson's voice bellowed:

"Yumpin' yee, Ay bet ve are too late!"

A heavy body crashed against the door, and it banged open.

"I really believe everything is all right," stated Henry's voice. "We do need a little light. Somewhere on that right-hand wall I believe you will fend a lantern."

"Yee-e-e-rusalem!" yelled Oscar. "Das is Hanry! Hallo, Hanry!"

"Hello, Oscar."

Someone found the lantern and managed to light it. There were Judge, Slim, Oscar and Frijole, Nick Borden and three of his men. Henry was leaning against the wall, wearing a strange coat and hat, a black mask dangling under his chin.

Only one of the guards was alive, but dying. Borden yanked away his mask, disclosing the gunman who had driven West away from Tonto City. Jack West was dead, a sneer on his face and a cocked revolver gripped in his right hand. Borden stepped over West's body and lifted Lola up in his arms, swiftly taking off the ropes, while Danny and Henry cut the bonds from Leila and her mother. They were crying from fright and exhaustion.

Tom Silver, his back against the wall, a black stain seeping down his shirt, stared with tired eyes at nothing whatever. Oscar cut the ropes loose, but it meant nothing to Tom Silver.

"West shot him, Nick," said Lola. "West was going to kill all of us, I think. Tom," she said softly, "do you—are you hurt bad? Can you hear me?"

"Yes, Lola, I can hear you. But my number is up. West is dead?"

"Henry Conroy got him, Tom," she answered.

"Conroy? Conroy got him? Good."

"We'll get you to a doctor, Tom," she said.

"Don't bother—it's too late. I'm glad that West went ahead of me. You'll get West's fortune, Lola. There's witnesses. West robbed Parke Neal. Mrs. Harper is entitled to a share, Lola. Her husband was the third partner in the Three Partners mine."

MRS. HARPER, shaken badly, leaned over and looked at Tom Silver.

"You knew Tom Silver?" she asked hoarsely.

"In the old days," he replied. "I—I knew his story."

"Do you know what became of him?"

"A—man—shot—him," replied Tom slowly and painfully, spacing his words carefully.

"Jack West?" she whispered.

His eyes shifted to her and he nodded.

"What is your name?" asked Lola.

"Tom—Tom Jones—is—the—name—"

"He is gone," sighed Judge, as he straightened up and looked around. "My God, what a night! Henry Conroy, you nearly drove us crazy. Why did you do all this alone? By what right, sir?"

Henry, with one arm around Mrs. Harper, the black mask still dangling under his chin, replied soberly:

"By right of my official position as sheriff of this county, sir. And not only that, I—I"—Henry's voice broke a little—"I had a big personal interest in seeing it done properly. They were thinking of me when it was written, 'Fools rush in where angels fear to tread.' And Leila, may God bless her, told me where they were. That is, she told Danny—but I got the message."

"Leila told you in that letter?" gasped Judge.

"I told you?" gasped Leila. "Why, Henry, I never wrote a letter!"

"Thank God for a man who can think!" exclaimed Lola. "They forced me to write that letter. It was a mighty long chance, but I made it as plain as I could."

"Plain?" muttered Judge. "Plain? Why, I read that letter."

"When I saw the word 'gold,' and then the word 'lucky,' I felt that it meant something," said Henry. "Lucky Gold. Lucky Stake. And when you wrote P.S., you made the tall of an L on the P. It was L.S.—Lucky Stake. Jack West moved his crew away from here so he could finish things for us. He meant to bury all of you in that old tunnel, where he kept Danny. Only through the grace of God did that guard happen to be built somewhat to my personal specifications. His coat was tight—but the mask fit fine."

"We trailed you, Henry," said Judge wearily.

"We trailed you, too," admitted Nick Borden. "We nearly had a battle between your outfit and mine, before Oscar Johnson fell over a log, and told the world what he thought of logs. Then we got together and were trying to find somebody, when the Fourth of July celebration started in here."

"Well," observed Henry, polishing his nose a little, "I guess that is about all we can do around here, until the coroner can look things over."

"I'll send one of my men to town," offered Borden. "We'll need a wagon to take the ladies home."

HENRY NODDED. The three women were talking things over together; so Henry and Borden walked over near the doorway.

"Conroy, I never can be grateful enough to you," said Borden. "You've—well, I've got a future—now. I guess you know."

"By the way," said Henry seriously, "is there any gold in the Smoke Tree, Borden?"

"Not an ounce," whispered Borden. "There never was. It was only a blind to cover what we were doing."

Henry nodded and caressed his nose.

"I believe that things will be very good in this valley. You and Lola can take over West's interests. There will be no more cattle rustling, no water poisoning—and the gold thieves are gone—now."

"Yes, they have left the valley, never to return, Conroy; thanks to you. There is only one thing left; one thing to tell you. That Golden Calf mine of yours, Conroy. It—"

"No good?" queried Henry.

"No good. I staked Parke Neal to enough gold to salt it, and the loose ore is all from the Yellow Warrior. He was goin' to sell it to Jack West. But he blew himself up, tryin' to make it too good."

Danny came over and put an arm around Henry's shoulders. There was a smile on his dirty face, as he said:

"The women have—well, they've kinda decided—for all three of us."

"Decided what?" asked Henry.

"A triple marriage at the J Bar C, with everybody in Wild Horse Valley at a big fiesta. Yessir, they decided unanimous. And—take a look, will yuh? They're all cryin' together."

"Well," replied Henry soberly, "you can't blame them for crying, if they took one square look at the three of us."

From the other end of the room came Oscar's voice:

"And Ay said to Free-holey, 'Free-holey, since me and Yudge and Hanry ain't shoriffs no more, das Vild Hurse Valley is going to de dogs.'"

"Yuh shore did," agreed Frijole. "And she was, too."

"Yah, su-u-ure. And yust de minute ve are back on de yob again, Ay said, to Free-holey, 'Free-holey, you'll be surprised.'"

"And I shore was, Oscar. Did I tell yuh that Bill Shakespeare, the rooster, came home today? No? He shore did. Both spurs wore right down to the quick, and he was a-limpin' in his left laig. If that rooster could talk—man, could he tell a story!"

"He seems to have a fairly good interpreter," said Judge dryly.

"Yeah," agreed Frijole soberly. "But we're changin' his name tomorrow—to Henry. Who the hell did Shakespeare ever whip?"

Henry laughed and walked over to Laura.

"I felt that I was blessed above all men, Laura," he said. "With peace in Wild Horse Valley—and you. And now they are going to name a rooster after me. Such is fame I suppose."

"But, Henry," said Mrs. Harper, her eyes filled with tears, "you have always said that anything can happen in Arizona."

"And I believe it stronger than ever, my dear. God bless Arizona."

"Das right," agreed Oscar heartily, "but don't forget Hanry."

SUSPECTED BY HENRY

San Francisco crooks, invading Arizona rangelands, think they have an easy million dollars—but Sheriff Henry thinks otherwise

"KID, YOU'RE a queer egg," laughed Breezy Lemair, as he leaned back in an easy chair, sipping at a highball. "Doesn't it mean a thing to you—the fact that you saved my life tonight?"

Breezy Lemair was well groomed, immaculate. Almost too immaculate, while the other man, hunched in a straight-back chair, was unshaven, badly in need of a haircut, his linen soiled, his suit wrinkled and ill-fitting. Breezy was only twenty-two years of age, and the trampish-looking young man was about as old.

"It doesn't mean much," replied the other. "In fact, I didn't try to save your life; I came to buy a bowl of noodles. Give the credit to John Barleycorn, if you must give credit. I stumbled and fell against the man with the gun."

"You don't even care *why* he wanted to kill me, eh?"

"Why should I care? You don't mean anything to me."

"I like that part of it," laughed Breezy. "Drunk and broke, eh?"

"I am now—broke. A man got out of a taxicab at the St. Francis, paid his fare and dropped a dollar into the gutter. He didn't see it, but I did—and so did the driver. When the man walked away, me and the cabby did a swan-dive, cracked heads, and I got the money. Seventy-five cents for whisky, and twenty-five cents for enough noodles to keep my stomach from turning handsprings."

"Funny thing about the man with the gun," mused Lemair. "He resented the fact that I stole his girl."

"Things like that are almost incredible," agreed the frowzy one. "But that don't explain why you bring me up to your apartment. I look like an alley-cat in a palace."

"I thought you needed a drink."

"Thanks."

"What's your name?"

"Bert Lawrence."

"You're pretty young to be a tramp."

"The Legislature has never fixed an age limit."

"That calls for another drink, Bertie. Wait'll I—"

A telephone bell rang softly. Breezy reached across the table and lifted the receiver.

Oscar proved he was an expert with the guitar.

"Hello. Yes… that's right. You have, eh? Yes, they're right here on the table."

There ensued a long period in which the other party did the talking.

"Yes, I get all that," replied Breezy. "I do, eh? Well, maybe that is the best thing. Get it right on the spot. Sure. What's that name? Riggs? Edgar Riggs? That's right. Oh, sure. Listen. Jack Flood tried to gun me down tonight. Huh? He sure did. No, Helene don't know it. I'm meeting her at the Peninsula tonight. What? Oh, no, I won't. I'm off the stuff until this deal is settled. Uh-huh. Good-by."

BREEZY LAUGHED and replaced the receiver. He quickly mixed two more highballs, and shoved one over to Lawrence. Breezy studied Bert Lawrence as he sipped his drink, and he suddenly laughed softly.

"We're about the same size, Lawrence," he said. "This is my last night here for a while, and I owe you a good time. There's a good barber shop downstairs, and I've got extra dress clothes. I have plenty of money for a good blowout, and there are two swell girls at the Peninsula Club. How about being a swell for a night?"

"You mean—a clean-up and—" Bert Lawrence began.

"Sure. Shave, haircut, bath, tuxedo. Who knows what might happen? Tomorrow I'll be far away. Snap out of that funk, Lawrence. The old world is our oyster for tonight—let's crack it and see what's inside."

Bert Lawrence started to voice a protest, glanced at the half-filled glass in his hand, and lifted it to his lips.

"As I am not doing anything this evening, I accept," he replied soberly. "I hope the shoes fit, because I have a corn on the little toe of my right foot."

The transformation was remarkable. Breezy looked Lawrence over critically.

"Not a flaw," he declared. "I almost hesitate in introducing you to Helene."

"You don't need to worry," replied Lawrence rather bitterly. "Tomorrow I shall probably be—well, it doesn't matter."

They went down to the apartment garage, where Breezy kept his expensive coupé, a huge, powerful brute of a car.

"I'm careful tonight," explained Breezy, as they slipped along Mission Street at a modest pace. "One more traffic violation and they'll cancel my license and throw me in the hoosegow. This baby can run."

"This speed suits me," replied Lawrence. "I'm timid about fast cars. A yellow streak, I suppose. I mean—an extra streak. I've got a lot of 'em."

"Keep your chin up," advised Breezy. "Whisky is whipping you."

"You talk a fine example."

Breezy laughed. "Oh, I don't let it get the best of me."

The Peninsula was not a private club. It boasted a wonderful cuisine, floor show, dancing and cocktail service. And, if you were known at all, a gambling room, where they took suckers' money in a grand manner.

Helene was a singer, part of the floor show, a gorgeous blonde with cold blue eyes. Breezy introduced her to Lawrence, and they had a drink at the bar. Helene looked Lawrence over keenly and with distinct approval.

She ate supper with them on the balcony. Breezy asked her if she had seen Jack Flood that night.

"He was out here early in the afternoon," she replied. "He was drinking and acted rather nasty. But he's harmless, Breezy."

"Yes, I realize that, Helene," replied Breezy dryly.

AFTER SUPPER Helene left them. Breezy saw some friends, and left Lawrence in the lounge, where Helene found him an hour later reading a magazine.

"Oh, hello," he said. "Looking for Breezy?"

Helene sat down beside him, her eyes narrowed.

"Breezy is getting drunk," she said coldly. "He always gets drunk out here. What do you know about the trouble this afternoon between him and Jack Flood?"

"I believe," replied Lawrence thoughtfully, "that a man named Jack Flood attempted to shoot him."

"That is what I was told over the phone a few minutes ago."

Lawrence stifled a yawn. "He missed him a foot. Maybe it was more than a foot—possibly three feet."

"How long have you known Breezy?"

"Oh, ever so long, Miss Helene. You've no idea—really."

"I think you're a sap."

"Please correct that sentence, Miss Helene."

"Correct it? What do you mean?"

"Use the word 'know' instead of 'think.'"

"Listen to me, Lawrence," said Helene quietly. "You must get Breezy out of here and back to his apartment. Jack Flood is coming here tonight, and that means trouble."

"Perfectly agreeable with me," replied Lawrence. "You fix it up with Breezy, will you?"

"You come with me—I'll fix it."

They found Breezy at the bar, drinking with several other men. He was telling them in no uncertain tones that he was through with San Francisco.

"Leaving t'morrow," he declared owlishly. "When I come back, I'll buy thish whole town."

He voiced no objections when Helene drew him away from the bar, and he looked foolishly interested when she told him that Jack Flood was coming out to the Peninsula.

"You're leaving town in the morning," she explained patiently. "If Jack Flood finds you, you won't ever leave town. You and your friend are going to get in your car and go home—now."

"Well, 'f all things," replied Breezy. "Tha's right, too. C'mon, Lawrench; we're goin' home. When Helene shez for me t' go home, she means it. C'mon."

"Look out for the dumb egg," whispered Helene, and Lawrence nodded.

At the parked coupé Breezy emptied his pockets, looking for the ignition key. Lawrence picked up his apartment keys and put them in his own pocket, along with some miscellaneous change, which Breezy dropped. Lawrence was a bit dubious about Breezy driving the car after Breezy scraped several fenders on his way out of the big parking space.

"I'm as shober as a judge," declared Breezy. "Why, I could drive thish car home on a tight rope."

A heavy fog was rolling in, rank with the odors of tules, almost like rain. The headlights of an incoming car flashed directly into them as they skidded crazily on the asphalt roadway. There came a splintering crash, in which Breezy removed headlights and bumper from the oncoming car. It whirled the coupé sideways, its rear wheels plowing deep in the dirt of the road shoulder.

Lawrence knew that the fenders and running-board on his

side were smashed. He flung open the door to inspect the damage, supposing, of course, that Breezy would stop. With a roar of its powerful engine the coupé lurched back on the highway, throwing Lawrence headlong from the car, where he rolled over in the soft dirt.

Slowly he got back to his feet. Far down the highway he could hear the whining roar of that coupé, the motor wide open. He could see the faint glow of lights from the Peninsula, like tiny moons in the fog. Brushing the mud off his clothes as best he could, he walked back toward the club. It had been built near a road intersection, and here, under a feeble light, was the sign of a bus-stop.

Lawrence examined the money he had picked up when Breezy dropped it at the parking lot. It was sufficient to pay his bus fare back to town. He also had Breezy's apartment keys.

THE LOBBY at the apartment was empty when Lawrence went in. Instead of using the elevator he walked up the two flights. Breezy was not at the apartment. Lawrence found the liquor and took a stiff drink. Breezy was either in the hands of the police, or in the ditch, Lawrence decided.

"I probably was lucky to get pitched out of that car," he told himself, and proceeded to go to bed.

It was three o'clock in the morning when the telephone rang. In fact, it rang several times before Lawrence awoke. His voice, husky with sleep, growled into the transmitter.

"Is that you, Breezy?" asked an anxious voice.

Still confused and not wholly awake, Lawrence grunted, "Yeah."

"Good!" exclaimed the man's voice. "Some damn fool in a coupé, running a hundred miles an hour, went off a cliff over by Lincoln Park tonight, and burned to a cinder. Nothing left for identification. I phoned Helene at the Peninsula, and she said you left early."

"Yeah?" grunted Lawrence, trying to get things straightened out in his own mind as to what this was all about.

"Well, that's fine," said the voice. "Don't forget you're leaving on that six o'clock train. I'll phone Helene and tell her you're all right. Now, damn it, don't miss that train. Good night."

The phone clicked. Slowly replacing the receiver, Lawrence rubbed his eyes, took a deep breath and looked around. It suddenly occurred to him that Breezy had gone over a cliff and burned up in his car. Lawrence shuddered slightly, reached for the whisky bottle and drank heavily. An ornate clock on the mantel showed several minutes after three o'clock.

Lawrence lighted one of Breezy's cigarettes, and as he started to drop the match in a silver ash-tray on the table he noticed an unsealed envelope on which was the imprint of a railroad company. Curiosity impelled him to open it, and inside the envelope he found a railroad ticket to Scorpion Bend, Arizona, along with a Pullman reservation and five one-hundred-dollar bills.

He spread the five pieces of currency on the table, studied the ticket for several moments, smoking thoughtfully. He was trying to remember something of the telephone conversation Breezy had had early in the evening.

"Riggs," murmured Lawrence. "Edgar Riggs. And out at the club Breezy promised to come back with enough money to buy San Francisco. It must be a big deal."

Lawrence got to his feet and walked into Breezy's room. Two leather bags had been packed and locked, but the ring which held the apartment keys also contained the keys to the baggage. Lawrence was not a thief. The gods of luck had scorned him for so long that he was desperate.

With only a hazy idea of what it might mean, he selected a gray suit from the closet, where a dozen well-tailored garments hung. From a dresser he secured shirt and tie. A pair of black shoes, gray overcoat and a soft black hat completed his attire.

The clock showed four thirty when he locked the apartment, and, with a bag in each hand, started down the heavily carpeted stairs. There were voices in the lobby as he halted on the second floor.

Someone was getting on the self-operated elevator. Lawrence moved down the stairs as the elevator stopped at the second floor.

The night clerk was helping a drunken man to his apartment.

"The finger of luck is on me," Lawrence told himself, and went swiftly down to the deserted lobby, where he carefully opened the door and stepped out into the fog.

"I just wonder who the devil I'm supposed to be," he muttered as he hurried down toward Market Street. "But perhaps Edgar Riggs will have that information."

CHAPTER II

AS THE HORSE FLIES

"**YOU DAMNABLE BRUTE**, I'll kill you, if it's the last act of my life!"

Crash! Bang!

For the next moment or two everything was silent in the office of the sheriff of Tonto City. Two men were on the floor, one sprawled on a cot. Henry Harrison Conroy, the sheriff of Tonto, sat up and rubbed his nose, squinting one eye as he looked at his swivel-chair, which was sagging drunkenly.

Judge Van Treece, the deputy, slowly sat up, rubbing his head and looking ruefully at the chair over which he had fallen. On the cot, Oscar Johnson, the jailer, sighed contentedly and shoved the Colt .45 back into his holster.

"Ay yust don't believe in chasing hurse-flies," he declared solemnly. "Ay shoot 'em."

Henry Harrison Conroy got painfully to his feet. Henry was of tub-like proportions, with a moon-like face, squinty eyes, and the biggest nose in Arizona. His nose was famous. For many years that nose had been featured in vaudeville, with Henry as a background.

In fact, until a few months ago, Henry Harrison Conroy's life had been spent in the theater.

When the lean days descended upon the theater, and Henry's contract had been canceled, fate came in the form of a will in which Henry inherited the J Bar C ranch in Wild Horse Valley. There, as a joke, the voters had elected Henry sheriff, and Henry, his sense of humor undiminished, appointed Judge Van Treece as his deputy, and Oscar Johnson as jailer.

Judge Van Treece, christened Cornelius, was sixty, tall and gaunt, with a long, lean face and pouchy eyes. Whisky had ruined his career as a lawyer.

Oscar Johnson, erstwhile horse wrangler at the J Bar C, was, according to Henry, a throwback to Viking period. Oscar had the physique of a Hercules, a flat face, round blue eyes, and a buttonlike nose.

"So you shoot them, do you?" remarked Henry.

"Ay yust don't believe in chasing them," replied Oscar blandly.

"The damn thing bit me on the ear," said Judge painfully, rubbing the injured ear violently.

"Being asleep," said Henry, "I missed the opening act. It seems that I must have reared back, snapped the spring in my official chair, and—and kept right on going."

"You looked fonny as ha'al," said Oscar. "Yudge go dancing around ha'ar, vaving his hat, and fall over a chair."

Oscar walked over to the front wall near the window and critically examined a bullet hole.

"Ay got him oll right!"

"It is no wonder," declared Judge, "that the people refer to this office as the Shame of Arizona. With the street thronged with people, you, you vitriolic Viking, fire a pistol through the front wall. Have you no brains, Oscar? No imagination? Does your mind only function up to the performance of—"

"I really believe he did kill that horse-fly," interrupted Henry. "At the edge of the bullet hole is a slight discoloration."

"Yuice," explained Oscar soberly.

"I suppose," sighed Judge. "Perhaps a close examination outside would show blood spattered all over the main street of Tonto City; the blood of innocent women and children. That bullet—"

"There has been no outcry," reminded Henry.

JUDGE SHOOK his head wearily, straightened up his chair and sat down carefully. Henry was trying to repair his wrecked swivel-chair when two men walked in. One of them was John Campbell, the prosecuting attorney, the other a big, square-faced, prosperous-looking person who wore glasses attached to his vest with a wide black ribbon. In his right hand was a bulging brief-case.

"Gentlemen," said Campbell, "this is Mr. Edgar Riggs, an attorney from San Francisco, who has charge of the Jack West estate. Mr. Campbell, this is Henry Conroy, Judge Van Treece, and Oscar Johnson."

"De-lighted, I am sure," rumbled Mr. Riggs. "De-lighted."

"Except for the dental display—as Theodore Roosevelt might have said it," remarked Henry dryly. "Won't you have a chair, Mr. Riggs? Take mine."

"Well, thank you very much; I shall."

He sat down in Henry's chair.

"Relax and make yourself at home, Mr. Riggs," said Henry expansively.

"Thank you, sir."

Mr. Riggs relaxed, leaned back heavily; and the next moment he was on his head and shoulders against the wall, accompanied by the clang of a swivel-spring, which struck the wall and re-bounded to the center of the room.

Several busy moments ensued, in which Henry, Campbell and Judge managed to pry Mr. Riggs away from the wall and get him on his feet. Red-faced and spluttering, the attorney sought to recover his breath and dignity. Judge looked reprovingly at Henry, who seemed utterly dejected over the unfortunate incident.

"Alvays somebody breaking up our forniture," said Oscar.

"Well, I guess I'm not hurt," panted Riggs. "It *was* sudden."

"I regret it very much," declared Henry. "In fact, I believe that this will always remain as a milestone in my regrets. Take that other chair, Mr. Riggs. Less comfortable, but reliable."

Sitting down gingerly, the attorney placed his brief-case on his lap, adjusted his glasses.

"I—er—as Mr. Campbell has told you, I represent the estate of the late Jack West. For a number of years I have been handling the legal work of Mr. West. It was with sorrow that I learned of his death. I had always found him—"

"Just a moment," interrupted Henry. "If you came here to eulogize Jack West, you waste your breath, Mr. Riggs. Jack West was a murderer and a damned crook."

"Unproved," declared Riggs. "Absolutely unproved."

"We rarely try murderers and thieves after they are dead," said Henry. "We know that Jack West murdered his wife. He admitted it to his daughter as he was dying."

RIGGS SMILED slowly. "That would be difficult to prove in court. When a man is dying he might admit anything. As a matter of fact, this woman—Lola Borden, I believe her name is now—will have to prove these things. And there is another matter, the suit of Mrs. Laura Harper, seeking to recover a third of the selling price of a mine known as the Three Partners, which she claims was her property, her alleged husband claiming to have been one of the original locators.

"No one, except Mr. West, knew what this price might have been. There is no record of the sale, except the usual one-dollar consideration. For your own information I will say that Jack West's will leaves every cent of his estate to Lonny West, his nephew, living in San Francisco. I have sent for this young man to come out here. While I appreciate the fact that you feel these claims honest and just, I must warn you that, in my opinion, and I am one of the best in my profession, no court in the land will consider either of these claims."

"My dear Mr. Riggs," replied Judge solemnly, "it so happens that I am attorney for the plaintiffs in both cases. I have, in my many years before the bar, argued many cases. Some of them have been settled out of court, through the intervention of Judge Colt. But never in my whole legal career have I, as attorney for a plaintiff, settled a case on the opinion of the defense attorney."

"I am, sir," declared Mr. Riggs, "merely endeavoring to save you much wasted effort, and to save attorney fees for your misguided clients."

"Very kind and thoughtful of you, Mr. Riggs," replied Judge quietly. "Would you mind if I asked you to take your brief-case and go to hell? You see, I have a personal grudge against the devil for trying to tempt me to arise and whale the eternal tripe out of you."

Mr. Riggs got slowly to his feet, glaring at Judge. John Campbell was trying very hard to stifle a laugh. He placed a hand on Riggs' arm, gently trying to propel him out of the office, but Riggs jerked away angrily and turned to Judge.

"If you are foolish enough to imagine for one moment that Edgar Riggs would let such an insulting remark pass, sir," he rumbled, "you are eminently fitted to prosecute these two cases. I demand an immediate—"

Bang!

The little office fairly shook from the concussion of Oscar's forty-five again.

John Campbell was so startled that he leaped against Riggs, who went stumbling out through the doorway. Campbell only reached the doorway, but Riggs, his brief-case in one hand, his hat in the other, went galloping up the main street of Tonto City.

Oscar, his head cocked on one side, was looking critically at the ceiling, the big gun dangling loosely in his huge right hand.

"Ay am sorry to say Ay missed that von," he said slowly.

"You—you missed what?" blurted Campbell.

"Hurse-fly," said Oscar blandly. "Ay don't see any yuice around de bullet hole."

"My God!" gasped the prosecutor, and went up the street.

"I am very sorry," said Henry. "That bullet seemed to punch a very decided period in a brilliant and pleasant conversation, Judge. Our friend, Mr. Riggs, appears to be an artist at gay repartee."

"He has amazing egotism," nodded Judge. "But something should be done about this crazy jailer, Henry. He is going to murder someone if he isn't careful. The idea! Shooting holes in the walls and ceiling! Ridiculous!"

"Hurse-flies," corrected Oscar. "Ay don't like 'em."

"You have proved that, Oscar," replied Judge gently.

"I believe I shall take a walk, before I have a physical breakdown," said Henry gravely. "This office is getting to be a madhouse."

HE WALKED slowly up the street to John Campbell's office, where he entered. The lawyer craned his neck, looking past Henry.

"You didn't bring that damnable Swede, did you?" he asked.

"And still," replied Henry, ignoring the question, "I love every ounce of ivory in his square head, Campbell. The man is positively amazing."

"Damnably dangerous," said Campbell soberly.

Henry sat down, and they looked out at the activity of Tonto City's main thoroughfare.

"So Jack West willed his property to his nephew, eh?" said Henry.

"That seems to be the case, Henry."

"What is your personal opinion of Mrs. Harper's chances to get any money out of that estate?"

Campbell scratched his chin.

"Well, I'll tell you, Henry—"

"Neither do I," said Henry quickly. "Morally, she has a case—legally, no. Mrs. Borden's case is different. She can absolutely prove that Jack West was her father."

"Can she?"

"Well, damn it, Campbell, when West was dying he admitted it."

"He took her word for it," corrected Campbell.

"Yes, I suppose that is true. I wonder what the estate is worth."

"I asked Riggs," smiled Campbell. "He evaded the question. Of course, I imagine it is worth close to a million dollars. Both the Gold Plate and the Yellow Warrior are heavy producers. West must have had a lot of money in banks, possibly a lot of stocks and bonds, too."

Henry nodded and rubbed his red nose.

"I'm afraid Judge Van Treece has a job ahead of him, Campbell. Is Riggs the executor of the estate?"

"That is what he told me, Henry. He has been legal adviser for Jack West a long time. How is everything at the J Bar C?"

"Going very nicely, I believe. Frijole Bill's last batch of prune whisky was twenty-four hours old before he brought some in. You have no idea what age will do to that stuff. It was really mellow."

"Judge said it was half-sister to nitric acid."

"Well, I would not swear to the relationship," said Henry, "but I will admit the family resemblance. It burns nicely in a lamp. I hope that Mr. Riggs was not too upset over Oscar's untimely salute."

"I haven't seen him since," smiled Campbell. "If I were you,

Henry, I would explain something of the ballistics of a forty-five to Oscar."

"The worst of that is," replied Henry, "by the time I had made him understand it, even in its crudest form, my term of office would have expired. Oscar was born two hundred years too late."

"Does he ever do anything right, Henry?"

"Well, he hasn't—not since I have known him. I believe he is the most reliable person I have ever known."

"Reliable?"

"Absolutely. For instance, we all make mistakes and do things wrong, at times. Oscar never makes a mistake—he is always wrong. If I want Oscar to do anything for me, I explain how to do it in the *wrong* way; and I would bet a thousand dollars against a thin dime that it will be done right. The man is absolutely infallible. Would you consider doing me the honor of joining me in a drink?"

Campbell laughed and reached for his hat.

CHAPTER III

A NEW RÔLE

WITHOUT A SINGLE idea as to why he was in Arizona, Bert Lawrence, clad in Breezy Lemair's clothes, and carrying Breezy Lemair's luggage, climbed aboard the stage at Scorpion Bend. Old Mose Upshaw, the driver, stowed away the luggage and asked Lawrence to ride on the seat with him. Mose liked to have a strange passenger for conversational purposes. Lawrence looked like a drummer—from Mose's viewpoint.

"Ever been to Tonto City?" he asked as they drove out of Scorpion Bend.

"No, I never have," replied Lawrence. "Rather sketchy," he said, pointing at the rugged hills.

"I imagine," nodded Mose, who did not recognize the word "sketchy."

"Is Tonto City a big place?"

"Yeah, she's pretty danged big. Wasn't exactly a mee-tropolis until they struck gold there. Shore woke up the place."

"Gold mines?"

"Biggest since Solomon plastered his first location."

"Owned by Solomon?" queried Lawrence.

"By jing!" chuckled Mose, and spat explosively. "Didn't yuh ever hear of the mines of King Solomon?"

"I have never been greatly interested in mines; and the only Solomon I ever knew kept a hock-shop."

"Well, anyway, the Tonto mines are mighty rich. You don't happen to be a drummer, do yuh?"

"Sorry. I haven't even a good ear for music."

"Judas Priest! Ain't interested in mines, eh? I thought mebbe yuh was a minin' engineer. Ain't thinkin' of buyin' a mine, are yuh? Reason I mentioned it was 'cause I've got a mighty likely prospect, which I might sell. She'll run about eight hundred a ton."

"Is that supposed to be rich?" asked Lawrence.

"Well, it wouldn't put the owner in no poorhouse. I've got a million tons in sight, too."

Lawrence did some mental calculation.

"A million tons, at eight hundred dollars a ton? Eight hundred million dollars? Why are you driving a stage?"

"Well, I'll tell yuh about me." Mose spat out in space, his eyes narrowed against the bright rays of the desert sun. "When I uncovered that Bonanzy, it was so danged rich that I lost m' mind. Fact. Can't control m'self at all. Only time I'm normal is when I'm drivin' four horses hitched to a stage. Young man, it's jist as unfortunate as hell, but if I quit this job for twenty-four hours I'd be a ravin' maniac. Eight hundred million dollars layin' there, waitin' for me to dig her out, and I can't take the chance.

Money ain't no good to yuh when yo're crazy. Do yuh see the situation?"

"Well," said Lawrence soberly, "why not hire somebody to dig it out for you?"

"Allus the same question," sighed Mose. "Even the Governor of the State has asked me the same thing. I jist cain't answer it."

"Why can't you answer it?"

"Well, it's jist some peculiarity about me, I s'pose. Years ago I trusted a mule. Doctors down in Yuma took the mule-shoe out of my head. Had to go about a foot deep to git it. Must have kinda shook me up, 'cause since then there's certain questions I cain't answer."

"**DO YOU** happen to know a man named Edgar Riggs?" asked Lawrence. "Or can't you answer that question?"

"Edgar Riggs? Shore, I can answer that one—and it's no. I used to know a Jim Riggs down in Yuma. But he's been dead for years. Edgar Riggs? He don't happen to be a bartender, does he?"

"I'm beginning to hope so," replied Lawrence dryly.

"I ain't never been much of a drinkin' man," mused Mose. "After I drink a couple of quarts of whisky I git kinda mean. I go round squintin' at people."

"I don't believe I'm going to like this country," said Lawrence.

"I hate it," said Mose. "But I got in here, and I've got to stay until I make enough money to buy a ticket out."

"How long have you been here?"

"Twenty-three years next June."

"And you've never met Edgar Riggs, eh?"

"Are you still harpin' on him?" queried Mose. "Sa-a-ay! You don't happen to be a detective, do yuh?"

Lawrence laughed and shook his head.

"No, I don't happen to be."

"Well, I've made three guesses, and they're all ain'ts. You ain't a drummer, you ain't a minin' engineer, and yuh ain't a detective. It jist might be that yo're a gambler."

"It—might—be," replied Lawrence thoughtfully.

"Gimme enough guesses and I'll hit the mark," chuckled Mose.

EDGAR RIGGS met the stage at Tonto City, and looked approvingly at Lawrence.

"I'm Edgar Riggs," he said. "We'll take your luggage down to the hotel. Your room—such as it is—is ready for you. We'll talk there."

Lawrence had nothing to say. Riggs had accepted him, so he decided to let Riggs do all the talking. In the hot, dingy room Lawrence threw off his coat and hat, and sat down.

"How much do you know about this deal?" asked Riggs bluntly.

"Not enough to talk about it, but enough to keep my mouth shut," replied Lawrence.

"That's great! You are Lonny West—and nobody else."

Lawrence looked speculatively at the big lawyer.

"Go ahead," he said quietly.

"Here is the deal," continued Riggs. "Jack West was probably the biggest and richest crook that ever worked in this part of the country. He owns that big saloon and gambling house across the street, owns the Yellow Warrior and the Gold Plate, two of the biggest producing mines around here, and property in other places. That is, he owned it before he was shot and killed by a man he had defrauded.

"Over twenty years ago, Jack West and two other men, Tom Silver and Parke Neal, located the Three Partners mine. Silver was married, and it seems that he thought Neal was trying to steal his wife. He saw Neal give her some money. Silver trailed Neal to a hotel in Yuma, but went to the wrong room, shot a stranger, and went up for twenty years, under an assumed name.

Neal lost his share of the mine to West in a poker game, and West sold out for big money.

"Entirely unproved, but undoubtedly the truth, Jack West, living in an eastern town before he came west, beat his wife so badly that she died. There was a baby girl who grew up, became a dance-hall singer and faro dealer, and was known simply as Lola. For quite a while she was the big attraction over there in the Tonto Saloon. Does this sound interesting?"

"Just as though you got it out of a book, Riggs," replied Lawrence.

"Well, it's all true. I told you about Tom Silver, who had a wife. The money Neal gave her that night was sent by Jack West. There was to be a baby; so West gave her the money for her to go back to her home, somewhere in the Middle West, I believe. In reality, West wanted her out of the country because he had an idea of owning the Three Partners.

"Now, here is another queer angle. The woman and daughter who own the millinery store in this town, Mrs. Harper and Leila Harper, are wife and daughter of Tom Silver. They want their share, basing their claim on the fact that Tom Silver had never received a share of the Three Partners mine. Lola, as the daughter, demands everything."

"It appears that they have a claim," said Lawrence.

"Except for the fact that Jack West's will leaves everything to you."

"Oh, I see," said Lawrence quietly. "That is why I am impersonating Lonny West."

"Exactly. There *was* a Lonny West, a nephew of Jack West."

"Where is he now?"

"Dead. Killed over a year ago in a train wreck near Dunsmuir, California."

"I see. Jack West didn't know this?"

"I don't care whether he knew it or not. That doesn't matter."

"What about that will? Didn't he really leave—"

"That will is as good as the cleverest forger could make it. I'll defy anyone to detect it."

"All right; what's the deal—my end of it?"

"Didn't Buck Shelton tell you?"

"No," replied Lawrence calmly, "he didn't make any price. He said you'd settle that down here."

"Oh, well, hell!" snorted Riggs. "He makes me mad! I told him to get you to agree on a price before taking you in on the deal."

"And the price was how much?" asked Lawrence.

"I told Buck to offer you ten thousand dollars."

LAWRENCE LAUGHED at the big lawyer.

"Ten thousand pay-off—and me heir to a million?"

"Don't be a fool! I'm the one to collect that money—and I'm the one to make the pay-off. You fool, it will be the easiest ten thousand you ever got."

"Not enough," smiled Lawrence.

Riggs spluttered, mopped his face, and tugged at his collar.

"I wish I had Buck Shelton here," he muttered. "Now, don't you get any foolish ideas. Maybe we can make the pay-off bigger, but I've got to get in touch with Shelton. A few extra days won't hurt. In the meantime you're Lonny West—and don't forget it. Use your brains. One slip of the tongue and we might sink. And try to forget any crazy notions you might have about a hold-up, Lonny; it won't work."

"I'm the mainspring in this machine," smiled the young man.

"Mainsprings have been known to snap—and don't forget it. We're here to collect a million dollars—and no one man is going to block the deal. You'll either play the game, take your cut—or else—"

"Are you sure Lonny West is dead?"

"Don't be a damn fool. Of course I'm sure. Both Wests are dead, and with the set-up we've got, we can't lose.

"Buck said you were the one person who could act the part."

"West wasn't much good, eh?" said the young man.

"Lonny West? Of course he wasn't. Just a hell-raising young fool. You shouldn't have any trouble acting as his double."

"Oh, I can play a damn fool," assured Lonny. "But suppose we get caught in the act. What's the penalty?"

"Don't let that bother you, Lonny; not while I'm handling the legal end of this deal. Edgar Riggs don't make any mistakes."

"All right, Riggs; I'll be Lonny West. Is there anything else that I should know?"

"That's all you need to know now; I'll do the rest."

CHAPTER IV

PRUNE JUICE

DOWN AT THE sheriff's office, Mose Upshaw leaned against the doorway, masticating thoughtfully. "Thasall right," he told Henry. "Mebbe he *is* West's heir. But if yuh ask me, he's iggerent as hell."

"Full of questions?" asked Henry.

"Full of one question," declared Mose. "Kept askin' me 'f I knowed a feller named Edgar Riggs, and I kept tellin' him I didn't. I asked him if Edgar Riggs was a bartender, and he said he hoped he was."

Henry squinted thoughtfully and rubbed his nose.

"I had me quite a few hopes to sell him a mine," sighed Mose.

"What mine?" asked Judge.

"Oh, well, hell!" grunted Mose. "As far as that goes, I could dig me one in a couple of hours. But 'f he's gittin' the Yaller Warrior and the Gold Plate, he's plumb loaded with mines."

Footsteps were coming down the sidewalk, and Mose sagged out, spat violently, and said:

"Hyah, Danny."

"Hello, Mose," replied Danny Regan, the young foreman of Henry's J Bar C spread.

Danny was twenty-four, a lithe, well-built cowboy. He had red hair, freckles, blue eyes, and a wide, white-toothed grin.

"How are you, Danny?" asked Henry.

"If I was any better I'd have to be tied," replied Danny. "I've only been in town ten minutes, but I've shore had a lot of news poured into my two ears. What's this talk about Jack West's nephew bein' here to claim West's estate?"

"There seems to be a lot of truth in the report," nodded Henry. "He came in on the stage today, and seems to have made his headquarters at the Tonto Hotel, along with Edgar Riggs, his attorney."

"Well, that's kinda startlin', ain't it?"

"Startlin' and iggerent, Danny," interposed Mose. "I had him in on m' stage t'day. He dresses as slick as a wet spot in a clay road, but he ain't got no more brains than a Chihuahua dog has hair. I've hauled me a lot of dudes, but—"

Mose craned his neck to look up the street.

"Shh-h-h!" he hissed warningly. "Here he comes!"

"Hello, Jehu," said the young man, halting at the doorway.

"Mr. Upshaw to you, sir," replied Mose loftily.

"My mistake. Greetings, gentlemen. I am Lonny West."

Henry got to his feet and shook hands with the young man.

"I am Henry Harrison Conroy, the sheriff, and at your service, sir. This gentleman is Judge Van Treece. Over here we have Danny Regan, foreman of the J Bar C cattle outfit. That calm-appearing person on the edge of the cot is Oscar Johnson, waiting for a horse-fly."

"Well, I am very glad to meet all of you," smiled Lonny. "I have never seen a horse fly—really. But I have been told that anything can happen in Arizona. Cozy little office you have."

"Thank you," said Henry dryly. "Mr. Edgar Riggs spoke about

you. He said you were here to claim the estate of the late Jack West."

"Yes," replied Lonny gravely. "I am here to claim the estate of my lamented uncle."

"Lamented?" queried Judge. "Did you say lamented, sir?"

"Perhaps I should have said deceased."

"Yeah, and he didn't have no disease, either," declared Mose. "He jist got his earthly envelope slit with a hunk of lead."

LONNY LAUGHED quietly. Turning to Henry, he said, "Being a stranger here, I have no idea what is the right thing to do. While I am not exactly temperate myself, I hesitate to—"

"Are you," queried Henry soberly, "trying in a roundabout way to invite us to have a drink?"

"Well, I wasn't sure—"

"Allay all doubts, my dear boy. The last abstainer in Tonto City died a horrible death years ago. I am sure that all of us accept your kind invitation, Mr. West."

"Yes, indeed!" exclaimed Judge, jerking to his feet. "It is a real pleasure to—"

Bang!

With a convulsive leap Mose Upshaw crashed into Lonny West, and they fell out through the doorway together. Danny ducked low, jerking out his gun, while Judge sagged against the wall. Henry looked reprovingly at Oscar, who sat on the cot, gun in hand, staring critically at the punctured ceiling.

"Ay had das one oll set," complained Oscar, "when Yudge yoomp oop and scare ha'al out of him."

"Missed again?" asked Henry weakly.

"Va'l, of course, Ay might have hit him dead center, Hanry; but Ay don't count 'em unless Ay can show some yuice around the edge."

"Of all the damn fools I've ever knowed!" exclaimed Danny, holstering his gun. "Shootin' horse-flies!"

"At them, Danny," corrected Henry calmly. "I can't say that

I am overly enthusiastic about it as an indoor pastime. In fact, I may be obliged to legislate against the practice, which is rather too ventilating."

"I should hope so," agreed Danny dryly.

"I don't quite understand," faltered Lonny West nervously.

"The subject is a little too damn deep for me, too," said Henry, putting on his sombrero, "but it hasn't quenched my thirst."

"Yuh ort to take that gun away from that dad-burned Swede," advised Mose Upshaw, looking nervously at Oscar. "He might shoot himself, don'tcha know it?"

"That thought opens possibilities," said Judge. "Oscar, you better keep that gun handy."

"Das ha'ar gun goes with me," declared Oscar. "Ay am de yailer."

"You will note," said Henry, "that Oscar feels the full responsibility of his position. Perhaps a drink will relieve the situation."

"Ay don't vant any saloon liquor," declared Oscar.

"I know," said Danny. "Frijole is comin' in later, and I happen to know he has a fresh supply of prune whisky. Oscar is savin' his thirst for some of that distilled dynamite."

"You bat you!" snorted Oscar. "Das saloon visky is yust pink lemonade. Ay vant hord liquor."

They went over to the Tonto Saloon, where Danny had one drink, and left them. Rarely did Danny ever take more than one drink.

"As a matter of fact," stated Judge, "you own this saloon, Mr. West. This is part of Jack West's estate."

The bartender became affable at once.

"While I ain't been told nothin'," he confided to Lonny, "yo're credit is shore plenty good here, Mr. West. The sky's the limit."

AN HOUR later they were still at the bar.

"Is there some—somet'n' wrong with the back of my coat?" asked Lonny.

"The coat is perfec', m' lad," assured Henry. "I was merely looking to see what was holding you up."

"He's good two-fis'ed drinker, awri'," declared Mose Upshaw. "Does anybody know any shongs worth shingin'?"

Mr. Edgar Riggs entered the saloon, halting near the doorway, where he looked with amazement upon his client. He settled his glasses upon his nose and looked closer, so that there be no mistake. ·

"If you please, Mr. West," he said coldly, "I would like a word in private with you."

"Mr. Riggs," replied Lonny, a trifle thickly, "have you ever done any public speaking?"

"I certainly have, sir."

"Are you good at it?"

"I believe I am capable of making a public address."

"Well, cut loose," said Lonny. "If it is good, I'll buy a drink."

"Good!" exploded Judge, hammering a bony fist on the bar. "Good! I have never heard a better one. Proceed, Mr. Riggs."

"I did not come here to bandy words with common drunks!" snapped Riggs angrily. "If you think you can prey upon the weakness of my client—"

"Weakness!" exclaimed Henry. "If that is his weakness, I would shudder to see his strength."

"West, I demand you to come out of there," said Riggs. "As your legal adviser, I demand that you obey. Of all the asinine actions! Don't you realize that Van Treece is bringing two suits against your estate? Don't you realize that, in getting you inebriated, they are—"

"In other words," Judge interrupted, "whatever you say, Lonny, may be used against you."

"Exactly!" snapped Riggs. "You have probably said too much—now."

"It seems to me that we could all be good little friends together," said Lonny. "Come and have a drink, Riggsy. Why,

there's no use of friends suing each other. We can settle everything nicely."

"Settle!" roared Riggs. "You poor fool, they're suing for the
entire estate!"

"Oh, they want it all, eh? No, I don't believe it. I'll bet I can
make a deal with 'em. We'll split it up—and everybody have a
good time. Come and have a drink."

"Can I speak privately with you for a moment?" asked Riggs.
He was trembling with anger. This pseudo heir was getting out
of control and needed a warning.

Lonny thought it over for a minute.

"Well, not longer," he said. "We are about to sing. I'll be right
back, boys."

HE FOLLOWED Riggs outside, and they halted near the
hitch-rack.

"You drunken young fool!" rasped Riggs. "Are you trying to
queer this whole deal? Drinking whisky with those men! They'll
get you drunk, and you'll talk too much—if you haven't already.
Don't you realize that this is a million-dollar deal, you fool?"

"Not for me," replied Lonny calmly. "Make it worth my while
and I might play the game with you."

"Blackmail, eh? Listen to me! I'll—"

"You listen to me," interrupted Lonny. "You brought me in
here as Lonny West. Without me—you're gone. You can't say
you made a mistake—that I was the wrong man. Your threats
are empty. Kill me—and what is left for you, Riggsy? You big
fat-headed crook, you've got to play the game my way. Go away
and quit bothering me when I'm drinking with friends."

"I'll send for Buck Shelton," threatened Riggs. "You'll play
the game for him, or he'll kill you."

Lonny laughed. He knew that Buck Shelton was one of San
Francisco's most notorious gamblers, but had never met him.

"Send for him," advised Lonny. "And you might tell him for
me that anything might happen in Arizona."

Riggs shook his head impotently.

"Shelton said you didn't have an overabundance of brains, but he didn't say you were damn fool enough to kick away a fortune. If you ruin this deal, you'll rue the day. Shelton said he had enough on you to put you away for a damn long time."

Lonny was seventy per cent drunk and thirty per cent mad. He walked up to Riggs, who drew back a little.

"You don't need to dodge," said Lonny quietly. "I'm not going to sock you in the nose—not yet. But if you make another crack about my mental capacity, I'll go across the street to the prosecuting attorney and tell him the whole game."

"All right, all right!" blurted Riggs quickly. "Get drunk, if you want to. But keep your head. Realize what it means, kid. I'm only talking for your own interests. Play the game with me. Hell, I'll see that you get more than the cut I promised you. I'm not cheap."

"All right, Riggs," laughed Lonny. "Forget it. I'll keep my head."

Riggs turned and walked swiftly away. Lonny chuckled softly.

Frijole Bill Cullison, the J Bar C cook, rode up to the sheriff's office and dismounted, carrying a jug wrapped in a burlap sack. Frijole was sixty years old, five feet, three inches tall, and would weigh about a hundred pounds, fully dressed. He had a skinny face, big eyebrows and a huge mustache.

Oscar came out to meet Frijole, and he waved at Lonny; an invitation to join them. Walking slightly erratically, Lonny went over there. Oscar had secured some tin cups while Frijole uncorked the jug.

"Free-holey," said Oscar, "das ha'ar yent's name is Vest."

"How are yuh?" greeted the little cook. "Git yore insides all primed for a surprise, pardner. Here yuh are."

"A tin cup full?" queried Lonny.

"Well, it's the only thing we've got to drink out of. It's a little slow, I'll admit—but yuh can drink out of the jug, if you'd ruther."

"Ay vouldn't do too much smelling, if Ay vere you," said Oscar. "Das liquor vars made for stummicks and not for noses. Va'l, ha'ar's to you, Mr. Vest."

Three tin cups were lifted to lips. Lonny took one big swallow, lost his breath, dropped the cup, and went out through the doorway, wheezing like an asthmatic.

Oscar and Frijole lowered their empty cups, listening to Lonny's uneven but departing footsteps on the wooden sidewalk.

"That dude must have weak tonsils," said Frijole huskily.

Oscar was smacking his lips, his forehead puckered thoughtfully.

"Free-holey," he said, "what in de ha'al is dis ha'ar stuff?"

Frijole tasted audibly, squinted at the jug closely, and wiped the back of his left hand across his mustache.

"Da-a-aw-gone it!" he blurted. "Oscar, I wondered why in hell that there jug wouldn't hold all I had in that can. I plumb forgot that Danny had a quart of hoss-liniment in a cracked bottle and poured it into my jug."

"Va'al," smiled Oscar broadly, "de label alvays says it is good for man or beast. Fill 'em oop again."

CHAPTER V

THE FIGHTING SWEDE

NICK BORDEN AND his wife were a handsome couple. Nick was tall and slender and addicted to severe black raiment. His handsome face was swarthy of skin, his hair as black as the proverbial raven's wing, except at the temples, where it was brushed with silver. Nick had been a gambler most of his life, but since his marriage to Lola West, erstwhile queen of the Tonto, he had made great efforts to develop his Smoke Tree mine.

Lola was twenty-three, with blue eyes and golden hair.

Leila Harper, engaged to Danny Regan, was twenty years of age, very slender, with wavy brown hair and dark eyes. Her mother was a buxom woman, middle-aged and very capable. She had been a beautiful girl, and that beauty still remained, in a matronly way.

Henry and Judge were sober when they came to the Harpers' rooms that evening to talk over the situation with the Bordens and the Harpers. Danny Regan was there, too.

"Judge," said Nick Borden, "just what is your impression of the present situation?"

"I am afraid of complications," admitted Judge. "Jack West willed everything he owned to this Lonny West, a nephew. I am afraid we shall have a devil of a time proving that Lola is—or was—West's daughter. I know just how you feel. I haven't the slightest doubt that Lola is the daughter of the man who was Jack West.

"It had been a great many years since Lola saw Jack West, until she found him here. I have been unable to discover a single photograph of Jack West which might positively identify him as the man who beat up Lola's mother. The man is dead quite a while. I don't know just what we can do to establish correct facts. This appearance of a will is damned inconvenient, if you will excuse my profanity."

"And my claim?" queried Mrs. Harper.

"Your claim, my dear," interposed Henry, "is more of a cripple than Lola's. Edgar Riggs merely snorts with disdain at such a claim."

"What sort of a person is this Lonny West?" asked Borden.

HENRY RUBBED his nose reflectively, glancing sharply at Judge.

"Lonny West," replied Henry, "according to Mose Upshaw, is a very ignorant young man."

"Iggerent," corrected Judge soberly.

"I welcome the correction, Judge," smiled Henry. "Mose says that Lonny West's appearance is as slick as a clay spot on a wet road, but he hasn't any more brains than a Chihuahua dog has hair. Beautiful similes. However, that all remains to be discovered. Judge and I accepted the young man's invitation to assimilate a modicum of rum, hoping thereby to learn more about this seeming upstart. You see, when a young man absorbs an undue amount of alcohol, he is liable to so far forget himself as to—well, show us the family album, as you might say."

"Did he talk?" asked Lola anxiously.

"I wish I could remember," sighed Henry. "We were nearing a crisis, if I remember correctly. Mose Upshaw had suggested a song. But Mr. Riggs, the enemy attorney, appeared and finally convinced Lonny West that he should speak in private with his legal adviser.

"If I remember correctly, we had a song. It was not so well rendered, because Mose Upshaw, who sang the lead, went to sleep on the first chorus. Judge and I finished, I believe. If the expression on the bartender's face was any criterion, the song was not well rendered."

"He has no ear for music," sighed Judge.

"I hope that is an explanation, Judge. At any rate, Lonny West came back, knocked over a card table, fell against the bar, and announced in no uncertain tone that he had been shot. For a moment I thought perhaps that Oscar had mistaken him for a horse-fly. But he managed to explain that he had swallowed a bomb, which Oscar gave him in a tin cup. He said it exploded inside him three times between the sheriff's office and the Tonto Saloon."

"But there was no information brought out, eh?" said Borden.

"Yes, there was," declared Henry. "Judge told most of his past life."

"I did not, sir," denied Judge.

"What became of Lonny West?" asked Leila.

"Well," laughed Henry, "he got pointed toward the hotel

finally. And as he reached the doorway he turned and held up four fingers. I do not know what he meant, unless it was that the bomb had exploded for the fourth time."

AT THE same time that this conference was in progress Edgar Riggs sat in Lonny West's room at the hotel. Lonny was stretched out on the bed, a wet towel across his forehead, a picture of utter dejection.

"I hope this will be a lesson to you," said Riggs. "You made an ass of yourself, and nearly ruined everything. Now, I've explained things to you a dozen times; things you have got to know. See how much you can remember. Go ahead and tell me."

"My name is Lonny West," replied the young man. "I am twenty-four years of age and a perfect ass."

"That last assertion was not included."

"Merely explanatory, in case I meet a stranger," replied Lonny. "I am the son of Howard and Virginia West. I was born in Chicago, but moved to San Francisco when I was ten. I was kicked out of two high schools, but finally graduated. Went to the University of California for one term, and was dumped out on my ear."

"Correct. Very good, Lonny."

"As far as it goes, Riggs. But suppose somebody wants to know what I've been doing since then. Do I make up my own sad tale?"

"You might evade that part of it."

"I see. How well did I know this uncle of mine?"

"You never saw him in your life."

"One of those non-irritating relations, eh? All right. I hope the real Lonny West don't show up."

"He's dead, I told you. Positively identified by his clothes and personal effects. As legal adviser for Jack West, I handled all this information. Lonny's mother died several years ago. No one knew what became of his father."

"Jack West knew the real Lonny was dead, eh?" queried Lonny.

"Well, it didn't affect him. He remarked that he knew he had a nephew somewhere in the world; and let it go at that."

"No tears for little Lonnie, eh? But if anything ever happens to prove you forged all this stuff, Riggs—"

"Drop that talk! If this estate was to be settled in a city, I'd hesitate. But out here—why, it's a cinch. Cow-town judge, who will never question a thing. Court convenes next week. Ten days from now it will all be settled. You sign everything over to me, take your ten thousand and go back to civilization."

"What about those two claims, Riggs?"

"I'll handle those claims. You watch my smoke."

"All right. Leave me alone; I want to sleep."

"A little sleep won't hurt you, kid. What in the devil smells so funny around here? Antiseptic?"

"Horse-liniment."

"Horse-liniment? Where's the horse?"

"No horse; just a jackass, Riggs. Good night."

NO MATTER what others thought of prune whisky, flavored with horse-liniment, Oscar and Frijole liked it. While Henry, Judge, Mose and Lonny sobered, Frijole and Oscar had no such temperate ideas; at least, not as long as anything remained in the jug.

"That liniment shore gives her a bite," declared Frijole.

"Yust damn goot visky," agreed Oscar. "Das ha'ar stuff inwigorates me, Ay ta'al you. Free-holey, do you know a Norvegian miner named Olaf?"

"I ain't never had no truck with Norwegians, Oscar."

"Va'al," confided Oscar, "he is a big yigger. Ay vish to meet him."

"Are you aimin' for to kinda bend him out of shape, feller?"

"Das Norvegian talk too damn much, Free-holey. He says

dere is a crazy damn Svede in Tonto City, and Ay am going to bust him in de yaw."

"Meanin' you?" queried Frijole.

"Yah, su-re. Ay am de only crazy damn Svede in Tonto City."

"Yeah, that's right," agreed Frijole soberly. "Let's me and you go out on a huntin' expedition."

It was dark when they left the sheriff's office. Arm in arm, they went looking for Olaf. Oscar's description was rather vague, because he had never seen Olaf. The town was full of miners.

"Ay vill know Olaf," declared Oscar. "Yust give me time."

After their own concoction ordinary whisky was like water— but they drank it, more to be sociable than for the effect. When Frijole seemed to be passing out on him, Oscar would grab the little cook, shake him violently, steady him for a moment, and then go on.

"You bet'r go eashy, you crazy damn Svede," warned Frijole, after a particularly hard shaking. "I'm li'ble to come unbolted. Then where'd yuh be? I 'preciate yuh t' beat hell, Oshcar, but I'm beginnin' to dish—dish-inte—beginnin' to come apart."

"Ay yust vant you to be ha'ah ven Ay meet Olaf, Free-holey."

They were not offensive. People merely smiled at the hulking Swede, leading his little companion about.

"You see, Free-holey," explained Oscar, propping the little cook against a bar, "das ha'ar Norvegian talks too much."

"I've noticed that," gulped Frijole. "He's gotta big mouth. He's gotta be sus-sus-smit'd hip'n thigh."

"Yah, su-u-ure," agreed Oscar owlishly. "How you feeling?"

Frijole was still upright, but snoring violently. Oscar looked around helplessly, shook Frijole violently, but only succeeded in causing the little cook's lower jaw to vibrate.

"You big, fat-headed Svede," remarked a voice beside them, "why don't you dust him with insect powder and sweep him out?"

Oscar turned slowly. It was undeniably Olaf. Under cover of

the bar, Oscar closed his huge left fist. He shifted his left shoulder, taking out any possible kink. And then, with no false motion, he whirled that hamlike fist in an overhead swing, and his knuckles connected square on the wide chin of Olaf, the Norwegian.

"My Gawd!" gasped a miner. "He knocked Olaf cold enough to skate on!"

No referee was needed to indicate that Olaf was out. The bartender threw a glass of cold water in his face, but it did not register. A miner moved in close to Oscar, speaking quietly.

"Look out for him when he wakes up. He's a bad boy. You knocked him out this time—but he'll git yuh—if yuh ain't careful."

"Yah?" queried Oscar. "Good! Ven he vakes oop, you tell him Ay am at my office. Come on, Free-holey."

He put one huge arm around Frijole, bent him in the middle, and went out of the Tonto Saloon, carrying the little cook with no more effort than he might have carried an extra shirt.

AFTER EDGAR RIGGS left Lonny West's room he went back to his own quarters in the hotel, where he wrote several letters. Riggs was still afraid of what Lonny West might do to their scheme; so he wrote Buck Shelton a résumé of things as they were in Tonto City.

He was starting to undress, when the door opened softly and a man stepped into the room. Riggs started violently.

The intruder was tall, clad entirely in black, his face covered with a black cloth. And in his right hand was a very business-like Colt revolver.

"A trifle late," agreed the masked man, "but I work late."

"Wh-what do you want?"

"Sit down, Riggs," ordered the man. "I want a word with you."

"A word, eh?" queried Riggs, regaining some of his composure. "What is the idea of the mask and gun?"

"Rather a dumb question, coming from a lawyer," observed the man.

Riggs sat down, trying to appear calm.

"I suppose this has something to do with the West case," he said.

"Mind reader," said the masked man. "I dropped in to warn you that we play a square game in this country. You may be a big-town lawyer, but that don't count out here. There are two legitimate claims on the West estate; and you'd better recognize them."

"If you've got any brains behind that black mask," snarled Riggs, "you'd know that the claims, just or unjust, will be thrown out of court. A dance-hall girl claiming a million-dollar estate! A woman making a twenty-year-old claim on a share of a mine because her husband was one of the locators. Rubbish!

"What actual proof has this female faro-dealer? None—and you know it. What proof has the other woman—proof that will stand in court? Not a damn iota of proof—and you know that, too. And you can't come into my room at night, wearing a black mask and flourishing a gun, trying to frighten me. Now, get out, you damned hoodlum!"

Slowly the masked man got to his feet. Riggs jerked upright, his jaw clenched tightly. The masked man stepped over to the little table, where Riggs' brief-case had been left.

"Damn you, if you—" Riggs made a sudden dive for the leather case. Shifting his feet with all the speed of a cat, the masked man's left hand shot out, in a fending motion, splatted against Riggs' jaw, and flung him off balance. For a moment he hung, as though suspended, arms outstretched, and then fell flat on the floor, his head bumping against the foot of the bed.

Riggs was dazed for a moment. As he sat up, the door was closing quietly, and the brief-case was gone.

With a grunt of rage Riggs climbed to his feet. Making a frantic grab for his hat, he went into the dimly lighted hallway. It was empty. Down the stairs he went, surprisingly fast for a man of his size. The little lobby of the hotel was empty. Riggs raced outside, cursing Tonto City for its lack of lights on the main street.

There was no sign of the man in the black mask. Riggs' one hope was to get help from the sheriff. Walking swiftly, rubbing his sore jaw, he headed for the office. Someone must be in there, he reasoned, because there was a dim light. He had seen a cot in the office—evidence that one of the force slept there.

With both his big hands he hammered loudly on the door. There was no response; so he repeated the operation.

"Wake up in there!" he roared huskily. "Wake up and come out!"

At his back was a narrow alley, which led around to the rear of the office. Except for that dim light in the office, everything was very dark at that spot.

Suddenly he heard the slither of a footstep behind him, and started to turn around.

It was then that the world became very chaotic for Mr. Riggs. He was smashed against the office wall under a fusillade of sledgehammer blows which drove the breath from his huge body. He tried to call out, to lift his hands, but it was no use. The air seemed filled with skyrockets, each one going in a different direction. Then he seemed to be in a vise, which whirled him around and around, and flung him far out into space, where he received the sensation of a final shock.

And then, as though from a great distance, a tiny voice said, "Yust remember, Olaf, that Ay may be crazy damn Svede, but Ay can fight like ha'al."

CHAPTER VI

A KILLER COMES TO TOWN

HENRY HARRISON CONROY sat on the edge of a chair in Edgar Riggs' room, next morning, and watched Dr. Bogart wrap several yards of tape around the ribs of the lawyer, who groaned dismally.

"I don't believe that any ribs are broken," said the doctor. "You may thank an excess of fat for that, Mr. Riggs."

"If you have finished," groaned Riggs, "get out of here. I want to talk to the sheriff."

The old cow-town doctor smiled grimly at Henry as he picked up his bag and walked out, softly closing the door.

Speaking slowly and with many groans, Edgar Riggs told Henry exactly what had happened to him.

"Remarkable," murmured Henry.

"Damnable," groaned Riggs.

"Peculiar," added Henry.

"To hell with adjectives!" mourned Riggs. "I'm dying, I believe."

"Faith in oneself is a wonderful thing," sighed Henry. "How many men do you think assaulted you?"

"At least six," replied Riggs huskily. "Not less than six."

"Working in relays, I suppose," murmured Henry, wondering just what did happen to the lawyer. There was no doubt that Edgar Riggs had been thoroughly beaten.

"I want that brief-case," panted Riggs. "Do you understand? I want it!"

"Was there anything incriminating in it?" asked Henry blandly.

"My private papers dealing with the West estate."

"Only of value to you, I suppose, sir."

"My God!" Riggs jerked upright, in spite of his misery.

The letter he had written to Buck Shelton was in that brief-case!

"A sudden twinge?" queried Henry solicitously.

Riggs swallowed painfully. Someone knocked softly on the door. Henry walked over and admitted Tom Rickey, owner of the hotel. In his right hand he carried the missing brief-case.

"I found this beneath the counter in the office," said Rickey, "and I wondered if it belonged to Mr. Riffs."

"It's mine!" panted Riggs.

Henry handed it to him, and with trembling fingers the lawyer opened it. A swift examination proved that the papers were there. Yes, that letter was there, too.

Riggs sank back on his pillow, his face beaded with perspiration.

"Everything is all right," he said wearily.

"I'll see if I can find those six men," said Henry, and walked out with Rickey.

Henry found Oscar at the office.

The big jailer was still redolent of horse-liniment, but very sober.

"Did you and Frijole have a celebration last night?" asked Henry.

"Yah, su-ure."

"I noted that your knuckles were skinned up a trifle, Oscar."

"Ay vipped Olaf last night."

"And who on earth is Olaf?"

"Olaf is a big Norvegian from de Yallow Varrior mine. Ay vipped him twice."

Henry rubbed his nose and squinted thoughtfully at Oscar.

"Twice, did you say?"

"Yah, su-u-ure. Ay knock him cold as ha'al in de Tonto Saloon. He must be tough yigger. Ay coom over ha'ar, and after vile Olaf coom over ha'ar and knock on de door. He say, 'Coom out of dere!' So Ay go out back door and coom in behind him. By yimminy, I knock ha'al out of him, and I t'row him out in de dort."

OSCAR'S STATEMENT was illuminating. The mystery of Riggs' assault was no longer a mystery.

"Have you seen Lonny West this morning?" asked Henry.

"Ay ain't seen him, Hanry. Ay don't like that yigger—much."

"You do not like him—much, eh?"

"Ay like good drinking man. Das Lonny Vest has stommick like a hommingbirt. Veak people like him should drink soda vater."

Henry blinked violently, peered closely at Oscar, and leaned back in his chair.

"I must tell that to Judge and Mose," he murmured. "The stomach of a hummingbird."

Later in the forenoon Henry met Lonny in front of the hotel, and they were discussing the strange assault of Edgar Riggs, when Mrs. Borden drove in. Henry tied her horse to the hotel hitch-rack and helped her from the buggy.

"Lola," said Henry, "I believe it is about time for you two to meet. Cousin Lola, meet Cousin Lonny."

"Great Scott!" exclaimed Lonny. "You are my cousin?"

"It seems to be a fact," smiled Lola. "You seem surprised—and yet you knew that such a thing existed."

"Yes, I—" Lonny faltered. "But I didn't know she was so mighty good-looking," he said frankly.

Lola laughed quietly.

"Honestly, I mean it," declared Lonny. "You are Mrs. Borden?"

"Yes, I am Mrs. Borden."

None of them had noticed Leila, who came up from the millinery shop, until she joined them.

"My dear Leila," said Henry quickly, "you must meet Lola's

cousin, Lonny West. Lonny, this is Miss Harper, whose mother is suing for part of your estate."

Leila flushed quickly, but Lonny laughed heartily and held out his hand to her.

"I am very glad to meet you, Miss Harper," he said.

"I know how you feel, Lonny," said Henry. "Every time I meet either of them on the street I fully expect to see a ballet sweep out from the wings and go into their dance."

"I—I believe you are right, Mr. Conroy," agreed Lonny. "I hope I am not considered an enemy. That would be terrible."

"Your father's name was West?" asked Lola.

"Howard West," replied Lonny. "He was Jack West's brother."

"Is he still alive?"

"Who knows? He deserted my mother a long time ago, and no one knows where he went."

"It must he a family trait," said Lola quietly.

"I—I hope it isn't an inherited curse," said Lonny.

Leila and Lola went together to a store, and Lonny looked after them with undisguised admiration.

"There is one thing to be remembered," said Henry quietly. "Leila Harper is engaged to Danny Regan—and Lola is married to Nick Borden."

"I'm sorry," replied Lonny, "I mean, I'm sorry I stared. Still," Lonny laughed, "I suppose one has a right to stare at one's cousin."

"I suppose," agreed Henry. "How do you like Frijole Bill's whisky?"

Lonny shuddered and shook his head quickly.

"Externally it may have curative properties, Mr. Conroy; but it is not a beverage. Will you join me in a drink?"

"I believe I will, Lonny. I haven't had my morning's morning yet. The sorry plight of your legal light—excuse me for being poetical—kept me from exchanging my usual morning pleasantries with the Tonto bartender. It is a rite, I assure you."

"We should have Mose, the stage driver," laughed Lonny. "He surely is quaint."

"Yes, he is—very, very quaint. He says you are ignorant. No, I believe he used the word iggerent."

"I don't believe there are any grounds for an argument," smiled Lonny. "And I still like Mose."

THAT EVENING, as Lonny ate his supper at the Tonto Hotel, listening to the strains of rattling crockery, Edgar Riggs surged in from the little lobby, looked anxiously around and came straight to Lonny.

"Look at this," he blurted, handing Lonny a telegram.

It was from San Francisco, signed by Buck Shelton, and read:

TELL LONNY FLOOD COMING STOP HELENE MISSING BUT PROBABLY ON WAY TO WARN LONNY STOP ADVISE IF YOU NEED ME.

Lonny read the message carefully, a puzzled expression in his eyes. He rubbed his chin and looked up at Riggs.

"Flood coming?" he inquired.

"Yes, he's coming," grunted Riggs. "And that woman, too."

Lonny remembered now. For the moment he had forgotten that man who had tried to murder Breezy Lemair in the chop-suey café.

Riggs sank down in a chair and leaned across the table, lowering his voice to a husky whisper.

"You've got to stop Flood," he said. "He's coming here to kill you. Buck said he'd handle Flood, but, as usual, he has failed. Flood will come here, with his nose full of snow, and kill you, unless you get him first."

"Such a beautiful sentiment," murmured Lonny.

"Self-defense," said Riggs.

Lonny's smile was frosty as he said, "I believe I'll tell the sheriff—and let him handle Flood."

"You can't do that! Handle Flood! In some way Flood knows

you are down here—and I'm betting that he knows something about this deal. Have him arrested, and he'll tell everything he knows. Flood has got to be burned down before he has a chance to talk."

"Helene is coming, too," said Lonny. "What about her?"

"She's in on our deal, and you know it. She's only coming to warn you. Maybe she didn't want to take chances on a telegram."

"Well, what's to be done, Riggs?"

"You take the morning stage to Scorpion Bend, and when Flood shows up, shoot him. Don't even let him start down here."

"Wonderful!" murmured Lonny. "Such a simple thing. Then I get hung for murder, and everything will be just fine. Riggsy, you've got some beautiful thoughts—with parts missing. For ten thousand dollars—maybe—I—yes, I said maybe. I wouldn't trust you as far as I could throw one of those loaded ore-wagons. If I—"

"You fool, he's coming here to kill *you*. He tried to kill you once before. He's a crazy hop-head. I can prove to the coroner that Flood—"

"Wait a minute," interrupted Lonny. "Why don't you shoot him? If he shoots me, you're shy one perfectly good heir. You harp about that million dollars you're going to get—why not protect it. I'm damn sure that I'm not going to Scorpion Bend to shoot Flood. That's final, Riggs."

"Are you going to let him come down here and shoot you?"

"Well, I'm not anxious to meet him."

"Buck is certainly a good picker," sneered Riggs. "He told me you had guts. He said you'd shoot. What I'll tell *him!*"

"You've almost ruined my meal," sighed Lonny. "If you don't get out of here, Riggs, I'll crown you with that platter."

"I could almost hope he shoots you," gritted Riggs, getting to his feet.

"But not quite, Riggsy; I'm your marked cards."

LONNY WAS not worried about Jack Flood. No doubt Flood

would be looking for Breezy Lemair. Lonny did not remember what Flood looked like, except that he was flashily dressed and had sleek, black hair. Lonny was willing to take Riggs' word for the fact that Flood was a cocaine addict.

Helene was a different proposition. She would remember him. One way to stop all this foolishness would be to tell the whole tale to the prosecuting attorney. Lonny walked nearly to the lawyer's office, but changed his mind and came back. The whole thing had an element of danger, plus humor; and Lonny decided to let things ride for a while.

In front of the sheriff's office he met Oscar and Frijole. The cook of the J Bar C was driving the ranch buckboard.

"Hyah, Delicate," said Frijole soberly. "How do yuh like prune whisky?"

"Without horse-liniment," laughed Lonny. "How are you, Frijole?"

"Finer 'n frawg-hair. Oscar's ridin' out to the ranch with me. Why don'tcha come along? Won't be nobody out there but us."

"I think I'd like to do that," replied Lonny. "I have never been on a ranch."

"Yeah? I'll betcha Mose Upshaw was right. You shore are iggerent."

"Yust stay around ha'ar a vile, Lonny," advised Oscar. "Ay vill drive de team, Free-holey."

"Over my lamented re-mains," retorted the cook. "I wouldn't let you drive a nail—unless yuh used yore own hammer."

"Ay am de best driver in Vild Hurse Walley," declared Oscar.

"Yo're a great help to the blacksmith. There's been seven sets of new wheels on that buckboard—and you only drove it seven times. C'mon, Lonny; we'll show yuh a ranch."

JACK FLOOD, erstwhile lieutenant of Buck Shelton, came to Scorpion Bend, where he hired a buggy team and driver to take him to Tonto City. Flood had been replaced by Breezy Lemair in Shelton's organization. Breezy had proceeded to steal

Helene from Flood, which was a case of adding insult to injury. Somebody in the organization had told Flood something about the West deal; so Flood came to Arizona with blood in his eye.

Jack Flood was of medium height, sallow of skin, with coal-black hair and a tiny mustache. Sartorially, he was splendid. Ben East, the driver, tried to carry on a conversation, but Flood refused. Ben went with him into the Tonto Saloon, where Flood asked the bartender if he knew a young fellow named West.

"Lonny West? Shore, I know him. I seen him not more'n an hour ago, ridin' out of town with Frijole Bill and Oscar Johnson. They was goin' out to the J Bar C ranch."

They finished their drinks and walked outside.

"Do you know where that ranch is?" asked Flood.

"Shore. I've been out there lotsa times."

"We'll go out there."

About thirty minutes later Edgar Riggs entered the Tonto Saloon, and looked around carefully before coming up to the bar.

"Have you seen Lonny West this evening?" he asked the bartender.

" 'Bout an hour and a half ago I seen Lonny West ride out of town, with Oscar Johnson and Frijole Bill, the J Bar C cook. I reckon they went to the ranch."

"He did, eh?" muttered the lawyer.

"Yo're the second one that's been lookin' for him," offered the bartender.

"The second?" queried Riggs quickly.

"Yessir. 'Bout a half hour ago a feller was in here, askin' for him. There was two fellers. One was Ben East, who works for the livery stable in Scorpion Bend. I reckon Ben drove him down here. Mebbe they went out to the ranch, too."

"What did this man look like?" asked Riggs eagerly.

"Awful slick looker. Kinda pale, with black hair and a mustache 'bout the size of a sickly eyebrow. Had a big diamond in his tie and a bigger one on his finger."

"My Gawd!" breathed Riggs, and almost ran from the saloon. The bartender's description covered Jack Flood. There was a light in the sheriff's office. Riggs hated to ask for help, but in this case he needed swift action.

HENRY WAS seated at his desk, one booted foot on the desk top, an unlighted cigar between his lips. He looked mildly surprised at the excited, panting lawyer, who blurted:

"You've got to get out to the J Bar C ranch right away, unless you want a murder on your hands, sheriff!"

Henry tried to cuff his hat back on his head, but sent it spinning off.

"Unless I *want* one?" he queried.

"Unless you hurry!" panted Riggs. "Do something, can't you?"

Henry managed to drag his foot off the desk, grimaced from the exertion, and drew a deep breath.

"Who is going to die?" he asked.

"Lonny West."

"Oh! And who is going to kill him?"

Riggs flapped his arms dismally.

"Don't argue! Do something—quickly. A man came all the way from San Francisco to kill Lonny West. Lonny, the damn fool, went out to your ranch tonight. This man has gone to the ranch to kill Lonny."

"Well!" exclaimed Henry. "That is a long ways to come, merely to kill a man. Still, he—he picked nice weather for it, Mr. Riggs."

"Nice weather! Oh, have you one scintilla of sense? Don't you realize what it means? Are you going—"

"Wait a moment," interrupted Henry. "How long has this killer been gone from here?"

"Over half an hour."

"Thirty minutes? Must be about there by this time. Giving

him ten minutes for arguments, five minutes for aiming purposes—" Henry shook his head. "Lonny will have been dead at least fifteen or twenty minutes before we could possibly get there. The road ends at the J Bar C, Mr. Riggs; so the killer will have to come back. Our best bet is to catch him when he goes through town."

"But my client will be dead!"

"Yes, I realize that. But we will do our very best to hang the murderer."

"I suppose that is all I could expect from such peace officers as we have here," groaned Riggs. "Can't you, at least, make a sincere effort to prevent a murder?"

"What makes you think this man came to kill him?"

"I received a telegram from San Francisco, saying that this man was on his way."

"And you never told me. That places the blame on you, Mr. Riggs. Did you tell Lonny West?"

"Yes, damn it, I told him!"

"I see. After the horse is stolen, you ask me to rush out and slam the stable door. You knew it, and Lonny West knew it. Why was I kept in ignorance?"

"Oh, what's the use of debating about it?" sighed Riggs. "I came for help and all I get is an argument. I suppose Lonny is dead by this time."

Henry nodded, glancing at his watch.

"It wouldn't surprise me one bit, Mr. Riggs. Can you furnish me with a description of the killer?"

But Edgar Riggs had walked out, and was crossing the street toward the Tonto Saloon. After a moment of indecision, Henry buckled on his gun, closed the office and went out to saddle his horse.

CHAPTER VII

MILD MURDER

LONNY, OSCAR AND Frijole sat in the main room of the J Bar C, with a demijohn and three tin cups. Oscar had his boots off, and was sitting almost on his shoulder-blades in an old rocker. Thirty minutes of sampling Frijole's distillation, and all three of them were looking at the world through rose-colored glasses.

"Gen'lemen," said Lonny, "it's like thish. The firsh drink—"

"I know," interrupted Frijole. "It allus does to a stranger. But when you drink it reg'larly, yore tonsils get petterfied, and you can't enjoy anythin' weaker'n thish stuff. Ain't it true, Oshcar?"

"Yust like Ay vars saying," replied Oscar. "My great grandfadder vars a Wiking. Ay vars born at Norrkoping. Ay can remamber—"

"You can't even remember where yuh left yore boots," interrupted Frijole. "My gran'father was a Cullison. What was yours, Lonny?"

"I think mine was a Republican," replied Lonny. "Shay! What 'n earth do you put in that liquor? I'm getting stiff."

"Prunes," replied Frijole.

"Prunes? Oh, those black things you eat for breakf'st?"

" 'F there's any left," said Frijole. "How 'bout shom music?"

"Ay vars yust thinking Ay might sing," grinned Oscar. "Do you vant to hear me sing, Lonny?"

"Do I, Frijole?" asked Lonny.

"Have you," queried Frijole owlishly, "an ear for music?"

"I don't know one tune from another."

"Good! Neither do me and Oscar. Oscar, go out to the bunkhoush and get my gittar."

"Ay vill do it."

Oscar went shuffling out.

"There's one of the grea'est fellers yuh ever met, Lonny," said Frijole. "Not a brain in his head to interfere with him. Hones' as the day is long. Fact. He ain't got brains 'nough to figger out a lie. Jus' a diamond in the rough—and, boy, how rough he can be! Have a drink."

Lonny shook his head. "Tha' stuff's bottled paralysis. I—uh—huh!"

The front door had opened and Jack Flood stepped into the room. A blued automatic covered Lonny and Frijole, while Flood's black eyes darted around the room. Then he came slowly, circling the room. A sharp glance showed that the kitchen was empty, and he turned on the two men.

"One move and I'll blast the both of you," he hissed.

"Well, 'f all things!" exclaimed Frijole.

"Where's Breezy Lemair?" gritted Flood.

"Didn't you git in the wrong stall?" queried Frijole. "I never heard the name before, did you, Lonny?"

"Lonny?" queried Flood. He jerked forward, staring at Lonny.

"Who are you?" he asked coldly.

"He's Lonny West," interposed Frijole.

"Lonny West?" Flood's eyes were puzzled. "*You are Lonny West?*"

"He shore as hell is!" snorted Frijole.

None of them heard Oscar come back. In his sock-feet he made no noise at all. Jack Flood's back was to the doorway, which led to the kitchen.

"Wait a minute," said Flood icily. "I want to know something. If you are—"

Crash!

A heavy guitar, swung by two powerful hands, landed square on top of Jack Flood's head; and Jack Flood's head went through the guitar body. The blow knocked him down, the gun flew out of his hands, and a moment later he was sitting on the floor.

FRIJOLE KICKED the automatic across the room, choking with unholy glee as he looked at Flood.

"Vat de ha'al is dis faller doing in ha're?" queried Oscar.

"I was jist a-wonderin' about that m'self," said Ben East, from the front doorway. "Hyah, Frijole. Hyah, Oscar."

"Hallo dere, Benny," greeted Oscar. "Coom and have a drink."

"What in hell happened?" asked Jack Flood blankly, pawing at the guitar strings.

"Benny, do you know anythin' about this yere critter?" asked Frijole.

"Not much, Frijole. He done hired me to drive him to Tonto. He was a-lookin' f'r a feller named West. The bartender at the Tonto sent us out here. Hell, I didn't know he was on the prod thataway."

Oscar reached down and yanked the ruined guitar off Flood's head. One string caught under Flood's nose and he howled miserably. His face looked as though it had been clawed by a cat.

"You was lookin' for Lonny West?" queried Frijole coldly.

"I—I guess not," replied Flood weakly. "There is some mistake."

"Yeah, and yo're the mistake," declared Frijole.

"Where-at is that afore-mentioned drink?" asked Ben East.

"I'll git a couple more cups," offered Frijole, and went into the kitchen. Jack Flood mopped his skinned features with an expensive silk handkerchief, his eyes puzzled, as he studied Lonny.

He looked up blankly when Frijole handed him a cupful of the powerful home-made whisky. He sniffed at it and started to put the cup aside, but Frijole's gun clicked sharply, and he looked up.

"We're all goin' t' have a drink," said Frijole meaningly. "I made that stuff m'self—and I'd drink, 'f I was you, feller."

Jack Flood looked at the gun, shifted his eyes to Frijole's skinny little face—and drank. His eyes snapped wide, and he made queer noises with his throat, but he emptied the cup.

"The second one's a cinch," declared Frijole, filling the cup.

"I—I've had plenty—thank—you," whispered Flood.

"Don't be so damn perlite," said Frijole. "We've got plenty."

CONSIDERABLE TIME had elapsed since Henry left Tonto City. He was not a fast rider. Lights glowed in the ranch house. Out in front was a team and buggy. Henry dismounted and walked over to an uncovered window, where he peered inside at the scene of carnage.

Lonny was sitting on the floor, his back against the wall, snoring serenely. Sprawled on the old couch was Ben East, sound asleep, his hat clutched in his right hand. Seated together on an old bench were Oscar and Frijole, while Jack Flood, the killer from Frisco, was hunched over in the rocker, a cup of liquor in his right hand.

"All ri'—let 'er go!" exclaimed Flood thickly, waving the cup.

And from the throats of Frijole and Oscar, the two worst singers in Wild Horse Valley, came wailingly:

"Oh, where is my wa-a-a-a-andering boy tonight;
Th' bo-o-oy of my ten'erest ca-a-a-are—"

And as they mistreated the old song Jack Flood, using the cup of whisky in lieu of a baton, led the singing.

Henry walked carefully back to the front of the house, unhitched the team, stabled the two horses and rode back to Tonto City. Edgar Riggs saw him ride up to the office, and came hurrying down there.

"You've been out to the ranch?" he asked anxiously.

Henry tied his horse and went into the office, where he unbuckled his gun-belt and tossed it aside, before he replied:

"Yes, I was out there."

"Lonny—is he—"

"Stiff as a board," replied Henry soberly.

"Dead?" whispered Riggs huskily.

"Drunk."

"Drunk? I—I don't—Where's Flood—the man I told you about?"

"Drunk."

"Drunk. Why, I—I don't understand, sheriff."

"I cannot exactly explain it," replied Henry seriously, "But I might make you understand if you would drink a couple of cupfuls."

"Cupfuls of what?"

"Prune juice."

"One of us," declared Riggs soberly, "must be crazy."

"Well," smiled Henry, "I doubt very much if either of us would pass a halfway examination. Good night, sir."

"I think I know who is crazy," said Riggs savagely, turning to the doorway.

"I am sure it is all right with me, as long as you do not get criminally violent," said Henry. "Please close the door."

EDGAR RIGGS was thoroughly mad. He went straight to the hotel, marched up the stairs, and almost collided with a woman. It was Helene, the blonde from the Peninsula Club.

"You?" gasped Riggs. "Where—"

"Not here," warned the woman. "My room is back here."

In the room, Helene's lips twisted angrily as she said:

"Where's Breezy?"

"Breezy? Oh, you mean Lonny. He is out at the J Bar C ranch."

"Did you know Jack Flood came here tonight?"

"Yes, I know he did. Sit down and quit pawing at me, Helene."

"What happened when they met?" she asked anxiously.

"I don't know. They were both out at that ranch before I knew that either was there. Buck wired me that Flood was coming, and I warned Breezy. The damn fool didn't seem to take it seriously. Why didn't Buck send me a man with some brains?"

"Breezy has plenty of brains," declared Helene.

"He's drunk half the time, and running around with the enemy."

"But what happened?" demanded Helene.

"I had to get help from the sheriff," said Riggs. "I knew that Flood was out there to kill the kid. Well, the sheriff just got back, and he said that both Flood and Lonny were drunk—stiff as a pair of boards."

"Together?"

Riggs nodded dumbly.

"I don't believe it," declared the woman. "There has been bad blood between them for months. Jack tried once to kill him. You can't tell me he'd come all this distance merely to get drunk with Breezy. Riggs, there's something decidedly fishy about this whole affair."

Riggs adjusted his glasses and looked at Helene closely.

"Fishy?" he said. "Why, what could be fishy about it?"

"Riggs," she said slowly, "did you know Breezy Lemair?"

"Only by reputation. Buck Shelton said—"

"You had never seen him?"

"No, and I wish I never had seen him."

Helene walked the length of the room and came back to Riggs.

"Bring him to me as soon as he comes to town," she said.

"I'll do that. I'd like to turn him over to somebody else. You didn't know he kicked on his cut, did you? Of course you didn't. He laughs at me. Helene, he would double cross all of us if he had a chance. Laughs at me and threatens to tell the prosecuting attorney about the deal."

"That doesn't sound like Breezy," said Helene. "Breezy likes his liquor; but he's no rat."

"I wish Buck would come out here to handle him."

"We don't need Buck; I can handle him. Bring him to me."

"I certainly will," replied Riggs grimly. "It will be a pleasure to see somebody handle the young fool."

Some time during the early morning hours a team and buggy rattled through the dark streets of Tonto City, heading north. It was Ben East, taking Jack Flood back to Scorpion Bend.

"What place is this?" asked Flood wearily.

"Tonto City," replied Ben.

"Stop the deal," ordered Flood. "We'll stay here tonight."

"Yo're payin' the bills," replied Ben.

CHAPTER VIII

THE UNBREAKABLE JUG

BECAUSE OSCAR WAS out at the ranch, Henry slept in the office that night. Early in the morning a man came down from the stage station, awoke Henry and gave him a telegram.

"This here is a copy," he told Henry. "I think it's what you asked me to watch out for, Mr. Conroy."

"Thank you very much," said Henry sleepily. "If I ever inherit a million, I'll give you a mahogany telegraph-key."

Edgar Riggs was an early riser, especially when he had a sleepless night. Merely out of curiosity he looked at the dog-eared register on the hotel desk. The last name on the book, written in a bold hand, was Jack Flood, San Francisco. Riggs made a nervous gesture with his right hand, caught a finger in the ribbon of his glasses, and sent them flying across the lobby, where they shattered against the wall.

As he stood there, staring at the ruined glasses, the man came in with the telegram.

"I wonder if Lonny West is up yet," he said.

"Lonny West? No, I—did you wish to see him, sir?"

"I've got a telegram for him."

"Oh, I see. Well, I am Lenny West's attorney. I can sign for the telegram, and give it to him."

"Well, I suppose that's all right."

When the man left the lobby, Riggs unfolded the telegram, which was from Buck Shelton. It read:

YOUR LETTER RECEIVED STOP HOLD EVERY-
THING UNTIL I GET THERE.

Riggs scowled and rubbed his chin. This telegram was puzzling. The man came back and stepped into the lobby.

"I forgot to tell you about that telegram," he said. "We've had a lot of wire trouble between here and Scorpion Bend. You'll notice that the wire was sent twenty-four hours ago. Sorry."

"That is perfectly all right," replied Riggs coldly, although he was paying no attention to what the man said.

Why on earth had Lonny West written to Buck Shelton, he wondered? What could Lonny have said to him that would cause Buck to send such a telegram? What did Buck want him to hold, until he could get there? Riggs leaned against the counter, puzzled beyond words.

"Jack Flood and Helene here in the hotel, and Buck Shelton on his way here," he muttered. "Flood hates Helene for quitting him, and he hates Shelton for kicking him out of some big money. And Lonny, the damn fool, out there at the ranch—drunk."

Recovering his composure somewhat, he examined the telegram. It had been sent twenty-four hours ago. Why, Buck Shelton would likely be in on the afternoon stage from Scorpion Bend! Riggs remembered now that the man had said something about wire trouble.

Slowly he went up the stairs and knocked softly on Helene's door.

"Who is it?" she asked.

"Edgar Riggs, and I must see you."

"Wait until I can get a robe, Riggs," she said.

A FEW moments later she admitted him, listened to what he had to say, and read the telegram.

"That's funny," she said grimly. "What have you done that would cause him to send letters to Buck?"

"Not a thing," declared Riggs. "The telegram sounds crazy."

"Buck wouldn't come here unless it was urgent."

"I don't know," sighed Riggs. "Everything was going along. Now you are here, Jack Flood is here, and Buck will soon be here. It is a swell set-up. I came here quietly to settle up this deal. There was no need of all this fuss. The first thing we know, the deal will be all off, and we'll be in that cute little jail down the street."

"Well, I'll tell you frankly," said Helene. "I'm not going out while Jack Flood is here."

"Afraid of him, eh?"

"I'm not taking any chances, Riggsy."

"Do you still want me to bring our heir up here when he comes?"

"I certainly do. But steer him away from Jack Flood, if you ever want to use him further."

"He and Jack were drunk together last night."

"I believe that, just like I believe in Santa Claus. Bring him up here."

Down at the office, Henry Harrison Conroy was saying to Judge:

"You might ride out to the Smoke Tree and ask Nick Borden to come in this morning, Judge. I was around at the rear of the hotel talking with Rickey a few moments ago. There's a beautiful blond lady in the hotel, and she knows Mr. Riggs. Also, that killer from San Francisco is at the hotel. Unless I'm mistaken, Mr. Shelton will arrive on the stage today. Yes, I think Nick should be here."

BUCK SHELTON was a tall, well groomed man of about forty years of age. In the parlance of the sporting world, he had a "dead-pan." That is, a face without expression.

His eyes were rather small, pale blue and as hard as ice. Being the only passenger, he climbed up on the seat with Mose Upshaw.

"What's yore odor?" asked Mose, as he sent the stage rocketing down the Tonto City road.

"My what?" asked Shelton coldly.

Mose adjusted the lines, spat over the wheel and replied:

"I asked yuh, what's yore odor. I use Lily of the Valley, myself. I used to smell m'self up with Jockey Club, but I wasn't satisfied."

Shelton turned his head and looked intently at the old driver.

"Are you trying to be funny, my friend?" he asked.

"Funny? Hell, no! I was jist wonderin' what yuh smell like. Everythin' and everybody has a smell. Now yuh take a polecat, f'r instance. It—"

"Oh, drop it!" snapped Shelton disgustedly.

"Well, don't take it. Hell, it's all right with me. Anyway, I like 'em."

"Like what?"

"Polecats."

After a mile or so, Mose said:

"They're makin' a lot of rich strikes around Tonto City. If yo're lookin' for somethin' to buy, I can shore let yuh in on a prospect that'll—well, you'd have to jist run one shift a day, or gold would git so plentiful that it wouldn't be worth as much as copper."

"I am not interested in gold mines."

"Gambler?"

"You seem to be full of questions, my friend."

"Yeah, that's right," admitted Mose, rubbing his cheek with a gloved hand. "When I went to school I was so blamed bright that when I was ten year old, I knowed everythin' that was in books. The teacher said:

" 'Mose Upshaw, the only way you'll ever learn anythin' further is to ask questions.' By golly, you'd be surprised at what I've learned."

"I suppose," replied Shelton. "No doubt you know what month the Fourth of July comes in."

"Yea-a-ah. Well, I did, when I was livin' in Nebrasky. But every State has different laws, yuh know. A feller has to ask—and it never did occur for me to ask in this here State."

"You are a newcomer, are you?"

"I shore am. Only been here twenty-three years."

Shelton glanced at Mose, but the old driver was watching the roads, his old face serious.

"Have you ever met a young man named Lonny West?" asked Shelton.

"That son-of-a-gun!" snorted Mose. "He can hold more whisky to the square inch than any man in Arizony. He's goin' to be worth a million dollars pretty soon. Why, he ain't drawed a sober breath since he come to Tonto City."

Shelton smiled grimly. "You haven't met a man named Jack Flood, have you?" he asked.

"Jack Flood? No-o-o, I don't reckon I have. The only Flood I ever heard about was in Jamestown. Oh, shore, I heard about the one Noah promoted."

"I see. Do you know a lawyer named Riggs?"

"Riggs? Oh, he's a big jigger, with a tie-rope on his specks. Yeah, I know him. Lonny said he was tempted to bust him on the beak."

"Lonny was, eh?" said Shelton grimly. "What for?"

"Oh, jist general principles, I reckon. You don't happen to be from San Francisco, do yuh?"

"Why do you ask?"

"Jist figgerin' there might be a rush on from Frisco. I was talkin' with the livery stable keeper this mornin'. Yesterday one of their drivers took a feller, from Frisco, to Tonto City, and a little while later another driver took a swell-elegant blond lady, from Frisco, to Tonto City."

Buck Shelton's jaw tightened, and his cold blue eyes stared out at the heat-scourged hills ahead.

NOON CAME, but no sign of Lonny West. Jack Flood was still in his room. Helene paced her small room, watching the main street from her window. The stage would be due about two o'clock. Edgar Riggs came up to talk to her.

"Can you drive a horse?" she asked him bluntly.

"Why, certainly I can drive, Helene."

"All right. Go over to the stable and hire a team and buggy. We are going out to that ranch and find Breezy. I want to have a talk with him before Buck comes here."

"Well, that might be a good idea. I'll have the outfit at the front door, where you can see it from the window. Jack Flood hasn't showed up yet."

"Make it snappy," ordered Helene nervously.

TWO HALF-BROKEN broncs, hitched to the ranch buckboard, were tied to the front porch of the J Bar C. In the back of the vehicle was a half-gallon jug, which was destined for the sheriff's office at Tonto.

Lonny West was sprawled out in an old home-made chair, his feet on the porch railing. Oscar Johnson was sitting on the top step, holding his head in his hands, as he moaned audibly a tuneless song.

Frijole Bill Cullison leaned against a porch post, puffing on a cigarette, which was so short it was scorching his mustache.

"I tell yuh, I'm right," declared Frijole. "Allus take a hair from the dog that bit yuh."

"Clear enough," sighed Lonny.

"You got bit by prune whisky; so take some more and git cured."

"I've had sh-shix," said Lonny thickly.

"Feller, I'm glad yo're to a point where sixes bother yuh. How 'bout me cookin' yuh a couple eggs?"

"I don' want any eggs."

"Oscar," said Frijole, "yore eyes look like two burned holes in a dirty blanket. Why don'tcha brace up and have a drink?"

"Say!" yawned Lonny. "What became of that gun Flood had last night?"

"I reckon he took it with him when him and Ben sneaked out on us. That shore was a funny deal. I ain't got it straight yet."

Lonny chuckled softly. "Oscar certainly crowned him."

"Yeah," agreed Frijole dryly. "And when you heir yourself into that million, don'tcha forget that it was my gittar that got busted."

"I'll buy you one for each hand," grinned Lonny.

"Dorling, Ay am growing o-o-old," crooned Oscar mournfully.

"Here comes somebody in a buggy," said Frijole.

They sat there and watched the driver bring the vehicle in a neat half-circle up to the porch. It was Helene and Edgar Riggs. Lonny's eyes popped wide at sight of her and he got slowly to his feet. Helene recognized him, too.

"Lonny, you fool, come down here!" snapped the lawyer. "We've got—"

"Lonny?" Helene fairly screamed the name. "Riggs, that isn't Breezy! We've been double crossed!"

"What? You mean—"

"Get out of here!" screamed Helene.

She made a frantic grab for the whip, yanked it from its socket on the dashboard, and slashed the horse viciously. With a lurch that nearly upset the buggy, they whirled away in a shower of gravel and dust.

Lonny sprang off the porch, yelling at Frijole:

"Come on, cowboys; we're going to town!"

In spite of his size, Oscar was into the buckboard ahead of Frijole and Lonny. Frijole yanked loose the tie-rope and barely leaped and caught the rear of the vehicle as Oscar whirled that half-broken team away from the porch.

"Have you got both lines?" yelled Frijole, crouched in the back, clinging to the jug.

"What the ha'al difference does that make?" howled Oscar. "Dis ha'ar road only runs von way."

IT WAS nearly stage time. Henry, Judge, Danny Regan, Nick Borden and John Campbell were all together in Harper's Millinery Store. Mrs. Borden was there, along with Leila and her mother.

"But why all this mystery?" queried Lola. "Nick won't tell me."

"Nick don't know anything to talk about," replied Nick seriously.

"What is it, Henry?" asked Mrs. Harper seriously.

"My dear Laura, I am very sorry, but—you see, I have been putting two and two together, which, in my simplicity, I believe might make four. But it hasn't made anything yet."

"Merely another of Henry's weird ideas," sighed Judge. "I feel that he is using a straw to try and poke an Ethiopian out of a wood pile."

"Oh-oh!" exclaimed Danny, peering through the window. "Here comes the stage!"

The four horses made a wide, sweeping turn, almost in front of the store, and drew up at the stage station.

"I believe our man is here," said Henry, and the five men filed out of the millinery store, while the three women crowded to the front windows.

"Before he has a chance to talk with anyone we will tell him that the whole plot is known," said Henry. "I hope he is impressed."

But before they could reach the stage a buggy rattled into town, the horse at a full gallop. Edgar Riggs, his hat long since gone, sagged back on the lines, fairly skidding the horse to a stop near the stage.

Buck Shelton had just dismounted from the stage, and was standing in the street, staring at Riggs and Helene.

"Get in here, Buck!" screamed Helene hoarsely. "Quick! Don't stand there! Get in here!"

"For Heaven's sake, what's wrong?" gasped Shelton.

"I tell you, he's still double crossing us, Helene," croaked Riggs.

Shelton started for the buggy.

"Get in, Buck!" choked Helene. "Lonny West isn't Breezy Lemair."

"What on earth do you—"

"Loo-o-o-ok out!" yelped a voice. "Yo're blockin' the street."

The yell came from over in front of the Tonto Saloon, as the J Bar C buckboard with the two running horses swept into the main street. There might have been plenty of room to pass, but the left-hand line had been broken.

Oscar was standing up, à la Ben Hur yelling, "Vhoa! Vhoa!" while Frijole was standing up in the back of the buckboard, clinging to the back of the seat with one hand, his precious jug in the other. Lonny was clinging with both hands. For a moment it looked as though the runaway might pass, but a cowboy sprang into the street and sent his sombrero sailing just ahead of the running team, which swerved a little.

The next moment the wheels on the right side of the buckboard connected with the wheels on the left side of the buggy. There was a terrific crash, and both vehicles erupted humanity, while wheels and parts of wheels seemed to fill both street and air. A huge cloud of dust obscured things for several moments. Both teams were galloping out of town, towing spare parts of the two vehicles, while the frightened stage four were up on the sidewalk, trying to get into the stage station.

BUCK SHELTON had been knocked backwards against the stage, where he sat in the dust. Helene had been flung out of the buggy, and was sitting a short distance away from Shelton, her hair over her eyes as she tried to paw the dust out of her face.

Lonny was on his feet, his nose skinned, one eye swelling shut, but with a grin on his dirty face. Riggs was flat on his back, his legs jerking, as he tried to pump air into his lungs. Frijole, still clinging to his jug, was walking around, like a pup, trying to find a soft spot to lie down.

Shelton got slowly to his feet, dazed and frightened. Helene had recovered quickly.

Lonny looked at her and said, "Sister, your make-up is ruined."

"You—you damn tramp!" she choked. "Buck, there's the—"

Riggs was on his hands and knees, spitting dirt.

"Buck, you double crosser!" croaked Riggs. "See what you've done!"

"Shut up, you fool!" snapped Buck.

"I won't shut up. You send this young fool here, instead of Breezy Lemair. He writes you letters and you wire him. Don't tell me you—"

"You crazy fool!" howled Shelton. "I don't even know him. Breezy wrote—"

Shelton's voice quit when he realized that he was talking too much.

"Go ahead and spill everything," said Helene. "You two—"

Shelton's hand jerked inside his coat and he yanked an automatic from a shoulder holster as he backed against the stage.

As he jerked his head around, surveying his situation, that half-gallon jug of prune whisky hit him square in the face.

The force of the blow knocked him back against the stage, and with a roar of battle on his lips Oscar Johnson made a flying tackle on Shelton, who was already half unconscious. Riggs started backing away from the scene, but Frijole tripped him, and he sat down heavily in the street.

"NOW," SAID Henry calmly, "that most of the folks are seated, you might tell us what this was all about, Lonny."

"Lonny!" exclaimed Helene huskily. "He's no more Lonny West than I am."

"Thank you, my dear," said Henry sweetly. He turned to Lonny.

"Just who are you?" asked Henry.

"Why, I'm Lonny West."

"I am very sorry," said Henry, "but it doesn't make sense."

"His name is Bert Lawrence—and he's a tramp," declared Helene.

"My name," said Lonny soberly, "happens to be Adelbert Lawrence West. I used the name of Bert Lawrence because the name of West did not mean a thing to me. My mother's name was Lawrence. Lonny was merely a nickname derived from Lawrence."

"Lonny West is dead!" croaked Riggs.

Lonny laughed. "A tramp robbed me of clothes and everything I had. I suppose he is the man who was killed in the train wreck. I never heard about it."

"Where is Breezy Lemair?" asked Helene weakly.

"I suppose he was in that car that went over the cliff that night. I got out, after we sideswiped another car, and he went on alone."

"And you," said Henry slowly, "were really the heir?"

"Not a chance," laughed Lonny. "Riggs told me the will was

just a clever forgery. But what was this about me writing Shelton?"

"You see," said Henry simply, "a bold, bad bandit robbed Riggs of his brief-case one night. In that case was a letter to Buck Shelton. It wasn't very well sealed, it seems. However, we won't go into that. The contents were illuminating, to say the least. In fact, Mr. Riggs gave us plenty to work on, in his explanations to Mr. Shelton. He mentioned many intimate details of the frame-up; so I kept the letter as evidence, and wrote one to Mr. Shelton, to which I signed the name of Breezy Lemair. I believe that is why Mr. Shelton sent that telegram—and why he came here."

"You—you damn thief!" wailed Riggs. "I'll swear—"

"You said the man was very tall and slender," interrupted Henry.

"I believe," said Campbell, "that it is time for me to come in on the case. You have plenty of room in the jail, haven't you, Henry?"

"The accommodations are adequate, sir," nodded Henry. He looked at Helene, his eyes squinted thoughtfully. Then he said:

"I woudn't like to have a woman in the jail, John. Don't you think she has been punished enough?"

"Well, yes, if you think so, Henry. I'll take her deposition and let her go, if you wish."

"I think so, John. Two out of three is a fair average."

"What about me?" asked Lonny.

"You are rather a problem, Lonny," Henry said.

"Ay t'ink," said Oscar expansively, "'ve ought to give him a yob at de ranch, Hanry. He is yust crazy enough to make good cowpuncher."

The three women from the millinery store were there, having seen most of the incident through a window. Lonny grinned at them, and Lola said:

"As far as I am concerned, Lonny is entitled to a share of the estate. None of us want to be mean about it."

"Well, I'll say that's daw-gone square!" blurted Mose Upshaw. "And when yuh git yore share, young feller, don'tcha forget what I told yuh about that mine I've got. A million tons in sight."

Helene was standing there, a queer expression in her eyes. She was looking at Jack Flood and Ben East, who had walked in close, and had heard much of the conversation.

"I'm going back to Scorpion Bend, Helene," said Flood quietly. "If you are ready, we'll be on our way. If the law don't want you—I do."

"Reminds me of a scene from the 'Music Master,'" said Henry, a suspicion of moisture in his squinty eyes. " 'If you don't vant her—I vant her.'"

"It all seems so wonderful," declared Mrs. Harper. "Everything cleared up in a few minutes, like this. Henry, I don't see how you did it."

"Just by being nosey, my dear," said Henry blandly. "When Lonny came down here, not knowing what Edgar Riggs' business was, I grew suspicious. I suspected Mr. Riggs of ulterior motives; so I made a deal with the telegraph operator to let me read all telegrams. I knew that Flood was a menace to Lonny, and that the lady was coming to warn him. It seemed that Mr. Shelton was the leading character in this shady little drama; so we secured Mr. Riggs' un-posted letter to Mr. Shelton, in which Mr. Riggs complained bitterly about the behavior of Breezv Lemair. So, we write a letter from Breezy, bringing Mr. Shelton."

"Ay yust vant to say, it is vonderful!" exclaimed Oscar. "Yust vonderful!"

"Thank you, Oscar," said Henry expansively.

"Yah, su-u-ure," said Oscar. "It vent all through de ronavay, hit dat yigger in de head, bounced off a veel, and never bruk."

"What in the devil are you talking about?" asked Judge.

"Das yug of prune yuice."

THE
ARGOSY™
LIBRARY

SERIES 4 INCLUDES:

* TUTTLE * ENGLAND * FARLEY *

* BRAND * BRENT * ROSCOE *

* GIESY & SMITH *

* RUD * PETTEE *

* CUNNINGHAM *

THE BEST FICTION
FROM THE FRANK
A. MUNSEY LINE

www.ingramcontent.com/pod-product-compliance
Lightning Source LLC
Chambersburg PA
CBHW022005010726
47494CB00003B/895